Yours
Truly

ALSO BY HEATHER VOGEL FREDERICK

Absolutely Truly

The Mother-Daughter Book Club
Much Ado About Anne
Dear Pen Pal
Pies & Prejudice
Home for the Holidays
Wish You Were Eyre
Mother-Daughter Book Camp

Once Upon a Toad

The Voyage of Patience Goodspeed
The Education of Patience Goodspeed

Spy Mice: The Black Paw
Spy Mice: For Your Paws Only
Spy Mice: Goldwhiskers

Hide and Squeak
A Little Women Christmas

Yours Truly

A Pumpkin Falls Mystery

HEATHER VOGEL FREDERICK

Simon & Schuster Books for Young Readers
NEW YORK • LONDON • TORONTO • SYDNEY • NEW DELHI

SIMON & SCHUSTER BOOKS FOR YOUNG READERS

An imprint of Simon & Schuster Children's Publishing Division

1230 Avenue of the Americas, New York, New York 10020

SIMON & SCHUSTER BOOKS FOR YOUNG READERS is a trademark of Simon & Schuster, Inc.

For information about special discounts for bulk purchases, please contact Simon & Schuster Special Sales at 1-866-506-1949 or business@simonandschuster.com.

The Simon & Schuster Speakers Bureau can bring authors to your live event. For more information or to book an event, contact the Simon & Schuster Speakers Bureau at 1-866-248-3049 or visit our website at www.simonspeakers.com.

Also available in a Simon & Schuster Books for Young Readers hardcover edition

Cover design by Krista Vossen

Interior design by Hilary Zarycky

The text for this book was set in Fournier.

Manufactured in the United States of America

0621 OFF

First Simon & Schuster Books for Young Readers paperback edition January 2018

4 6 8 10 9 7 5 3

The Library of Congress has cataloged the hardcover edition as follows:

Names: Frederick, Heather Vogel, author.

Title: Yours Truly / Heather Vogel Frederick.

Description: First edition. | New York : Simon & Schuster Books for Young Readers, [2017] | Series: A Pumpkin Falls mystery | Audience: Ages 8-12. | Summary: When someone tries to sabotage the maple trees on her friend Franklin's family farm, Truly Lovejoy rallies the Pumpkin Falls Private Eyes to investigate. | Sequel to: Absolutely Truly

Identifiers: LCCN 2016031402 | ISBN 9781442471863 (hardback) | ISBN 9781442471887 (eBook)

Subjects: | CYAC: Mystery and detective stories. | Families—Fiction. | Farm life—New Hampshire—Fiction. | New Hampshire—Fiction. | BISAC: JUVENILE FICTION / Mysteries & Detective Stories. | JUVENILE FICTION / Humorous Stories. | JUVENILE FICTION / Family / General (see also headings under Social Issues).

Classification: LCC PZ7.F87217 Yo 2017 | DDC [Fic]—dc23

LC record available at https://lccn.loc.gov/2016031402

ISBN 9781442471870 (pbk)

For my maple buddy, Jonatha

PROLOGUE

It takes roughly forty gallons of sap to make a gallon of maple syrup.

How do I know this? Welcome to life in the sticks.

I never expected to become an expert on maple syrup, that's for sure. Then again, I never expected to become a middle school private eye, either, or to spend Spring Break hunting for Bigfoot and wind up tangled in cobwebs in a long-forgotten tunnel. A whole lot of unexpected things have happened to me ever since my family left Texas and moved to Pumpkin Falls, New Hampshire.

This isn't a story about maple syrup, though. Not really. It's the story of how I stumbled onto a secret in my grandparents' house and unraveled a mystery dating back to the Civil War. And it all started the week I finally spotted an owl and celebrated the worst birthday of my life.

CHAPTER 1

"Knock it off, Lauren!" I stuffed my pillow over my head, trying to block out the noise on the other side of my bedroom door.

Sunday was just about my only day to sleep in, thanks to swim team. I was usually up and in the pool by zero dark thirty. Which was fine—no complaints. The pool had always been my happy place. But ever since my younger sister discovered a box of our aunt's old Nancy Drew books up in the attic and started reading *The Hidden Staircase*, she'd been wandering around the house at odd hours tapping hopefully on the walls.

It was driving us all crazy.

"Lauren!" I hollered again, and this time the racket finally stopped.

Burrowing down under the covers, I squeezed my eyes shut and willed myself to go back to sleep. It seemed like I was tired all the time these days. My mother said it was a symptom of impending teenage-hood. Maybe she was right, because my older brothers would sleep all day if she and my father let them. And I was turning thirteen soon.

Soon?

My eyes flew open. I sat bolt upright, flinging my pillow aside. How could I have forgotten? My birthday was *today*, not *soon*!

I swung my legs over the edge of the bed, toes scrabbling for the slippers that waited on the hardwood floor. Reaching for my bathrobe, I slipped it on and sniffed the air expectantly. Lovejoy family birthdays always started with one of Dad's special breakfasts: scrambled eggs, bacon, and homemade sourdough waffles with real maple syrup. I'd been looking forward to it all week.

I shuffled across the room and out into the hall. There was no sign of Lauren, except for the fact that Miss Marple was sitting by my door, wearing a University of Texas T-shirt. Miss Marple is my grandparents' golden retriever. We were taking care of her while my grandparents were in Africa.

"Hey, girl," I said, and leaned down to give her a pat. She looked up at me and whined. Lauren loved dressing her up, but Miss Marple was not a fan.

I extricated her from the T-shirt, and she wagged her tail gratefully and followed me across the hall into my bathroom.

I still wasn't used to having one of my very own. It was pretty sweet, especially after having to share one with my brothers and sisters for so many years. Two older brothers—Hatcher and Danny—and two younger sisters—Lauren and Pippa, to be exact, putting me smack-dab in the middle. My dad was retired military, and for as long as I could remember we'd lived in base housing—Alabama, Colorado, Germany, Texas. Now, though, we were living in my grandparents' house, the one my dad grew up in. How we ended up here was kind of complicated, but the short version was, my father lost an arm in the war in Afghanistan, and because of that he lost his chance to be a commercial airline pilot, and partly because of that and partly because they wanted to, Gramps and Lola joined the Peace Corps and moved to Namibia so my dad could have a job running the family bookstore with his sister, and we traded our home in Austin for living here in their house. Complicated, right?

As Miss Marple settled happily onto the rug by the radiator, I got in the shower, humming the "Happy Birthday" song to myself and wondering if my parents had gotten me any presents. My cousin and best friend, Mackenzie, was my main gift—she was flying in from Texas tonight to spend Spring Break with me—but I'd spotted my mother sneaking a big bag inside the house yesterday, and I was pretty sure there was something for me inside.

Hopefully, it was the new feeder I'd been eyeing in one of my grandfather's birding catalogs. I'd placed the catalog strategically on the kitchen table a couple of weeks ago, open to the page in question. There was no way my parents could have missed it.

I was planning to put it outside one of the windows in my room. I figured it would be almost like having pet birds.

A person couldn't have enough bird feeders. Especially when that person was as crazy about birds as I was.

The house was still quiet when Miss Marple and I emerged from the bathroom.

"They're probably in the kitchen already, waiting to surprise me," I whispered to the dog as I got dressed and then tiptoed downstairs. Correction: I tiptoed; Miss Marple galumphed. She wasn't exactly the daintiest of dogs.

The only surprise waiting for me, though, was an empty kitchen. There was no sign of my family, no sign of any presents, and, tragically, no sign of waffles.

Disappointed, I glanced out the window. The driveway was empty too. Was there a wrestling tournament today that my parents and sisters had taken my brothers to? I'd almost forgotten my own birthday; maybe I'd forgotten about one of Hatcher's and Danny's wrestling matches as well.

Just then I heard the door to the garage open, and a moment later my father walked in.

Finally, I thought happily. *Waffles.*

"Why are you dressed like that?" He eyed me, frowning.

"Um . . . ," I replied, looking down at my clothes. I'd made an effort for once—I was always getting scolded for not dressing up enough for church—and picked out what I thought was a pretty nice outfit.

"Go get changed, Truly!" My father sounded impatient. "We haven't got all day."

I looked at him, bewildered. "Aren't we going to church?"

"Not this morning. We're needed at Freeman Farm."

My mother came into the kitchen behind him. "They have a syrup emergency," she said, like that explained everything. "We just dropped your brothers and Lauren off to help, and Pippa is waiting in the car. You were in the shower when we left—didn't you get our note?"

I turned around and looked to where she was pointing. Sure enough, right there in plain sight leaning against the salt and pepper shakers was a tented piece of paper with *TRULY* written on it.

"Don't worry, honey, we haven't forgotten you," my mother promised. "We'll have your special birthday breakfast tomorrow, after Mackenzie gets here."

Tears sprang to my eyes. We weren't going to celebrate my birthday until *tomorrow*?

Seeing the expression on my face, my mother bit her lip. "It's the right thing to do, Truly. The Freemans are swamped, what with the Maple Madness rush."

Maple Madness! I was sick of hearing about stupid Maple Madness. Our whole town had gone maple syrup crazy. The minute the weather conditions cooperated, all the farms and small backyard operations around town had begun scrambling to harvest the sap from the trees and turn it into liquid gold. And now, with April just around the corner, all anyone could talk about was Maple Madness.

Every autumn New Hampshire flung its doors open wide for the leaf peepers—tourists obsessed with fall foliage—and every spring they did the same for the maple maniacs. All over the state there were special events and tours and other celebrations during "sugaring off" season, including Pumpkin Falls' own week-long Maple Madness.

And this year my birthday had the misfortune of falling right in the middle of the kickoff weekend.

"But Mom, it's my *birthday*," I said, trying not to whine. *An extra-special one*, I wanted to add. The one I'd been waiting for forever, because today I was finally a teenager, which was practically a grown-up.

"Truly." My father's voice had the warning note in it that meant business.

I sighed. "Yes, sir."

My mother stretched up on her tiptoes and gave me a quick kiss on the cheek. At six feet tall, I towered over her. In fact, I pretty much towered over everybody in my family, except for my aunt.

"Thanks, sweetheart," my mother said. "And don't worry—we'll make it up to you tomorrow."

Fat lot of good that does me today, I thought bitterly, and went upstairs to change my clothes.

CHAPTER 2

By the time we arrived at Freeman Farm, the line of cars waiting for the parking lot to open stretched halfway down Lovejoy Mountain.

I still got a kick out of the fact that everybody around here called it a mountain. It was more of a molehill, really—and the ski run was a joke, compared to the ones we used to live near in Colorado.

"Good thing we took the back way," said my father, scowling at the traffic. "It's practically at a standstill over by Maynard's Maple Barn."

The farm next door to the Freemans was what's called a "hobby farm." It belonged to my swim coach. Like many people across New England, Coach Maynard and his wife had a small-time maple operation that they cranked up this time of year for fun and a little extra income. For the Freemans, though, maple syrup was their main business.

My father tooted the horn to announce our arrival, and Mr. Freeman trotted over to move one of the sawhorses blocking the entrance to the lot.

"I can't thank you enough for coming," he called, directing us into a parking spot. We all piled out of the minivan. A crowd of volunteers in orange aprons milled around nearby, including my brothers and two of my classmates from seventh-grade homeroom, Scooter Sanchez and Romeo Calhoun, who just went by "Calhoun" because he hated the name Romeo. I couldn't blame him. Truly was bad enough—I was named for one of my ancestors—but Romeo? He and Scooter and I waved at one another.

"Happy to help, Frank," said my mother with one of her sunny smiles. "Where do y'all want us?"

"Grace is hoping you'll join her in the Snack Shack." Mr. Freeman pointed toward a small shed at the far end of the puddle-strewn parking lot. "She's been up since before dawn making donuts, and by the look of things she's going to be busier than a one-eyed cat in a fish market today."

My mother laughed. "That busy, huh?" She took Pippa by the hand. "Come on, sweetheart, you can be my helper."

Mr. Freeman turned to my father. "J. T., how do you feel about taking over the parking detail? I need to prep the sugarhouse for the first tour."

"I'm on it," said my father.

Mr. Freeman frowned at the line of waiting cars. "I'm not

sure how we're going to squeeze everybody in. I can't ever remember having a kickoff weekend this busy before."

"Good problem to have," my father told him, and he brightened.

"You've got a point." Mr. Freeman started to go, then paused. "You'll probably need to open the satellite lot in the field across the street soon. Franklin and I cleared the last of the snow away this morning, so it's good to go. He and Annie know the ropes if you have any questions."

Annie Freeman detached herself from the gaggle of volunteers and came over to us as her father headed for the sugarhouse, a small wooden cabin beyond the barn and the Snack Shack.

"These are for you," Annie told my father and me, handing us each one of the bright orange aprons. On the front was the outline of a giant maple leaf with the words FREEMAN FARM printed inside. "My mother designed them—aren't they cute? They're for sale in the barn shop. Only you'll probably get to keep yours for free, as a thank-you for volunteering. But act surprised when my mother tells you, okay? Volunteers have to wear them at all times," she continued, without pausing to take a breath. "My father says it's safer that way, and safety is our top P-R-I-O-R-I-T-Y during Maple Madness."

Annie Freeman was in the same fourth-grade class as my sister Lauren. She never stopped talking—or spelling. Annie was the reigning queen of the Grafton County Junior Spelling

Championship, as she was quick to tell anyone who stood still long enough to listen.

Lauren emerged from the barn just then, clutching a stack of orange flyers. Annie motioned her over and took a bunch. She thrust them into my hands. "One per car," she told me.

"Got it," I replied, glancing down at the piece of paper on top of my pile.

WELCOME TO MAPLE MADNESS!
Tour the sugarhouse!
Grab a treat at the Snack Shack!
Stop by our barn store for more maple goodness
and our special MAPLE MADNESS SALE!

"Madness" is definitely the right word, I thought, wincing. Could this whole thing possibly be any more lame?

My father checked his watch. "Okay, troops, it's oh-nine hundred hours," he announced crisply. "Time to get this show started!"

Annie's brother Franklin grabbed Scooter Sanchez and Calhoun and my brothers, and they all began moving the sawhorses that blocked the entrance to the parking lot. A moment later cars started streaming in.

"Scooter and Calhoun, I'm stationing you two here with Franklin," my father told my classmates. "Danny and Hatcher, you boys get the satellite parking lot across the street ready. By the looks of it, we're going to need it for overflow soon."

He doled out a few more assignments, then turned to me. "Truly, you're my floater. Look for anyone who needs extra help, cover for anyone who needs a break, take coffee to Mr. Freeman and any of the volunteers who look like they could use something hot to drink, that sort of thing."

I held up the orange flyers, and he nodded.

"That too. Hand them out to the incoming—I mean the customers."

In thirty seconds flat, Lieutenant Colonel Jericho T. Lovejoy had slipped back into his element, barking orders at everyone in sight. As I headed off to do as he'd asked, I glanced back over my shoulder at him. With his leather flight jacket and glove covering his titanium arm and hand, my father looked like anybody else's dad.

He wasn't, though. He was still adjusting to his "new normal," as he and my mother called it. A new normal that for him meant no more military and no more flying helicopters and airplanes. Grounded by his injury, he'd traded that life for a new life in this teeny town where he'd grown up. I could tell he still missed the old life, though, even though he was doing a really good job running the family bookstore with his sister.

"Where's your aunt?" asked Annie, who apparently had a gift for mind reading as well as spelling.

"Holding down the fort at the bookshop," I told her. "It's kind of a busy weekend, in case you haven't heard."

Annie grinned. "Too bad Jasmine and Cha Cha aren't here. They love Maple Madness."

Jasmine was Scooter Sanchez's twin. She and Cha Cha Abramowitz were my closest friends in Pumpkin Falls. The two of them were in Florida for Spring Break, visiting Cha Cha's grandparents. I'd been invited to go along, but I couldn't because of Mackenzie.

Who would be here in just a few more hours! There was one bright spot in this dud of a birthday, at least.

"We'll take that half of the parking lot; you take this half," said Annie. She ran off to join my sister Lauren, her bouquet of dark braids bobbing.

I made my way slowly toward the Snack Shack, passing out orange flyers as I went.

"Need any help?" I asked when I reached my destination.

"Thanks, Truly, but I think we're okay for now." Annie's mother nodded toward Pippa, who was perched on a box behind the window counter, flirting with one of the customers as only a kindergartner can flirt. "This one's quite the lucky charm."

I had to smile at that. With her gap-toothed grin, pink sparkly glasses, and halo of strawberry blond curls, my baby sister had the world wrapped around her little finger.

"I don't think I've ever seen this many people turn out for Maple Madness kickoff weekend before," Mrs. Freeman continued as she boxed up a dozen donuts for a waiting customer.

"I think people are just grateful for a reason to celebrate spring, after the winter we've had," my mother told her, adding hastily, "Not that they aren't eager to sample your maple products too."

Pumpkin Falls and the rest of New England had just emerged from the coldest winter on record. It made the national news and everything. The snow in our town was epic—even the famous waterfall froze, which it hadn't done for a hundred years. Spring was finally on its way now, though, and the ground, so recently blanketed in white, was a patchwork of brown as the remnants of the last snowstorm faded away.

Of course, the beginning of spring also meant the beginning of what locals call "mud season." We didn't have that back in Texas, and it was just another in the long string of strikes against Pumpkin Falls, if you asked me, which nobody ever did.

"Now that I think of it, we could use more paper plates and napkins," Mrs. Freeman said. "Would you mind, Truly? They're in the kitchen, on the bottom shelf in the pantry."

"No problem," I told her, starting back across the parking lot. The sun felt good on my face, and my grumpy mood began to melt right along with the last of the snow. From all the weather reports I'd been hearing, conditions couldn't be more perfect for a successful sap run—the weeks when the maple trees released their sugary liquid. "Cold nights plus warm days make for a busy season in the sugar bush," one of the radio announcers had said just this morning on the drive over.

I can't believe I even pay attention to news like that, I thought in a rush of embarrassment. I'd have to watch my step once Mackenzie arrived. She'd never let me hear the end of it if I started spouting random facts about maple syrup.

"Isn't this a beautiful farm?" my mother asked me a few minutes later when I returned with the plates and napkins.

I shrugged. "I guess."

"You guess! Truly Lovejoy!" She took me by the shoulders and spun me around. "Just look at that view, darlin'!" Shading her eyes, she gazed out across the road at the long sweep of meadows that sloped down toward the Pumpkin River. She turned to Mrs. Freeman. "How long has it been here?"

Mrs. Freeman laughed. "The view or our farm? I suspect the view has been here longer."

My mother laughed too.

"The farm was built shortly after the Civil War, by one of my husband's ancestors," Annie's mother told us.

Annie's family were the first African Americans to settle in Pumpkin Falls. I knew this because we'd learned about them in school a few weeks ago, during Black History Month. Our social studies class had even taken a field trip to the old Oak Street Cemetery. Oak Street paralleled Maple Street, where my grandparents' house was—the house we were living in now. At the far end of our backyard there was an overgrown cut-through to the cemetery. Hatcher and I had discovered it one summer when we were visiting Gramps and Lola.

On our field trip my classmates and I had wandered around looking at the graves of long-departed Freemans and learning a bit about their history. For instance, Franklin's grandfather had marched with Martin Luther King during the Civil Rights movement back in the 1960s, which was pretty cool. I took a bunch of pictures of the tombstones. I still had some of them on my cell phone, including Fanny Freeman's (because who doesn't love the name Fanny?), an earlier Franklin Freeman (I took that one because of the awesome owl carved into the headstone), and, of course, the tomb of Frank Freeman, the original ancestor who had built Freeman Farm. That particular grave was one of the most famous in the Oak Street Cemetery.

"The whole namesake thing is as bad for Franklin's family as it is for mine," I'd remarked to Calhoun as the two of us had stood there looking at it.

He'd flashed me one of his rare smiles. "No kidding. Way too many Franklins, Franks, and *F*'s in general. But the epitaph is pretty sweet."

Two hearts forever entwined, one forever yearning to be free. I looked at it again, then slanted my friend a glance. Calhoun was a bit of a puzzle. He had this übercool exterior, but underneath he was smart as a whip and knew a ton about Shakespeare, of all things, thanks to his Shakespearean scholar father, and he could be funny and really nice when he wanted to. Which had been a lot more than usual lately. He'd even asked me to dance at the Valentine's Day party. I was beginning to think that maybe he liked me.

We'd both taken photos of the sculpture on top of the lid to the tomb and agreed that a mother cradling her infant was kind of a weird thing to have on a guy's grave. But then, there were a lot of weird things on the tombstones in the old Oak Street Cemetery, including a stone pumpkin on the one belonging to my ancestor Nathaniel Daniel Lovejoy. *Way to represent the Lovejoys, Nathaniel,* I'd thought, staring at it.

"You folks certainly ordered up some fine weather for the Maple Madness kickoff," commented one of the customers standing in line at the Snack Shack.

My mother nodded. "Couldn't be prettier."

A pretty day for a birthday, I almost blurted out, but didn't. Even I had to admit that helping the Freemans was the right thing to do. Still, being a Good Samaritan didn't completely erase the sting of missing my birthday breakfast.

I swear, moms must have radar that tells them when their kids are unhappy, because just then mine handed me a maple donut and a cup of hot chocolate. "I know it's not sourdough waffles," she whispered, "but maybe it will tide you over until tomorrow."

"Thanks, Mom," I said, and we smiled at each other.

"That'll be two dollarth," my little sister announced smartly, holding out her hand. Her front teeth are finally starting to grow in, but she still has a bit of a lisp.

My mother arched an eyebrow. "You drive a hard bargain, young lady," she said, reaching into her pocket for some coins. "But I'm happy to pay for the birthday girl."

As she plunked a pile of quarters into Pippa's palm, I bit into the donut. It was so good I groaned out loud. "Oh man, these are *fantastic*, Mrs. Freeman."

Annie's mother handed me another one. "Why, thank you, Truly! It's an old family recipe." She winked. "This one's on the house, since it's your birthday."

Scooter Sanchez, who was walking by just then, turned and looked at me in surprise. It seemed like he was about to say something, but before he could, my father bellowed at him to double-time it back to his station. He sketched a wave and ran off.

Scooter was a lot nicer to me now than when we first moved here. He was still kind of a pain, though. It was really, really hard for him to resist teasing people, for one thing. On my first day at Daniel Webster School, we got off on the wrong foot when he called me "Truly Gigantic." Things got worse for a while, especially after he discovered that my brother Hatcher's nickname for me was "Drooly." It's one thing for your brother to call you something like that, and another when a complete stranger does it.

"Truly?" Mrs. Freeman handed me a cardboard box containing two cups of coffee and a paper plate piled with donuts. "Would you please take these to Ella and Belinda? They're manning the barn store for us this morning, and I'm guessing they could use a break about now."

Picking my way around the puddles, I headed toward the barn. I was more than a bit curious to see how our former postmistress and the local cat rescue lady were getting along. Things had been a little tense for a while between Ella Bellow and Belinda Winchester after last month's Valentine's Day dance, where Belinda had slipped a kitten into Ella's coat pocket. Of course she never admitted to it, but who else had a ready supply of kittens and handed them out like popcorn at a movie? Maybe Belinda had sensed that Ella was lonely and needed a friend—Ella was widowed a few years ago—or maybe Belinda was just being Belinda. Whatever prompted it, Ella had not been happy about the kitten surprise, at least not at first. She and Belinda had since patched things up, mostly. It helped that Ella had quickly fallen head over heels in love with little Purl—the name she picked for the kitten, to go with the new knitting shop she'd opened as a retirement project.

"Having fun yet?" Hatcher loped up behind me and slung an arm around my shoulders.

"You've got to try a maple donut," I told him. "They're amazing."

My brother reached for the cardboard box I was carrying,

but I whisked it out of his reach. "Go get your own. These are for Ella and Belinda."

"C'mon, Drooly," he coaxed, following me into the barn.

"Quit it, Hatcher!" I scowled at him. The Scooter Sanchez fiasco was still a bit of a sore spot between us.

"Sorry." He grinned, obviously not sorry at all. "Can't you let me have just one? Ella and Belinda will never notice."

"Aren't you supposed to be in the satellite lot?" I replied, keeping a firm grip on the donuts.

My brother shrugged. "I'm just taking a break."

"Better not let Dad catch you slacking."

"He won't. Cross my heart and hope to fly."

I gave him a rueful smile. That particular family saying had been off-limits for months after Black Monday—our name for the day Dad had been injured. I'd gotten into huge trouble earlier this winter for accidentally using it. The catchphrase was something my father and his best friend Tom Larson made up a long time ago when they were in flight school. But when Dad returned from Afghanistan and Mr. Larson didn't, the words stirred up too many bad memories for my father. Recently, though, the ban had been relaxed, and I'd even caught Dad using it himself a few times. Another sign that he was on the mend, according to Aunt True.

"Whoa," said Hatcher, looking around the store. "This is over the top."

The Freemans had pulled out all the stops for Maple

Madness. I had no idea there were so many maple products in existence. In addition to the usual jugs of every size filled with maple syrup, the shelves were crammed with a bunch of other stuff: maple sugar, maple candy, maple coffee and tea, maple-scented candles—even maple-scented soap. *Who in their right mind wants to smell like breakfast?* I wondered.

But that wasn't all. There was also maple hot sauce, maple fudge, maple cookies, maple cotton candy, and maple pepper, along with maple leaf key chains, maple recipe books, stacks of Mrs. Freeman's orange aprons, matching T-shirts, bumper stickers, and, I noted with chagrin, tote bags with MAPLE SYRUP—APPEARING SOON ON A BREAKFAST PLATE NEAR YOU! emblazoned on the side.

Not on one near me, I thought with a stab of self-pity, thinking wistfully of the sourdough waffles that had gone AWOL—military-speak for "absent without leave."

"Kids!" cried Belinda, waving at us from the far side of the store. Belinda Winchester looked a little less like a bag lady than she had when I first met her—Aunt True's recent wardrobe makeover had helped, sort of—but Belinda was still a few tacos short of a fiesta platter, if you asked me, which nobody ever did. Belinda had been on kind of a purple streak lately, but today she'd traded that in for head-to-toe orange. Not just any shade of orange, either, but fluorescent hunter-in-the-woods orange. I was guessing this color scheme was inspired by the apron that Mrs. Freeman had designed, which

Belinda was wearing over orange overalls, orange turtleneck, orange socks, and orange plastic clogs. With the bright green beret she'd plopped on her snowy owl white hair, Belinda looked like a carrot—an observation I whispered to Hatcher. He laughed.

"How's it going out there?" Belinda asked, trotting over and reaching for a donut. Hatcher gave me a mournful look, which I ignored.

"Busy," my brother and I replied at the same time.

Belinda nodded, sending the wires to her ever-present earbuds swinging back and forth. "Busy in here, too. Oh, happy birthday, by the way. Your aunt told me."

"Thanks."

"You having a party?" she asked hopefully as I handed her a cup of coffee. Belinda loved parties. Correction: Belinda loved the *food* that accompanied parties. "I have a great playlist I could bring."

She bit into the donut, her earbuds leaking the tinny strains of "Surfer Girl." Out of the corner of my eye I could see Hatcher grinning broadly. He got a huge kick out of Belinda. I did too, as a matter of fact. The thing was, you couldn't help but like her. As odd as she was, she had a lot of spunk for an older lady, along with a mischievous streak a mile wide.

Still, a senior citizen DJ-ing my birthday party wasn't exactly my idea of a fun time. Not that there was anything wrong with her oldies mixes. Belinda always played them during her bookstore shifts, and I liked the Beatles and the Beach Boys as much as anybody.

I shook my head. "Nope. No party. My cousin's coming tonight, though. She's going to spend Spring Break with me."

"Your aunt said something about that." Belinda took another bite of donut, then reached into the pocket of her orange apron and pulled out a kitten. "Would you like a present?"

I had to admire her persistence. "My mother would kill me, Belinda. And so would Lauren—she's been begging for one for months now."

"You could keep him at the bookstore."

Belinda worked part-time for us now—or maybe we worked for her, I wasn't exactly sure which. When the book-shop was teetering on the verge of bankruptcy earlier this winter, she'd saved our bacon by becoming a silent partner. She might look like a slightly crazy cat lady, but it turned out she was a shrewd investor, too, and those deep pockets of hers contained far more than just kittens. Anyway, Aunt True put her in charge of the mystery section, since that was Belinda's favorite genre and she knew pretty much everything there was to know about it.

I shook my head. "A resident kitten wouldn't go over well with Memphis."

"He'd get used to it."

Fat chance. My aunt's cat didn't like anyone except my

aunt. As for other animals, well, he'd made it his job in life to make Miss Marple as miserable as possible.

"Are you sure you don't want him? He's awful cute," Belinda coaxed, holding out the little bundle of gray fuzz. "So are his six sisters, if you'd rather have a girl. They're in a box behind the counter."

"Oh, look, honey, a KITTEN!" shrieked a woman wearing an orange I WENT MAD FOR MAPLE MADNESS sweatshirt. She dragged her husband over to where we were standing.

Belinda pulled out her earbuds and smiled. "They're free with a purchase," she told the customer. "Better act fast, though—we're almost out."

My mouth fell open. Belinda winked at me. She was never above stretching the truth when it came to finding homes for her furry charges.

"Going, going, gone!" added Ella Bellow, materializing just then.

I handed the former Pumpkin Falls postmistress a cup of coffee and a donut, and she gave me a chilly smile. Tall and rake thin, Ella had thawed a bit since I'd falsely accused her of stealing a rare book from our store, but despite my public apology we were hardly pals.

"I'd better get back," said Hatcher, who'd been watching for an opening and finally managed to swipe the last of the donuts.

"Yeah, me too," I said. "Bye, Belinda. See you later, Ella."

"You certainly will," Ella replied, her mouth pruning up in a smug I-know-something-you-don't smile.

"What was that all about?" my brother whispered as we headed out of the barn.

"No idea," I whispered back.

As we emerged into the sunshine, Hatcher trotted off toward the parking lot. I rounded the corner of the barn and nearly flattened Scooter Sanchez.

"Watch where you're going!" he said, startled.

"Like I did it on purpose!"

We stood there awkwardly for a moment, glaring at each other, and then all of a sudden Scooter lunged at me. Before I realized what was happening, his face loomed close to mine and he kissed me.

On the *lips*.

I stepped back, too astonished to speak.

Scooter's face flamed. "Happy birthday," he mumbled, and loped off.

That's when I spotted Calhoun. I could tell by the look on his face that he'd seen everything. Before I could say a word, he spun on his heel and stalked off.

It's not what you think! I wanted to shout in protest. *I didn't have anything to do with it!*

But he was already gone.

I slumped against the side of the barn. I never used to give boys a second thought. They were just there, like my older brothers. Now, though, they were kind of on my radar screen. Not the way they were on my cousin Mackenzie's radar screen—she was totally boy crazy. At the moment, she was head over heels in love with Cameron McAllister. They were both on the same swim team in Austin. Behind Mackenzie's back, I call him Mr. Perfect.

The thing was, though, it had recently begun to dawn on me that not only was there a chance Calhoun liked me, but that maybe, just maybe, I liked him back.

Except now, thanks to the kiss he'd just witnessed, he probably thought I liked Scooter.

Running behind the barn, I grabbed a handful of snow and scrubbed my lips. Why did my first kiss have to be from Scooter Sanchez, of all people? And why did Calhoun have to be there to witness it?

My birthday couldn't possibly get any worse.

CHAPTER 3

Actually it could, as it turned out.

That bag I saw my mother sneaking into the house? There was a gift for me inside, just as I'd suspected, but it wasn't what I'd been hoping for.

At breakfast the next morning after swim practice—waffles! finally!—I found a pile of presents waiting for me on my chair. On top was a big blue gift bag covered in sparkles.

"What's this?" I asked.

"Must be something for the birthday girl," said my father, setting a loaded plate in front of me and planting a kiss on top of my head.

"But it ithnt her birthday anymore," said Pippa.

"A technicality," my father told her.

Pippa's forehead furrowed.

"He means you're right, but she gets presents anyway," said Hatcher.

I opened the envelope taped to the bag. Inside was a birthday card containing a slip of paper. I pulled it out and read it aloud: *"This gift certificate enrolls the bearer in 'Spring Break Socks!' at A Stitch in Time."*

Hatcher's eyes met mine across the table. So this was what Ella had been all mysterious about at Freeman Farm yesterday.

"We're going to take knitting lessons!" my mother said, her Texas twang growing twangier as her excitement bubbled over. "The class starts tonight. I thought it would be something fun we could do together. You know, a little mother-daughter bonding time."

My eyes slid over to where my cousin Mackenzie was sitting. We'd barely had time to say hello since she'd arrived late last night. She smirked at me. Mackenzie had turned thirteen just last week, and when I called to wish her a happy birthday, she told me that her mother had enrolled the two of them in a yoga class as part of her present. The whole mother-daughter bonding thing must kick in automatically when you become a teenager, like zits or something.

"You and I haven't had much time to spend together since the move," my mother continued.

She was right about that. I'd been busy with swim team and school and helping out at the bookshop, and between her full-time college classes, part-time job as receptionist at the Starlite Dance Studio, plus the fact that there are five of us Lovejoy kids, my mother had been spread a little thinner than usual lately.

I reached into the gift bag and pulled out two skeins of pool blue yarn and a pair of knitting needles.

"I thought it would be a nice way to support Ella's new business venture too, Little O," my mother added, her voice trailing off as she sensed my lack enthusiasm.

Little O was what she used to call me when I was, well, little. Which I hadn't been for a long time. It's short for "Little Owl," because I was a night owl back then and never wanted to go to bed. My mother even knitted matching sweaters for us with owls on the front and our initials on the back: L. O. for me, and M. O.—Mama Owl—for her.

Across the table, Hatcher was frowning at me.

"Uh, yeah, mom, I'm sure it will be fun," I chirped as brightly as I could. But knitting was her thing, not mine. On a scale of one to ten, my interest in learning how to rub two sticks together and make socks was about minus a zillion.

"The class meets in the evenings," my mother continued. "I figured that would give you and Mackenzie plenty of time together during the day. And Ella says we'll each have a finished pair of socks by the end of the week."

"Awesome!" said Mackenzie, and I shot her a look.

My mother turned to her. "Why don't you join us, sweetheart? My treat."

My cousin's fork paused halfway to her mouth. "Uh, that's okay, Aunt Dinah. I'm happy just to hang out here with Lauren and Pippa."

"Yay!" cried Pippa, bouncing in her seat.

"Nonsense," my mother said. "I'll call Ella right away. I'm sure there's room for you in the class. It will be fun!"

Now I was the one with a smirk on my face.

"I wish I could take knitting lessons," said Lauren enviously, looking up from her book. Breakfast was the only time my bookworm sister was allowed to read at the table. Another Nancy Drew, I noticed: *The Secret of the Old Clock.*

"You're taking dance right now, sweetie," my mother told her. "We can do a knitting class together another time."

"Open my prethent next!" Pippa demanded, plucking a package wrapped in bright pink paper from the pile and handing it to me.

"Wow, thanks!" I told her when I opened it. She'd given me a photo of herself in a homemade frame made of Popsicle sticks covered in purple glitter.

"Belinda helped me," Pippa explained. "You can put it on your drether, and that way you won't ever forget me."

Hatcher kicked me under the table. I studiously avoided looking at him.

"No chance of that, Pipster," I said solemnly.

Lauren gave me a bookmark with an owl on it—she must have overheard me admiring it at the bookshop—and my brothers had pooled their resources on a gift certificate to the sporting goods store in West Hartfield.

"For those new swim goggles you've been wanting," said Danny.

I beamed at my family. "Thanks, everybody!"

"Wait, there's one more," said Mackenzie, and passed me a small box she'd been hiding on her lap.

"Owl earrings!" I cried happily. I don't wear much jewelry—it's too much of a pain taking it on and off all the time, what with swim practice and everything—but these were really pretty. The flat, round disks were made of sterling silver, and each one had a great horned owl etched onto it, tufted ears and all.

"Nice," said my mother as I put them on and showed them off. "Your cousin knows you well."

"Maybe they'll bring you luck in finally spotting one," Mackenzie added.

"I hope so." Adding an owl to my life list—the list all birders keep of the different species they spot—was something I'd been trying to do practically forever.

My father placed another platter of sourdough waffles on the table, and my brothers and I dove for them. I managed to snag two.

"Truly!" scolded my mother. "Leave some for the rest of us."

"How come you aren't yelling at Hatcher and Danny? They've had, like, four each already!"

Across the table from me, Hatcher held up five fingers and grinned.

My mother sighed. "I swear, it's like feeding a pack of

wolves." She spiked a fork into one of my waffles and whisked it onto Mackenzie's plate.

"Hey!" I protested.

"You have a guest," she said.

"It's just Mackenzie!"

"Truly, you know better than to sass your mother," my father chided.

"Sorry," I mumbled, not feeling sorry at all. This was my birthday breakfast, and I'd been a good sport—well, sort of—about postponing it. What was wrong with making the most of it now that it was finally here?

"What was that?" my father replied, cupping his hand behind his ear.

"Sorry, *sir*," I corrected myself. Lieutenant Colonel Jericho T. Lovejoy was a stickler for protocol.

I slathered my waffle with butter, then drenched it with syrup.

Hatcher pretended to look shocked. "Have a little waffle with your syrup, why don't you?"

My mother took the pitcher away from me and passed it to Mackenzie. "This is real maple syrup from Freeman Farm."

"The place where you guys helped out at yesterday?" my cousin asked, perking up. She glanced over at me. "The one where—"

"*Yeah*," I said, giving her the stink eye. I could feel my face growing pink.

On the way home from helping the Freemans out yesterday, I'd texted Mackenzie about Scooter's ambush. She was at the airport in Chicago waiting for her connecting flight to Boston, and had called me back immediately demanding the gruesome details.

"Can't talk now. I'm in the car. I'll tell you more when you get here," I'd whispered, and hung up.

"Tell who what?" asked Hatcher, who had ears like a bat.

"Nothing."

I hadn't had a chance to tell Mackenzie more last night, though, because her flight ended up being delayed. She didn't arrive until nearly midnight, and thanks to daily doubles—the Spring Break camp I'd signed up for that had me at swim practice both morning and afternoon—I hadn't been allowed to go pick her up at Logan Airport.

"Are you kidding me?" I'd blurted when my father told me the news.

"I am not," he'd replied. "You made a commitment, and Lovejoys always honor their commitments. Coach Maynard is expecting you at the pool at oh-six hundred, and we won't get back until the wee hours."

Most of the time I didn't think swim practice was stupid. Swimming was one of my favorite things in the entire world, and usually there was no place I'd rather be than in the pool. But when it's your birthday, and your cousin who's your best friend and whom you haven't seen since Christmas is coming to visit, trust me, you'd think it was stupid too. My father's decision was a supreme act of parental unfairness, and I told him so. Then I asked—begged—him to make an exception for once.

"Sorry, Truly," said Mr. Military. "No means no."

"But Dad, it's my *birthday*."

"You girls will have all week to visit," he'd said stubbornly.

I'd tried to stay awake anyway until Mackenzie arrived, but between running around all day at Freeman Farm and the whole drama of my close encounter with Scooter Sanchez, my eyes slammed shut the minute my head hit the pillow.

When I woke up, it was morning, and Mackenzie was snoring lightly a few feet away. My grandparents' house was huge, and there were actually two extra bedrooms for guests, but we'd wanted to be together so I'd set up the air mattress for her in my room instead.

I'd pulled on my swimsuit and sweats, then tapped her on the shoulder. "Hey."

One of Mackenzie's eyelids had fluttered open. "Huh?"

"I'm going to swim practice."

"S'nice," she'd murmured, then rolled over and went back to sleep.

And now here we were at the breakfast table, and she was about to spill the beans about my first kiss. But she took the hint, thank goodness.

"—the one where you spent your birthday?" she finished smoothly.

"Truly was a good sport," my father said, patting my shoulder.

"She sure was," said Mackenzie, grinning broadly. I gave her the stink eye again.

"Happy day-after-your-actual-birthday, fellow namesake," said my aunt, breezing in through the back door just then. She leaned down to kiss my cheek. The two of us are both named after the first Truly Lovejoy, and one of the best things about moving to Pumpkin Falls had been getting to know Aunt True better. She'd always been the family free spirit, a world traveler who rarely stayed anywhere very long, but ever since Black Monday she'd given up her "wandering ways," as Gramps and Lola put it, and moved here to Pumpkin Falls to help run the bookshop with my father. She was totally in his court.

"Nothing's more important than family," she'd said simply, when I asked her about it once.

Leaning down again, my aunt took my empty plate away and replaced it with two brightly wrapped packages.

Across the table, Pippa started bouncing in her seat again. "Open them! Open them!"

I did. Inside the bigger of the two was the bird feeder I'd wanted. I looked up at my aunt, mystified. "How did you—"

"A little bird told me," she quipped, and everyone groaned. "Sorry, I couldn't resist. It was your mother."

"Did you think we didn't notice all the hints?" said my mother, and suddenly I felt ashamed of the way I'd reacted to her present.

"Thanks, Aunt True—and thank you for the knitting lessons too, Mom," I said, jumping up to hug them both.

The second package was from Gramps and Lola. It was a book, of course. When your grandparents own a bookstore, you pretty much know what to expect every time Christmas and birthdays roll around.

"*Owls of North America*," Mackenzie read the title aloud over my shoulder in her Texas twang. "Sounds like a real page-turner."

I grinned. "Shut up."

Mackenzie loved to tease me about being a birder, but I didn't really mind. She said it was an obsession, and she was probably right. I couldn't help it, though—birds fascinated me, especially owls. The fact that I hadn't yet spotted one wasn't for lack of trying. The last time there was a full moon, I'd dragged my father out into the woods to look for owls. We'd had fun, but unfortunately that's all we'd had, and I returned home without anything to add to my life list.

My father checked his watch. "Boys, you'd better hit the road if you don't want to be late to wrestling practice." As Hatcher and Danny got up from the table, he turned to me. "Truly, you and Mackenzie may be excused as well."

"Why don't you show Mackenzie around the house, and

then take her downtown," my mother suggested. She crossed the kitchen and kissed my father. "Thanks for breakfast, handsome. I'll be at my desk if anyone needs me."

My mother's "desk" these days was the dining room table. She'd pretty much taken it over since going back to college.

"Be sure and come see me at the bookstore," Aunt True told my cousin and me.

"We will," I assured her.

My father looked over at my little sisters. "And you two young ladies have KP this morning," he said, which was military shorthand for "Kitchen Patrol."

"But it's Truly's turn to do the dishes!" Lauren protested.

"The birthday girl doesn't do dishes," I reminded her.

Pippa frowned. "No fair! Yethterday wath your birthday, not today!"

Leaving them to argue their case to Dad, I escaped to the front hall. Mackenzie was right behind me. She grabbed my arm the second we were out of earshot. "Now, tell me about the kiss!"

CHAPTER 4

"Please," I groaned. "I just ate."

"That bad, huh?" Her blue eyes sparkled with anticipation. "I want all the gory details! Scooter's the one you had to dance with at that cotillion thing, right?"

Of course she had to bring that up. "That cotillion thing" was the mandatory dance class at Daniel Webster School that I'd been forced to enroll in right after we moved to Pumpkin Falls. It was part of this stupid town tradition that had its grand finale at the annual Winter Festival, when the whole school participated in an exhibition dance. I'd gotten stuck with Scooter for my partner. In the end, it wasn't all that horrible, especially after the two of us won the "most improved" award, which came with a cash prize of $25 each. And of course there'd been that dance with Calhoun. . . . Still, dancing would never top the list of things that I was good at, or that I liked to do. Especially not with Scooter Sanchez.

"So c'mon, Truly, what happened?" Mackenzie begged.

I made a face, then gave her a play-by-play account of Scooter's surprise ambush behind the Freeman's barn. I left out the part where Calhoun saw us, though. If Mackenzie suspected that I maybe, even a teeny tiny bit, might like Calhoun, she'd pounce on it like an owl on a field mouse. I'd never hear the end of it.

"So that's it?" she said when I finished. "Scooter just walked away?"

"Uh-huh."

"He didn't try and talk to you later, or call you?"

I shook my head.

"Weird! Well, we have all week to get to the bottom of it."

"Or not," I said. Analyzing Scooter Sanchez's romantic intentions was not my idea of a fun way to spend Spring Break. "How about we drop the whole subject instead, and I give you a tour?"

She sighed. "Fine."

We started in the living room.

"Mom told me to be sure and take lots of pictures," my cousin told me, pulling out her cell phone and snapping one of the baby grand. "Nice piano. Are you taking lessons again?"

"Maybe this summer. I haven't had time yet, between swim team and everything else that's happened."

"Everything else" meaning uprooting from Texas and moving across the country, starting over at a new school, stupid cotillion, stupid math tutoring, helping out at the bookstore, solving two mysteries, and falling into a frozen river. It had been a busy winter.

"Are those the ancestors you told me about?" asked Mackenzie, pointing to the oil portraits that flanked the piano.

"Yep. That one's Nathaniel Daniel Lovejoy, and the other is his wife, Prudence."

"Nathaniel's the one who founded Lovejoy College, right?" said Mackenzie, taking another picture. "The one with the big stone pumpkin on his grave?"

I nodded. I'd sent her a picture of it that day of the field trip to the cemetery. Mackenzie loved all the oddball stuff here in Pumpkin Falls.

"Yeah, and he named a mountain and a lake after himself while he was at it," I added. "It's kind of embarrassing."

"At least he used his last name," my cousin pointed out. "It could have been worse." She struck a pose and summoned her fake radio announcer voice. "And now, a word from Nathaniel Daniel Lovejoy, founder of Nathaniel Daniel College."

We both burst out laughing. My ancestor's parents must have been total morons to pick a pair of rhyming names like that. Didn't it occur to them how much the poor kid would get teased at school? Even Pippa called him "Nathaniel Daniel looks like a spaniel."

Mackenzie stared up at the painting. "You weren't kidding when you said he has a big nose."

The "Lovejoy proboscis," as Gramps had dubbed it, was a topic of great concern at the moment for my brother Hatcher. Gramps inherited Nathaniel Daniel's nose, and so did Dad, and now Hatcher was convinced that he was starting to follow in their footsteps. At least once a week he asked me if I thought his nose had gotten bigger. I said yes, of course, just to torture him, but to be honest I didn't think it looked any different.

"This is such a cool house," Mackenzie said, gazing around.

I nodded. Coming here for our annual visits used to be the high point of the year for me. When you grow up in a military family, you move a lot, and this was the one place I could count on never to change.

My cousin gave an envious sigh as we started upstairs. "You're so lucky you get to live here."

"Except for the fact that it's in Pumpkin Falls, not Austin."

"What's so bad about Pumpkin Falls?"

I shrugged. "It's not that it's bad, it's just—not Austin."

I still really missed Texas.

I skipped the squeaky stair, but I'd forgotten to warn Mackenzie about it, and it let out a screech as she stepped on it. "That's the original Truly," I told her, pointing to the portrait hanging above it.

"J. T.!" my mother called from the dining room before I could continue.

My dad emerged from the kitchen, frowning. "What?"

"Could you maybe find time this week to fix that stair, darlin'?" my mother asked, poking her head out into the hall. "I hate to keep nagging you, but it's driving me crazy. I'm trying to work in here, and every time anyone goes upstairs or down, all I hear is *squeak squeak squeak*."

My mother was working on a research project for her American History for Educators class at Lovejoy College. Professor Rusty was the instructor. Professor Rusty's real name was Erastus Peckinpaugh, and he was my Aunt True's boyfriend. At least we suspected he was her boyfriend. Nobody was really quite sure. Ever since the Valentine's Day dance, when my friends and I delivered his long-lost love letters to Aunt True, Professor Rusty had been spending a lot of time hanging around the bookstore with a hopeful expression on his face, and my aunt had been acting a little odd.

My father flapped his good hand. "Put it on the honey-do list, and I'll get to it soon, I promise," he told her. "I'm late for a meeting at the bookstore."

"It's been on the list for weeks," my mother grumbled as he disappeared back into the kitchen.

"What's a 'honeydew' list?" asked Mackenzie.

"Oh, you know, 'Honey do this, honey do that.'" My mother smiled. "I'm guessing Teddy has one too."

Teddy was my uncle Teddy, Mackenzie's father. He was one of my mother's six Texas brothers.

Mackenzie smiled back. "Yeah, I'm pretty sure he does too."

My mother went back to her research, and I turned to the portrait again. "So, as I was saying, that's the original Truly Lovejoy."

"The one you and your Aunt True are named after?"

I nodded.

"She's pretty."

"You think?"

"She kind of looks like you."

I knew she meant it as a compliment, but I didn't see the resemblance at all. The original Truly and I were both tall, a fact I know because it said so on her German passport, a faded document that was hanging in a frame in the upstairs hall. Aside from her name, though—which clearly said "Trudy" and not "Truly," so the idiot at U.S. customs had no excuse for messing it up and forever changing her legal name—I couldn't decipher the German script. Aunt True could. She'd lived all over the world and spoke half a dozen languages, and she translated the passport once for me. The original Trudy/Truly came from a town called Lutterhausen in Germany, shortly before the Civil War. She had just turned eighteen when she arrived in the United States. Aunt True and I both beat her by two inches, heightwise, but she was still nearly six feet, which was really tall for a woman back in those days. The passport described her as "*schlank*," which my aunt told me means "slender," and her hair and eyes were listed as "*braun*"—"brown," like both of ours. There was no mention of freckles, though, and I hadn't detected any on her portrait. I, on the other hand, had a generous helping of them.

Mackenzie took a selfie of the two of us standing in front of the portrait.

"Perfect!" she said, showing it to me. "We look adorable."

Adorable? More like an ostrich and a finch, I thought. If my cousin were a bird, she'd be something small and cute, for sure. Definitely a finch, or better, a painted bunting, like the one I'd spotted last year in Texas and that had birders in New York City all atwitter a while back when one was seen in Brooklyn. Colorful as a box of crayons, the painted bunting was one of the most eye-catching species in North America. It fit Mackenzie to a tee.

"Cameron will love this," my cousin said, tapping on her cell phone as she sent off the picture. "He still can't believe your name is actually Truly."

Her phone vibrated almost immediately in response. She read the incoming text and smiled. "Cameron says hey."

I rolled my eyes. "Hey back."

We climbed up a few more steps.

"Who's that?" Mackenzie asked, pointing to another portrait. My grandparents' entire stairwell was lined with long-gone Lovejoys.

"Matthew Lovejoy," I told her. "He was Truly's husband.

She met him just a few weeks after she arrived in New York. He was staying at the hotel where she got a job as a maid, and it was love at first sight. At least Gramps told me once that's how the story goes."

My cousin sighed. "That's so romantic! I can see why she fell for Matthew. He's really cute." She took another picture. "Is that a uniform he's wearing?"

I nodded. "He was a soldier in the Union army." Our family's military tradition went way back, lots farther than just my dad. Matthew fought in the Civil War, and there were Lovejoys who fought in the Revolutionary War too.

Mackenzie wrinkled her nose. "The Union army was the Northern one, right?"

I grinned. History had never been my cousin's thing. "Yeah."

We continued upstairs, pausing at each of the remaining Lovejoys so Mackenzie could take their pictures. "What's that jingle you told me that you made up, to help remember their names?"

"Obadiah, Abigail, Jeremiah, Ruth," I singsonged, pointing to each one in turn. "Matthew, Truly, Charity, and Booth. But it only works going downstairs."

We decided that Mackenzie should finish unpacking before I gave her the rest of the tour. I'd cleared out a couple of drawers and made space in my closet for her stuff, but there still wasn't enough room.

"You're only here for a week!" I exclaimed, emptying another drawer. I jammed the clothes it contained under my bed. "Did you have to bring everything you own with you?"

"Just because you always dress like you're on your way to a wrestling match doesn't mean I have to," she said loftily.

I glanced down at the ratty sweats I'd thrown on after swim practice this morning. She had a point.

The corner of her mouth quirked up in a smile. "Your room looks good, at least."

Up until now Mackenzie had seen my bedroom only on her computer screen, when the two of us videoconferenced. It was Aunt True's bedroom when she was growing up, and it had always been called the "Blue Room," since it was decorated in blue and white. I had a blue bedroom at our old house back in Austin, too—our old new house, really, because we'd only lived there for a few months before we moved here to Pumpkin Falls. Mackenzie had helped me pick out the perfect shade of aqua for its walls: Mermaid. I still dreamed about that color sometimes, and I'd been thinking of asking Gramps and Lola if they'd let me repaint my room here, too. *If* we stayed, that was, which it looked like we were going to, now that the bookstore was on more solid footing.

After Mackenzie finished unpacking, I showed her the rest of the second floor.

"Six bedrooms and three bathrooms?" she said, incredulous. "This place is huge!"

"And that's just the second floor," I pointed out. "There are more in the attic."

"Really? Wow."

"People had big families back when they built the house. At least that's what Gramps told me."

Mackenzie gave me a sidelong glance. "Even bigger than the Magnificent Seven?"

That was what my father called our family. It was the title of his favorite old movie, and the theme song was the ringtone on his cell phone. I nodded. "Even bigger than the Magnificent Seven."

Mackenzie was an only child, and I knew sometimes she envied the fact that I had so many brothers and sisters. That was because she didn't actually have to live with them.

We made a quick detour to Lauren's room so my cousin could say hi to all of my younger sister's pets.

"I'd forgotten how many you have!" Mackenzie said as she made the rounds.

"Nibbles is my hamster—" Lauren began.

"And Thumper ith the bunny, and Methuthelah ith the turtle," Pippa finished.

"I want a kitten too, but Mom and Dad keep saying no," Lauren said.

"No kittens for me, either," Mackenzie sympathized. "Hooper wouldn't like it."

Hooper was my cousin's beagle. He was old as the hills

and always rolling in gross things, but she loved him anyway.

Pippa tugged on her sleeve. "Want to play Barbieth with me?"

"Um, we've got plans, Pipster," I said. "Maybe later."

We finally managed to extricate ourselves, and I led Mackenzie to the door at the end of the hallway that led to the third-floor stairs. "If you thought Lauren's room was kind of stinky, brace yourself. This is where Hatcher and Danny live."

Mackenzie followed me up the steep, narrow staircase that led to my brothers' lair. "Whew!" she exclaimed, waving her hand in front of her face when we reached the top.

"Told you so. Total man cave. That's why I mostly don't come up here. What is it about teenage boys, anyway? Their rooms always smell like a cross between sweaty gym socks and wet dog."

My cousin giggled.

"So Aunt True told me that back in the old days, the maids and hired help lived up here," I continued. "Check out their bedrooms."

I showed her a row of closet-size rooms that branched off the big, central, open area my brothers had commandeered for their headquarters.

"Are you kidding me?" Mackenzie's eyes widened. "Where are the closets?"

Nowadays, my grandparents used the tiny rooms for storage, but back when there were servants living in the house, there would have been just enough room for a twin bed and a small chair or night table. At least there were windows.

"People in those days didn't have many clothes, and servants had even fewer," I explained. "Gramps said they just hung everything on hooks." I pointed to a trio lining one of the walls next to the door.

I watched as my cousin absorbed this information.

"Not exactly Mackenzie-friendly, right?" I said with a grin.

She stuck out her tongue at me. "Hey, I can't help it if I've gotta have my closet space." Looking around, she added, "Where are the bathrooms?"

I held up a single finger, and she gave me another incredulous look. "Are you kidding me? *One?* For all those servants?"

"There probably wasn't even indoor plumbing back in the early days," I told her. "Gramps said that when he was a kid, there was still an old outhouse behind the barn."

"Eew."

"No kidding."

"So is there an attic too, or is this it?" Mackenzie asked.

"This is it, mostly. There's a little more storage space through there." I waved a hand at a door at the far end of Hatcher and Danny's lair.

"Can I see?"

"Sure."

Someone had left the light on inside. Lauren, most likely. She'd been spending a lot of time up here lately, rooting

around through all the old stuff. There was a lot of it—
Lovejoys hated throwing anything out. The attic was where
Lauren had found all of Aunt True's childhood books,
including the set of Nancy Drew mysteries, and a bunch of
other relics belonging to earlier generations of ancestors. She
kept showing up at the dinner table dressed in the strangest
outfits. White leather gloves that nearly reached to her arm-
pits, moth-eaten shawls, hats with veils, that sort of thing.
Mom thought it was funny, but my brothers and I thought it
was weird, and told Lauren so.

Mackenzie surveyed the scattered jumble of boxes and
trunks and moldering magazines and random pieces of broken furniture that littered the cramped space. A dressmaker's
dummy sporting a sun hat leaned against an old armchair
with the stuffing hanging out of it; a battered table covered
with dust held an old birdcage, one of those ancient record
players you had to wind up to play, and some fishing tackle;
off in the shadows toward the eaves were a bicycle and an
ancient wicker baby carriage and more boxes than I could
count.

"Look at all this cool old stuff!" Mackenzie took another
picture.

I snorted. "You and Lauren should start a club."

"How old is this house, anyway?"

"1769. It was built the same year that Nathaniel Daniel
founded the college."

"This is seriously amazing," she said. "I can't wait to tell Cameron all about it."

Cameron will love this, Cameron will love that, I thought. I could tell I was going to get really sick of hearing about Mr. Perfect by the end of the week.

It was getting close to lunchtime, so I decided to save the rest of the house, including the barn turned garage and my grandmother's art studio above it, for later. "We'd better get going, if you want to see some of Pumpkin Falls before afternoon swim practice."

We stopped by my room to pick up our gear. Since Mackenzie was on a swim team back in Austin, I'd been given special permission from Coach Maynard to bring her along to practice this week at Spring Break camp.

"We can leave our stuff at the bookshop and pick it up right before practice," I said. "That way we don't have to come all the way home for it. Oh, and I have one more thing to show you," I added as we fished our jackets out of the front hall closet.

"What?"

I led my cousin to the tiny phone booth under the stairs and opened the door. "This."

My grandparents were just about the only people on the planet who still had a landline, and the dank closet with the faded, peeling wallpaper was where they kept their ancient rotary phone. My dad claimed it was the same one that was there when he was a kid.

"Gramps and Lola are true Yankees," he liked to tell us. "Thrifty to the core. You know your grandfather's favorite saying, right? 'Use it up, wear it out, make it do, or do without.'"

The phone booth was one place in the house that I could certainly do without. "I hate it when I have to take a call in here," I told Mackenzie.

She poked her head in and wrinkled her nose at the musty smell. "Yeah, but it's still kind of cool. That phone is totally retro—check out that vintage dial!"

I closed the door. "Um, yeah. My point exactly."

Glancing over at another door just beyond the phone closet, Mackenzie asked, "Where does that go?"

Now that I thought about it, there were two places in the house that I could do without.

"The basement," I replied. "Trust me, you don't want to go down there."

"Sure I do! I want to see everything!"

I sighed. "Don't say I didn't warn you."

I watched from the safety of the hallway as she tiptoed down and took a quick peek around. Quick, because the basement was always freezing cold, for one thing—the house still had its original dirt floor and stone foundation—and quick, because, well, my brothers didn't call it the spider farm for nothing.

I wasn't afraid of a whole lot of things, but spiders

combined with my grandparents' dark, creepy basement? I shuddered.

"Okay, you were right," Mackenzie said, clattering upstairs again a moment later.

I closed the door firmly behind her. "We definitely don't need to go down there again."

CHAPTER 5

"This whole place is like a movie set," Mackenzie said happily a few minutes later, as we headed down Hill Street into town. "Fade in to Pumpkin Falls," she intoned, slipping into her fake radio announcer voice again, "a small, charming New England college town—"

"Emphasis on *small*," I added.

"—complete with historic houses," she continued, ignoring me, "a church with a steeple that I want a tour of, by the way, so don't forget, a village green, a world-famous waterfall—"

I snorted. "World famous? Right."

"—and crowning it all, a spectacular covered bridge."

Snapping pictures right and left, my cousin continued her breathless narration all the way to the bookstore, where she made me stand under the LOVEJOY'S BOOKS sign so she could take yet another picture for Mr. Perfect.

"It's Miss Marple!" she cried when we finally went inside.

My grandparents' golden retriever, who'd been napping on her dog bed by the sales counter, heaved herself up and trotted over, tail wagging.

"Take a picture of us," Mackenzie ordered, passing me her cell phone.

"Greetings and salutations, girls!" said Aunt True, emerging from the back office. "You're just in time for a snack."

"Pumpkin whoopie pies?" asked Mackenzie hopefully.

My heart sank. I'd sung the praises of our bookshop's signature treat to my cousin, but, to be perfectly honest, I was kind of tired of pumpkin whoopie pies. They'd certainly proven a success—my mother says Aunt True is a marketing genius, and one of her bright ideas was to create a treat designed to lure customers into the store. The strategy had worked, as people often stopped by for a whoopie pie and rarely left without buying something. But I'd eaten so many in the past month that I didn't think I could choke down another one.

"Sorry, Mackenzie, but I decided to switch it up in honor of Maple Madness," my aunt told her. "May I present . . . Bookshop Blondies!" She pulled a tray out from beneath the sales counter and whipped off the tea towel that was covering it.

"Mmm," said Mackenzie, reaching for what looked like a brownie, only lighter in color. I took one too.

"Oh man, these are *delicious*," said my cousin, grabbing a second one before she'd even finished her first.

"That would be the secret ingredient," Aunt True told her, looking pleased.

I paused midbite. One of my aunt's last secret ingredients had been yak milk.

"Maple sugar," she continued, and I relaxed. "I'm going to enter them into the Maple Madness Bake-Off."

The annual Bake-Off was another Pumpkin Falls tradition. From what I heard, the competition could get pretty heated, which was kind of ridiculous, especially since there weren't any prizes. Just a blue ribbon and stupid Maple Madness Bake-Off winner bragging rights. But that was Pumpkin Falls for you.

There was a commotion in the back corner of the store just then, and my aunt looked over and sighed. "If you have time, girls, maybe you could help Belinda," she said. "We're just about ready to send another shipment to Namibia."

A couple of weeks ago my aunt had come up with another marketing idea. One of my grandparents' Peace Corps projects was building a library for the school in the Namibian village where they're staying, and Aunt True decided that it would be fun to help fill its shelves—drumming up a little extra business for our store while we were at it.

The Buy a Book, Send a Book campaign invited every customer who bought a book to buy a second one to donate to the new school library in Africa. If they did, they got a 50 percent off coupon for their next purchase. My aunt downloaded photos of our grandparents with the village kids, and used the pictures to design a really cool flyer and poster for the window. She advertised the program on our website and in our newsletter, and she got the *Pumpkin Falls Patriot-Bugle* to write an article about it too. Everyone in town knew Gramps and Lola, and their faces, along with all those smiling village kids, had been like catnip to our customers. So far, we'd shipped off three big boxes of books for the new library.

"Add this to Miss Marple's Picks while you're at it, would you, Truly?" my aunt said, passing me a book. "Face out, please."

Miss Marple's Picks was another of my aunt's promotional ideas, a twist on the typical "staff picks" shelf that most bookstores offer. Not only had it increased sales, but it had also turned my grandparents' dog into a minor celebrity. Miss Marple had been profiled by newspapers all over the world, and she even had her own column in our bookshop newsletter (ghostwritten by Aunt True, of course).

Helping myself to another Bookshop Blondie, I made a quick detour to Miss Marple's Picks, where I shelved the book my aunt had given me. Then, trailing Mackenzie in my wake, I headed back to the children's section to help box up more books for Namibia.

"No, Harold, you may not go to Africa!" I heard Belinda

scolding as we approached. Her voice was oddly muffled, thanks to the fact that she was leaning so far down into an open cardboard box that only her bottom was visible. The bottom in question appeared to be covered with another pair of overalls—white ones this time.

"Um, anything we can do to help?" I asked.

Belinda straightened. Swiveling around, she removed one of her earbuds and thrust a kitten at my startled cousin. "Here," she ordered. "Hold Harold."

Mackenzie blinked in surprise, but did as she was told.

"Wait a minute!" Belinda peered more closely at her. "You're not Lauren!"

"Um, no," my cousin replied meekly. "I'm Mackenzie."

Belinda's eyes narrowed. "Mackenzie-from-Texas?"

My cousin nodded.

"Well, all right then." Fishing in the pocket of her overalls, Belinda pulled out a lint-covered breath mint and popped it in her mouth. Sucking on it loudly, she smiled. "Welcome to Pumpkin Falls."

"Uh, thanks?" said Mackenzie.

I smothered a grin, watching as my cousin got her first dose of Belinda Winchester. I'd told her lots of stories about our retired lunch lady turned bookseller, but it was nothing like having the full experience for herself.

Belinda had shucked off yesterday's orange and reverted to her purple phase. My cousin's eyes drifted from Belinda's white painter's overalls to the purple-and-white-striped turtle-neck underneath, then on down to the purple-and-white-striped socks and purple sneakers. For once, Belinda wasn't wearing a hat, and she'd combed her dandelion fluff of white hair into a semblance of neatness. Reaching into another pocket, she pulled out a long purple feather, which she twirled between her fingers, a thoughtful expression on her face.

To celebrate Belinda becoming a silent partner in the bookshop and taking over the mystery section—and to help her be a little more presentable to the public, I suspected—Aunt True had taken her on a clothes shopping spree a few weeks ago. This was a prime example of the blind leading the blind and a big mistake, if you asked me, which nobody ever did. Between the two of them, there was more "local color," as they called it in New England, here in our bookshop now than just about anywhere else in town.

"I have a gentleman caller," Belinda announced abruptly, with another twirl of her feather.

"Um, that's nice?" I replied, not quite sure what a gentle-man caller was. It couldn't be what it sounded like. Belinda was way too old to have a boyfriend.

The bell over the bookshop door jingled, and Belinda quickly thrust the feather behind her ear. She removed it just as quickly as my father came in.

He looked around as if he were expecting someone to salute. That rarely happened in Pumpkin Falls—never, actually—but my father hadn't completely transitioned out of military mode yet, even though he'd been a civilian for nine months.

"True?" he called, frowning.

My aunt emerged from behind the sales counter. "You rang?"

"Memphis is on the loose again," my father reported. "Lou said that Mr. Henry said that Ed Sanchez saw him just now sitting in one of the rocking chairs down on the General Store porch."

I was guessing that wasn't a sentence my father ever imagined coming out of his mouth back before Black Monday. Pumpkin Falls was the kind of place that did that to you, though.

Aunt True sighed. "Spring fever. Happens every year, no matter where we're living. I'll take care of it."

As she headed out to round up her cat, my father waved to Mackenzie and Belinda and me, then disappeared into the back office.

A few minutes later, as we were finishing up the shipment for Namibia, the bell over the bookshop door jangled again. Belinda's purple feather instantly swooped back behind her ear as someone bounded across the bookstore toward us.

"My angel!" cried the someone.

Beside me, Mackenzie gasped. "Is that—"

"Yep," I whispered. "Captain Romance, in the flesh."

Captain Romance was what Hatcher and I called Augustus Wilde. He was our town's resident celebrity, a romance writer whose books were published under his pen name, Augusta Savage. There were a whole bunch of his titles over in what my brother had dubbed the "shirtless men kissing beautiful women" section. Augustus liked to come in every few days and check on sales. He also liked to rearrange the shelves so that his books were facing out, and I'd caught him trying to sneak them in with Miss Marple's Picks too.

Augustus was kind of a pest.

"Purple becomes you, my sweet, like heather on the bonnie highland moors," he cooed to Belinda, who made a noise I'd never heard her make before. It sounded alarmingly like a giggle.

Wait a minute, I thought. Was Augustus Belinda Winchester's *gentleman caller*? No way! I turned toward my cousin and surreptitiously mimed sticking my finger down my throat. Mackenzie pressed her lips together, trying hard not to laugh.

"As I wrote in my latest *New York Times* best seller, *Sweet Savage Siren*, 'Spring is here, the sap is rising, and so is love,'" Augustus continued.

This time my cousin couldn't contain herself, and neither could I.

"Mock me if you must," said Augustus, clearly wounded by our laughter. He flipped back his mane of silver hair and struck a dramatic pose. Which was easy to do when you were wearing a purple cape. Eyeing it, it suddenly dawned on me why Belinda had been decking herself in purple lately. "But as the great poet Tennyson says, 'In the Spring a young man's fancy lightly turns to thoughts of love.'"

I stared at Augustus. Seriously? A young man's fancy? He had to be eighty if he was a day, and Belinda, well, Belinda had been ancient when my dad was a kid.

The bell over the door jingled once again. This time it was Aunt True, with Memphis tucked firmly under one arm. She crossed the bookstore to join us.

"Greeting and salutations!" she said to Augustus, then turned to me. "Truly, would you mind putting Memphis upstairs? I think there's less of a risk of him escaping again if I just keep him in my apartment for now."

I took the cat eagerly, glad for any excuse to be spared more senior citizen lovebird talk. Before I could head off, though, the bell over the door jangled yet again.

"Uh-oh," I muttered under my breath to Mackenzie, when I saw who it was. "Incoming."

"What is the meaning of this?" demanded Ella Bellow.

"Greetings and salutations to you, too!" Aunt True replied mildly. "What is the meaning of what?"

Ella shook a finger toward the front of the store. "That window, is what!"

Aunt True and I exchanged a glance. What could Ella

possibly find objectionable about our front window? The two of us had stayed up late Friday night to finish it in time for Maple Madness kickoff weekend, and we'd devoted an entire corner to welcoming Ella's new knitting shop to the neighborhood.

"You have *Maple Country Mufflers* on display!" Ella sputtered. "It's one of the exact same books I'm selling at A Stitch in Time—you're competing with me!"

"Have a Bookshop Blondie, Ella," my aunt said soothingly, scooping the tray off the sales counter and holding it out. "We'll take the book out of the window. It's nothing to get worked up about—I had no idea you were planning to stock it too. Competing with you is the farthest thing from our mind."

Somewhat mollified, Ella selected a treat. Her dark eyes gleamed as she spotted my cousin. "You must be Mackenzie."

My cousin nodded warily.

"I heard you were coming to town—"

"Told you this place was small," I whispered to Mackenzie.

"—and I want to know all about you."

Memphis squirmed in my arms as Ella began pumping Mackenzie for information. She might have retired as the Pumpkin Falls postmistress, but Ella Bellow was still in the full-time gossip business.

"I see Rusty has been spending a lot of time here at the bookshop lately," Ella said to my aunt when she was done extracting Mackenzie's age, height, grade in school, hobbies, favorite color (green), and parents' names and occupations.

Aunt True nodded. "Indeed."

My aunt likes to torment Ella by giving one-word answers to her "fishing expeditions," as she calls Ella's nosy interrogations.

"I suppose it's only natural, seeing as how he's still a bachelor and seeing as how you're still single. You two used to date back in high school, right?"

"Yes," said my aunt.

"The two of you aren't getting any younger, you know."

"No," agreed my aunt.

Ella's mouth pruned up, but Aunt True just smiled sweetly. I smothered a grin. My aunt was rapidly elevating her evasion technique to an indoor sport.

Ella tried a different tack. "Speaking of couples, you two aren't the only ones in town keeping company. I've noticed that Amelia Winthrop has been spending a great deal of time at the coin and stamp shop."

Really? I thought in surprise. I knew Lucas liked spending time with Bud Jefferson, but his mother did too?

"Interesting," was my aunt's only comment.

Nothing escaped Ella's eagle eye, it seemed. I was just glad she hadn't seen Scooter kissing me behind the Freemans' barn, or I'd be the one undergoing the third degree right now.

Before Ella could ask any more questions, the bell over

the bookshop door jangled once again, and Franklin Freeman came in hefting a large box.

"Need some help?" asked Aunt True.

As I started to follow her to the front of the store, Memphis twisted out of my arms and made a dash for freedom. In a furry flash of spring fever, he squeezed through the door just before it swung shut.

"Blast that cat!" My aunt put her hands on her hips and scowled.

"Mackenzie and I will round him up again, Aunt True," I told her.

My father emerged from the office. "What's going on out here?" he asked, then saw Franklin. "Oh good, more maple supplies. Those little jugs of syrup sold like hotcakes this weekend, and we're running low." Lovejoy's Books did a brisk business in "sidelines," the official term for all the stuff besides books that our store sells, and the merchandise from Freeman Farm was among our most popular. "Nice turnout at your place yesterday!" my father added, clapping my classmate on the back with his good hand. "Your parents must be pleased."

Franklin nodded. He didn't look pleased, though. He looked miserable.

"Is something the matter, son?" my father asked, peering at him.

"Someone's been stealing our sap!" Franklin blurted.

We all stared at him.

"You mean from the barn store?" I asked.

He shook his head. "Not syrup, *sap*! They're taking it right from our trees!"

Ella's dark eyes gleamed again. At last, a piece of gossip she could sink her teeth into!

"Bad blood—or should I say bad *sap*—right here in Pumpkin Falls," she said with a delighted shiver. "Imagine that!"

CHAPTER 6

Lucas Winthrop was in love with my cousin Mackenzie.

He might as well have fallen in love with my left shoe.

Mackenzie was oblivious, of course. She was too wrapped up in Mr. Perfect Cameron McAllister to notice someone else. Especially someone else like Lucas Winthrop.

Everything seemed normal at first when we got to the pool for afternoon practice. Mackenzie and I changed into our suits and went out onto the pool deck, where we started the warm-up stretches that Coach Maynard had posted on the whiteboard.

"Who's the kid who looks like a stalk of celery?" Mackenzie whispered as Lucas emerged from the men's locker room.

"Lucas Winthrop," I whispered back. "I told you about him, remember?"

I still sometimes felt the need to avert my eyes when I saw Lucas in a swimsuit. He was so skinny, it was painful.

"Oh yeah—helicopter mother."

Lucas went about seven shades of red when I introduced them.

"Uh . . . hi," he stuttered, then just stood there looking at Mackenzie, dazed.

"Okay, everyone in the water!" said Coach Maynard, clapping his hands. He flipped the whiteboard over to reveal the afternoon workout. I groaned. He obviously wasn't planning to go easy on us over Spring Break.

Everyone got into the pool except Lucas, who continued to stand rooted to the spot. He looked like he was going to throw up.

"What's the matter with you, Winthrop?" Coach frowned at him. "You'd better not barf on my pool deck!"

"I'm fine," Lucas squeaked, his voice shooting up an octave as he jolted out of his trance and scuttled into the water.

It was clear he was anything but, though. He kept lifting his goggles and peeking at Mackenzie, for one thing. He did it once right in the middle of one of his laps, and swallowed so much water that he almost choked. Coach Maynard had to fish him out with the pool's lifesaving hook.

When it finally dawned on me what was wrong with him, I almost laughed out loud.

Lucas was a nice guy and everything, but crushing on my cousin? There wasn't a girl on the face of the planet— well, in Pumpkin Falls, at least—who would describe Lucas as Mr. Perfect. Mr. Scrawny and Undersized was more like it. He didn't stand a chance.

Despite Lucas's erratic behavior, swim practice went well, and Coach Maynard singled Mackenzie out several times for praise. He told her he'd be proud to have her on our swim team if she lived in Pumpkin Falls, which I could tell pleased her.

"I think we can do something this week to put some polish on that flip turn of yours," he added with a wink. "We'll send you back to Texas all charged up and ready to go."

Later, in the locker room, Mackenzie brought up the subject of Lucas. "I know he's your friend and all, but what's with the way he stares at people?"

I smiled. At "people"? *You're the only one he was staring at*, I wanted to tell her, but we had a whole week together, and she'd eventually figure things out for herself. Meanwhile, there was no point depriving myself of the fun of watching the *Lucas in Love* show.

So all I said was, "He's actually really nice," and then changed the subject. "You want to stop by the General Store on the way home? We could get ice cream."

Lucas was lying in wait for us outside the rec center.

"Why, thank you," drawled Mackenzie, her voice all full of Texas honey as he sprinted over and held the door for us. "Aren't you the gentleman!"

I don't think Lucas's feet actually touched the pavement the entire length of Main Street.

When we reached Lou's Diner, the door flew open and Mrs. Winthrop popped out, like a bird from a cuckoo clock. She'd obviously been watching for her son. Lucas's mother kept him on a really tight leash and tended to panic if he was the least bit late for anything.

"There you are, sweetie!" she said. "I was beginning to get worried. You're usually so prompt."

Lucas looked like he wished the sidewalk would open up and swallow him. As Mackenzie and I said good-bye, his face flushed scarlet. His mother looked at him anxiously. "You're not coming down with a fever, are you?" She held the back of her hand to his forehead.

Spring fever, maybe, I thought, suppressing a smile. Could Augustus Wilde be right with all his poetic talk about springtime and rising sap? Was love bubbling up around Pumpkin Falls the way the sap was rising in the maple trees? The thought of maple trees made me think of Freeman Farm, and my smile faded. Between the sap theft and Scooter's ambush, I had plenty of reasons not to want to be reminded of that right now.

"We'd better get some chicken soup into you," Mrs. Winthrop added, hustling her son inside. "Bye, girls!"

Mackenzie and I continued on past the Starlite Dance Studio and Mahoney's Antiques and the Suds 'n Duds, then paused to look at the window display at the *Pumpkin Falls Patriot-Bugle*.

"This maple thing is a big deal around here, isn't it?" said Mackenzie.

"Everything's a big deal around here," I replied, eyeing today's headline: MAPLE MADNESS KICKOFF WEEKEND DRAWS RECORD CROWDS! From the newspaper's breathless coverage, you'd think alien life had been discovered on Mars.

We crossed the street to the General Store. Inside, I spotted Scooter and Calhoun at the ice cream counter. My stomach lurched. So much for not being reminded about Freeman Farm. I really wasn't ready to face either of my classmates again just yet.

Running into them was unavoidable, though, in a town the size of this one. *Might as well get it over with*, I thought glumly.

"Hey, guys," I muttered, and they turned around.

"Hey, Truly!" said Scooter, all smiles.

Calhoun didn't say a word. He didn't smile, either.

"This is my cousin Mackenzie," I told them, suddenly conscious of the fact that my damp hair was still plastered to my head. Mackenzie's hair was perfect, of course. She'd taken the time to blow-dry her strawberry blond Gifford curls—the very same kind that Pippa was born with—and they looked as perky as she did.

"Hello, boys!" My cousin's voice was dripping with Texas honey again, and she smiled the same Gifford sunflower smile at them that I see every day on my mother and Hatcher.

A funny expression settled over Scooter's face, somewhere between dazed and thunderstruck. It was a look I'd seen before. Quite recently, in fact. Lucas had been wearing it back at the pool. *Another one bites the dust*, I thought in amazement.

I didn't know whether to be annoyed, disgusted, or relieved. Annoyed, because even though I absolutely truly didn't care a speck for Scooter, it still hurt my pride a little to be passed over so quickly. Disgusted, because, well, Mackenzie and Scooter Sanchez? Eew. And relieved, because at least I wouldn't have to worry about Scooter trying to kiss me again. In the space of a split second, he'd transferred his affections to my cousin.

Mackenzie turned to Calhoun. "What did you say your name was?"

"Calhoun," he replied. "That's not my first name, though. My first name is Romeo."

My mouth dropped open. This was the first time I'd ever heard Calhoun voluntarily offer up this bit of information. He hated his real name.

Mackenzie laughed her breezy little laugh. "Romeo! I like it."

He smiled.

"Hey, did you guys talk to Franklin yet?" I asked, more by way of inserting myself into the conversation than anything else. It was becoming increasingly clear that with Mackenzie in town, I might as well be invisible. Which was kind of ironic, since for a long time after we first moved here I'd actually wished that I *were* invisible—"stealth mode," I called it. I didn't like sticking out, and stealth mode had always been my fallback position after one of our moves, which were numerous, since we were an active-duty military family until recently.

But I didn't like being ignored, either.

And if I were honest with myself, I'd have to admit I particularly didn't like being ignored by Mr. Romeo Calhoun.

At my question, my classmates managed to drag their eyes away from Mackenzie.

"No," said Scooter. "Why?"

I explained about the sap theft and how worked up Franklin had been about it.

"Sounds like a job for the Pumpkin Falls Private Eyes," said Calhoun, flicking me a glance.

My mouth dropped open again. Calhoun hated that name almost as much as he hated Romeo. He was the one who'd teased me the most about how dorky it was when I made it up last month after my friends and I got involved solving a couple of mysteries.

"Or not," he added coolly, looking away.

"I didn't know we were still a thing," I said. "The, uh, private eyes, I mean," I added quickly, when he glanced over at me again.

He shrugged.

"Great idea!" said Scooter, looking at my cousin to see what she thought. "It's pretty exciting, solving mysteries."

I could barely watch this. He was practically flexing his muscles for her.

"Cha Cha and Jasmine aren't here," I objected. "There is no Pumpkin Falls Private Eyes without the two of them."

"I could help," Mackenzie offered.

Scooter lit up at this suggestion. "Yeah!"

Everyone seemed to be looking to me to decide, even Calhoun. I stood there awkwardly, conscious of his gaze.

He's probably just eager to spend time with my cousin, I thought. *Same as Scooter.*

On the other hand, did it really matter, considering what hung in the balance? A major loss of sap—and the syrup it was turned into—could spell disaster for Franklin's family. Their farm really depended on all those maple sales. If there was something we could do to help, didn't we owe it to our friends to try?

"Well, okay, I guess," I said finally.

The four of us agreed to meet at my house the next morning after swim practice. From there we'd head to Freeman Farm to examine the scene of the crime.

"We'll tell Lucas on our way home," said Scooter as we took our ice cream cones outside and headed to the rocking chairs lining the General Store's porch.

The sun dipped behind the trees and the wind began to pick

up. Mackenzie shivered. "Y'all are nuts, eating ice cream in this weather," she said, but I noticed she didn't stop licking her cone.

"Maple *wal*nuts, " I quipped, and my friends all groaned obligingly.

A few minutes later Scooter and Calhoun took off for Lou's, and Mackenzie and I started up the hill for home.

"You're really lucky, you know, getting to live here," she said.

I grunted. "You told me that already. I'd still trade it for Austin in a hot second, though."

"Seriously? Why?"

It was hard to explain. I didn't hate Pumpkin Falls the way I did when we first moved here—it was growing on me, in fact—but it didn't feel like home yet, either. And life in Austin seemed so simple in comparison, especially right now. There were no mixed-up feelings about Romeo Calhoun in Austin.

We turned off Hill Street onto Maple, and Mackenzie suddenly stopped in her tracks. "Whoa!" she said, pointing at a tree branch overhead. "Is that what I think it is?"

I looked up. Peering through the dusk, I stared at the large bird perched on the limb above us. It stared back, unblinking. "Uh, yeah," I replied, stunned.

It was an owl.

Mackenzie whipped out her cell phone and began furiously snapping pictures. "Cameron won't believe this! What kind of owl is it?"

"A barred owl," I whispered. I'd seen only about a zillion pictures of them, including one in the new book that Gramps and Lola had given me for my birthday. "Scientific name *Strix varia*; native to North America; also known as the hoot owl. It's the only owl in the eastern United States whose eyes are brown, not orange or yellow."

Brown eyes just like mine, I thought, transfixed.

"Well, aren't you just a fountain of information," drawled my cousin, still snapping away.

The owl didn't seem in any hurry to leave. It posed obligingly as Mackenzie continued to take pictures, and then, after a minute or two, finally spread its wings. Flapping once, it swooped away over our heads.

My heart squeezed tight with happiness as I watched its silent flight. I'd never seen anything more beautiful in my entire life.

Mackenzie clutched my arm. "How cool was that?" she squealed as we watched the owl glide into a thicket of trees across the road and disappear.

"Unbelievably cool!" I squealed back. Even as I said the words, though, I could feel a sour aftertaste of disappointment curdling my joy.

Joy, because finally—*finally*—after so many years of trying, I'd seen an owl in the wild!

Disappointment, because Mackenzie was the one who'd spotted it, not me.

It shouldn't have mattered, but somehow it did. I followed my cousin home, feeling deflated.

This was almost worse than yesterday's kiss.

And being overlooked by a boy I might actually like.

I was pretty sure I wanted to go back to being twelve again.

CHAPTER 7

"Directly into the shower, boys," my mother said, pointing to the back stairs as Hatcher and Danny barged into the kitchen.

"Something smells good!" said Danny, sniffing the air appreciatively.

"It sure isn't you!" I retorted, backing away. There was nothing worse than post–wrestling practice brothers.

"I want your dirty clothes in the wash too," my mother continued. "All of them. I was upstairs earlier today and found things lurking under your beds that could have walked to the laundry room all by themselves."

My brothers laughed.

"I'm serious," said my mother, putting her hands on her hips. But she was smiling, too. She shook the wooden spoon she was holding for emphasis. "No roast chicken unless you—and your clothes—are spotless."

Hearing this threat, my brothers quickly trotted off.

"Whew!" Mackenzie held her nose as they wafted past.

"And you keep saying you wish you had brothers," I reminded her.

"Truly, would you mind popping next door and feeding Bilbo?" My mother turned back to the stove. She was stirring something. Mashed potatoes, from the looks of it. Dinner couldn't come soon enough for me, despite our recent ice cream break.

"Who's Bilbo?" asked my cousin.

"A ferret," I told her. "Our neighbors are in Bermuda for Spring Break and we're taking care of him."

"That's a funny name for a ferret," Mackenzie said.

"They named him after Bilbo Baggins in *The Hobbit*," I explained. "Because he likes to explore."

Technically, my sister Lauren was the one who was supposed to be ferret-sitting. She was the big animal lover in the family. Me? If it had feathers and wings, I was all over it. Fur or scales? Not so much—although I had to admit I'd taken a shine to Miss Marple. Probably because she'd taken a shine to me. I seemed to be her favorite Lovejoy, at least while Gramps and Lola were away.

"Where's Lauren?" I asked my mother. "She's the one in charge of Bilbo."

"She and Pippa are still at Belinda's."

Belinda's Spring Break camp kicked off this afternoon. My sisters both whined so much about the fact that I got to have

Mackenzie come visit that Belinda offered to do something just for them. Nobody was exactly sure what—arts and crafts projects like Pippa's glitter and Popsicle stick frame, maybe, or a little baking, maybe. A whole lot of kittens, that was for sure.

I turned to Mackenzie. "Want to come with me?"

She shook her head. "Mind if I skip it? I'm a little jet-lagged, and I should probably call my parents. I promised I'd check in today."

"No problem."

She headed upstairs, and I grabbed my barn jacket from its hook by the kitchen door and went back outside.

The house next door looked a lot like my grandparents' house, except that the shutters and front door were painted black instead of green. I was guessing it was built around the same time that Nathaniel Daniel built ours.

The Mitchells had been Gramps and Lola's neighbors for as long as I could remember. They both worked at Lovejoy College. They didn't have any kids of their own, but thanks to their jobs—they were both professors—there were always lots of students hanging out at their house.

Not this week, though.

I made a short detour to fill our bird feeders and top off the water in the birdbath. Gramps left me with a list of instructions for caring for his "feathered friends," as he called them, and I'd been really good about keeping up with everything.

Thinking about his list of instructions reminded me that I needed to add "barred owl" to my life list tonight. Mine was still pretty measly compared to my grandfather's, but then he'd been keeping his a lot longer than I had.

I collected the mail from the Mitchells' mailbox, then fished the spare key out from under the welcome mat by the back door. Not the most original place to keep a key, but the fact was, hardly anybody locked their doors here in Pumpkin Falls. Gramps and Lola went to Mexico for a vacation one winter a few years ago and accidentally left their house unlocked the entire month they were away! They were also the ones who kept the bookstore cash inside a hollowed-out trigonometry textbook—I guess they figured nobody in their right mind would think of stealing that. Dad about had a fit when he found out. One of the first things he did when he took over the store was open a proper bank account.

Inside, I plopped the mail into the basket on the kitchen counter, then crossed the room to the enormous cage where Bilbo spent most of his time. Mr. Mitchell was crazy about ferrets—"the smartest pet imaginable!" he liked to boast—and Bilbo was completely spoiled. He had all sorts of toys and plastic tubes to run around in, plus a little ferret-size hammock for sleeping.

I tapped tentatively on his cage. "Hey, buddy."

Bilbo was already pacing back and forth. He knew what was coming next.

"That's right, it's playtime," I said, gingerly unlatching the cage door.

I let out a screech and jumped back as the ferret darted past me. I watched as he ran in circles around the room, then began gleefully romping on the furniture in a way that would get us Lovejoy kids hollered at big-time if we did the same thing at home. Leaving the ferret to his fun, I changed his litter and fixed him a snack.

"Mmm, your favorite," I said, reaching into the container of ferret treats and holding one out to him.

Bilbo dashed across the room and snatched it from me, then made a beeline for the basement door.

Someone had left it open.

"Wait, no!" I cried. *My stupid sister! How could she have forgotten?* Lauren was the one getting paid for this, not me. I chased after the ferret, but he was too quick for me. He slipped through the door lickety-split. I heard his little feet pattering down the stairs, and then—silence.

I stood at the top, staring down into the darkness. Flipping on the light didn't help. The Mitchells' basement was just as creepy as Gramps and Lola's. Plus, the house was deserted, which made it extra creepy.

"Bilbo?" I called, embarrassed at how shaky my voice sounded. I descended the stairs reluctantly, every hair on the back of my neck standing at attention. Pausing at the bottom, I called the ferret's name again.

A moment later, something raced across my feet, and I nearly leaped out of my skin.

"Bilbo! Get over here!" I shouted.

There was no point trying to chase him. There were too many places in the basement to hide. I'd have to outwit him instead.

Running back upstairs, I grabbed the container of treats and stepped behind the open basement door. "Bilbo!" I called again, rattling the container enticingly.

Silence.

I gave it another shake, and this time there was a tentative scrabbling at the base of the stairs.

"Bilbo! Cookies!"

The ferret knew that word. In a flash, he came bounding up the stairs, and the second he was through the door I slammed it shut behind him. "Gotcha!"

Bilbo skidded to a stop and eyed me reproachfully.

"Sorry for spoiling your fun," I told him. "But I don't have all night."

Inching backward across the room toward his cage, I placed ferret treats on the floor like bread crumbs on a trail. "Come on, buddy," I coaxed. "This way."

He gave the first one a suspicious sniff, but the treats proved irresistible, and in a few moments he was back in captivity.

"You be a good boy now," I told him, latching the cage

firmly. "Lauren will be over to play with you tomorrow."

My pest of a sister owed me big-time for this one. Grabbing my coat, I locked the door, then slipped the key back in its hiding place and went home.

"There you are," said my mother as I came through the back door. "Right in time to set the table."

"But I just—"

"No buts, young lady. Your birthday is officially over."

"Yes, ma'am," I said meekly.

"I'll help," offered Mackenzie, reappearing in the kitchen just then.

"How are your folks?" my mother asked.

"Surviving without me."

"We're eating in the dining room tonight, girls," my mother continued. "I've cleared my books and things away. We'll need places for ten."

"Ten?" I frowned. "Who else is coming?"

"Your aunt and Professor Rusty."

I made a face at Mackenzie. "Prepare to be bored out of your gourd."

"Truly!" my mother frowned.

"Sorry, ma'am," I said.

It was true, though. Professor Rusty—a.k.a. Erastus Peckinpaugh a.k.a. Professor Punkinpie, as Pippa called him—was a full-fledged nerd. He was really nice and everything, and sometimes he could be funny, so I could see why my aunt liked him, but he was totally fixated on history. I mean *totally*. Especially the Civil War. He felt the same way about the Civil War as I did about birds, and swimming, and sudoku.

Last time he came to dinner, we were treated to a lecture on the Fighting Fifth, New Hampshire's most famous Civil War regiment. Professor Rusty belonged to a group of Civil War reenactors—excuse me, "living historians" was the proper term, according to him—who were named for soldiers in the Fighting Fifth. He was all excited that we'd moved here, because Matthew Lovejoy, the original Truly's husband, belonged to that regiment, and he was trying to talk one of my brothers into joining the group and portraying him. Danny wasn't interested, but Hatcher, surprisingly, was seriously considering it. When I gave him a hard time about it, he just looked at me and said "life list."

In other words, people who live in glass houses shouldn't throw stones.

I guess he had a point. Everybody has their obsessions.

My cell phone buzzed as we were finishing up setting the table. "It's Jasmine and Cha Cha," I told Mackenzie. "Check it out."

"No fair!" she cried, peering over my shoulder to see the selfie they'd sent of the two of them lounging on a beach. "Where are they again?"

"Key West."

"Sweet."

I texted back, telling them briefly about the sap theft at Freeman Farm and the resurrection of the Pumpkin Falls Private Eyes. CHECKING OUT SCENE OF CRIME TOMORROW, I added. WILL LET YOU KNOW IF WE FIND ANYTHING.

SAY HI TO FRANKLIN FOR ME! Jasmine texted back.

Franklin Freeman was Jasmine's Mr. Perfect. Except he didn't know it yet.

"Anything else we can do to help, Aunt Dinah?" Mackenzie asked as we returned to the kitchen.

"That's sweet of you to offer," my mother replied, "but I think I have the rest of it under control."

Hatcher and Danny and Lauren and I had been doing a lot of the cooking these past few months since our move to Pumpkin Falls. My father was the one who came up with that plan, as a way to help Mom now that she was going back to college full-time. She'd told us we were all off the hook for Spring Break, though.

"Y'all have been juggling a lot, and I appreciate it," she'd said. "You've earned a real vacation."

There was a knock on the front door just then.

"Truly, would you get that?" asked my mother, pulling the roast chicken out of the oven.

I watched Mackenzie's face as I introduced her to Professor Rusty. I could hardly wait to ask what she thought of him. They're kind of an odd couple, my hippie-dippie aunt and her absentminded professor.

Professor Rusty would almost be handsome, if it weren't for that wild hair of his, which was dark and bushy and way too long, in an Albert Einsteiny kind of way. He'd been perpetually underfoot ever since the Valentine's Day dance, when the Pumpkin Falls Private Eyes revealed him to be the author of some love letters that had never made their way to my aunt. In a classic case of missed connections, the two of them had gone their separate ways after high school, Aunt True to travel the world, and Professor Rusty to college and graduate school.

If Erastus Peckinpaugh was clearly interested in rekindling the romance, it was harder to tell with Aunt True. For as long as I'd known her, my aunt had proudly classified herself as a nomad and a rolling stone. Was she ready to settle down? I honestly had no idea. Aunt True was being completely close-lipped about it, and not just with Ella Bellow.

Dinner was the usual Magnificent Seven mayhem. My brothers held court, recounting their day at wrestling camp; Pippa spilled her milk twice; and Lauren, who was wearing another of her attic finds—a glossy black hat with a fishnet veil—got reprimanded for reading at the table, although Aunt True argued for leniency. "She has such excellent taste in literature, Jericho!" she protested, when my dad took the book away. "*The Westing Game* was one of my favorites when I was in fourth grade."

I didn't even bother trying to get a word in edgewise.

"How's your research going, Dinah?" Professor Rusty asked my mother. "Have you settled on a topic yet?"

"I can't decide between the Hatfields and the McCoys or the Underground Railroad," she told him.

"I know about the Underground Railroad!" Pippa piped up excitedly from the far end of the table. "Mr. Henry read about Harriet Tubman at library thtory hour!"

Professor Rusty nodded. "Indeed, Pippa. She was a very important conductor along those invisible rails, leading dozens of slaves to freedom." He turned back to my mother. "They're both excellent subjects, Dinah. Hmmm. Which would I choose? The famous feud that has entered both the annals of American folklore and our national lexicon, or one of the most exciting chapters in nineteenth-century history, featuring a network of brave souls and safe houses, secret tunnels and passwords, disguises and subterfuge? An organization that involved whites and blacks alike, men and women who risked everything to help some hundred thousand slaves to freedom? Slaves who faced danger at every turn as they risked recapture, punishment—even death?" He pretended to rub his chin, considering.

My mother laughed. "I think it's pretty clear which one you'd choose."

"You know my weakness for the Civil War era," he admitted. "It really is a fascinating subject, however. And did you know that the Underground Railroad may have a Pumpkin Falls connection? It's been the basis for much speculation over the years, although nothing has ever been proven."

"Is that so?" said my mother.

Professor Rusty ran a hand through his hair, warming to his theme. "Have you read about Henry 'Box' Brown, the slave from Virginia who mailed himself to freedom in a box?"

We looked at him blankly.

"Just one of many fascinating stories," he continued, turning to me. "Truly, you'll appreciate this one—there was a Canadian man by the name of Alexander Milton Ross, known as 'Birdman' to the workers on the Underground Railroad, because he traveled through the Southern states helping slaves escape while pretending to be an enthusiastic ornithologist."

"An orni-what?" asked Pippa, frowning.

"A bird watcher," I told her.

Across the table, my cousin gave me a frantic get-me-out-of-here-before-I-die-of-boredom look. Not that I wanted to sit through another of Professor Rusty's lectures, either, but history was so not Mackenzie's thing.

"May we be excused?" I asked politely. "Mackenzie and I set the table, so it's Hatcher's and Danny's turn to do the dishes."

"Don't go too far, girls," said my mother. "We'll be leaving for our knitting class in about half an hour."

Like I could forget.

"We'll be ready," I promised, forcing myself to smile sweetly, and I followed my cousin upstairs to my room.

CHAPTER 8

"Cute place," said Mackenzie, peering out the window of our minivan as we pulled up in front of A Stitch in Time.

Ella Bellow's new shop was carved from half of the building that housed Earl's Coins and Stamps. Bud Jefferson's business hadn't been doing too well—I guess people didn't collect that stuff the way they used to—and the two of them had struck a deal for Ella to take over part of his space. I examined the window display as I got out of the car. I was hardly an expert on store windows, but I'd been helping Aunt True with the one at our bookstore for a few months now, and I could tell that Ella had done a good job with hers. It was cheery and colorful, and she'd even managed a very un-Ella-like touch of whimsy: a near-life-size plush sheep in the center of the display, surrounded by baskets spilling over with skeins of bright wool. Decked out in a knitted hat and scarf, the sheep was wearing a sweater sporting a maple leaf design. A sign around its neck announced: MAPLE MADNESS IS BAAAAAAA-CK!

I couldn't help noticing the book propped up by the sheep's front hooves—*Maple Country Mufflers*, the one Ella'd had her gym shorts all in a twist about when she'd spotted it in our bookshop window.

"Ooo, that sheep is *adorable*!" Mackenzie squealed. "I have to get a picture. Go stand in front of it. You too, Aunt Dinah. Now smile!"

My mother slipped her arm around my waist and put her head on my shoulder. I rested my chin on top of her head. It still felt weird being taller than her, but I was getting used to it.

"Hey, Little O," she whispered as Mackenzie snapped the picture.

"Hey, Mama O."

"Happy birthday!"

"Thanks." I felt myself start to relax. Knitting might be my mother's thing, not mine, but that was no reason not to have fun.

"Come in, come in!" said a voice behind us. We turned around to see Ella holding the door open, beaming. Ella didn't usually beam, especially at me. I gave her a cautious smile in return and followed my mother inside.

A circle of chairs had been set up. Most of them were occupied. The other students in the Spring Break Socks class besides my mother and Mackenzie and me were Lucas Winthrop's mother; Alice Maynard, who was married to my swim coach; Belinda Winchester; Mr. Henry, the Pumpkin Falls children's librarian; and Annie Freeman and her mother.

Belinda jerked her chin at me and patted the seat next to her. I plunked myself into it. My mother and Mackenzie sat down on the other side of me.

"I'm so happy you all are joining me for the inaugural class in A Stitch in Time's knitting instruction series," Ella began rather primly. "As you can see, there's a snack table set up, and I hope you'll all help yourselves to tea and currant scones, my signature treat."

I elbowed my mother sharply. Ella had a nerve, making us take a book out of our window, when she was stealing Aunt True's idea for a signature treat!

My mother frowned and shook her head at me. "It's not a big deal."

I wasn't so sure Aunt True would feel the same way.

"Let's get started, shall we?" Ella continued. "We'll begin by winding our skeins of yarn into balls. It's so much easier to work with that way, I find."

Before she could show us how, there was a tap on the door in the new wall that divided her shop from Earl's Coins and Stamps.

"Got everything you need, Ella?" asked Bud Jefferson, poking his head in. "How's the temperature in here?"

"Such a thoughtful landlord!" Ella said. "It's just fine, thank you, Bud. There's an extra seat if you'd like to join us."

Across the circle from me, I noticed Mrs. Winthrop's cheeks turn as pink as the yarn she was holding. I remembered what Ella had said at the bookshop earlier, about Lucas Winthrop's mother and Bud Jefferson spending a lot of time together recently. Sap really did seem to be rising all over Pumpkin Falls these days.

"Uh, knitting isn't really my thing," he replied.

I could see why. Bud Jefferson looked like a bear, and he had hands like hams. It was hard to imagine them clutching a pair of knitting needles.

"Did you know that knitting used to be considered men's work?" Mr. Henry told him. "In fact, in some cultures women weren't even allowed to knit."

Mr. Jefferson's bushy eyebrows shot up. "Really?"

Mr. Henry nodded. "During the Renaissance, only men were allowed to join knitting guilds. The word 'knit' itself is derived from the Old English *cnyttan,* meaning 'knot'— probably because it grew out of the knots with which fishermen crafted their nets. They've been knitters for centuries, as have sailors and shepherds. The craft has a fascinating history. It started in ancient times, with the Romans and Egyptians."

It has been my experience that librarians know a lot of stuff.

"Huh," said Mr. Jefferson, digesting this information. "Interesting."

"Oh, come and join us, Bud!" said Ella. "You can at least

be sociable if you don't actually want to try your hand at knitting. I made some of those currant scones you like."

That clinched it. Closing the door behind him, Mr. Jefferson tiptoed in and looked around for a seat.

"Amelia could use your help." Ella's dark eyes gleamed as she gestured toward the empty chair next to Lucas's mother. "It takes two to wind wool, you know."

Beside me, my mother gave a quiet snort. I had a feeling that Ella was talking about more than just knitting. I wondered what Lucas thought about his mother and Mr. Jefferson. Did it freak him out that they might be "winding wool," as Ella put it?

"Here, Bud, hold your hands out straight," Ella directed. "Like a robot. Now, Amelia, untwist the skein. See how it forms a loop?" She placed the loop of wool over Bud Jefferson's hands and passed the loose end to Mrs. Winthrop. "Off you go—start winding."

I watched for a few moments as she wound and a ball began to form, then took my yarn out of my bag.

"We'll wind yours first," Belinda Winchester told me. I nodded, untwisted the skein, slipped it into place over her waiting hands, and started winding.

"Blue socks, they never get dirty . . ." Belinda sang softly to herself.

"What?"

She shook her head. "Nothing. Just an old camp song."

At least my mother had chosen my favorite color for the yarn she bought me, I thought as I wound. *Blue as water, blue as sky.* Thinking of water made me think of my Mermaid-hued bedroom back in Texas, and I made a mental note to ask Gramps and Lola about painting my room here in Pumpkin Falls. Maybe as an extra birthday present?

The work went quickly, and before I knew it I had a fat ball of yarn, ready to be turned into socks.

"My turn," said Belinda. She'd brought along purple wool, and I wondered if maybe she was planning to knit socks for her gentleman caller.

Purl the kitten skittered past just then. Belinda paused her winding and reached for the purple feather tucked behind her ear. She dangled it in the air, and Purl stopped in her tracks, then leaped up and batted at it with her paws. Belinda was too quick for her and whisked it out of her reach.

"Stop teasing Purl, Belinda," said Ella severely.

"Not teasing. Playing," Belinda replied, dangling the feather again.

"Her name's spelled P-U-R-L," Annie announced, just in case anybody was wondering. "It's a knitting stitch."

I smiled at Mackenzie. I'd told her all about the reigning junior spelling bee champion of Grafton County, but, like Belinda, Annie had to be experienced firsthand.

My mother leaned toward me. "Now that I know Annie's here, I'm feeling a little guilty," she whispered. "Should I call home and have your father bring Lauren down to join us?"

Lauren again! "But this was supposed to be *our* thing!" I protested. "You know, Little O and Mama O?"

I didn't want Lauren tagging along. I never got a chance to have my mother all to myself, and as it was, I was already sharing her with Mackenzie, sort of.

"I suppose you're right." My mother didn't look convinced, though, and she kept shooting guilty glances over at Annie.

Once we all had our yarn tamed into balls, Ella showed us how to cast on. "You'll want to look carefully at the patterns I've given each of you, and find the exact number of stitches you'll need," she said. "I've tailored them to your shoe sizes."

Great, I thought, with a rueful glance at my size-ten-and-a-half feet. I'd be casting on all night.

Sure enough, I had to cast on nearly twice as many stitches as Mackenzie. My cousin had feet like an elf.

Those of us who had never knit before—me, Mackenzie, Annie, Mrs. Winthrop, and Mr. Jefferson, who had succumbed to the spirit of the evening and was as busy casting on as the rest of us—were shown the two basic stitches, and instructed to practice several rows of each of them.

"When you alternate rows of these two stitches, which we'll be doing shortly," Ella explained, "you'll have what's called 'stockinette stitch.'"

"S-T-O-C-K-I-N-E-T-T-E," Annie couldn't resist whispering.

"Nice and smooth," Ella continued. "And when you alternate those stitches, or pairs of those stitches, within a single row, you create ribbing, which we'll all do at the top of each of our socks."

The more experienced knitters were already off and running. I watched in admiration as my mother's needles flashed. She could seriously go pro. The socks she'd chosen to knit were for my father, in a complicated pattern called "argyle." Mr. Henry was making red-and-white-striped ones, of course. Nearly his entire wardrobe was red and white, and Hatcher said he looks like an African American *Where's Waldo?* Mrs. Freeman was starting on an orange leaf design, and I wondered if maybe she were planning to sell the socks in the barn store at Freeman Farm.

After a few minutes I paused to inspect my progress. I'd made a hash of casting on, and somehow I must have managed to knit some of the stitches together, because now I had three fewer stitches than when I started. Seeing my dismay, Ella came over and helped me rip out the mistaken rows, and I started again.

I glanced over at Mackenzie. Her head was bent over her needles, and she was frowning in concentration. She was way ahead of me.

"No fair—you've done this before!" I said.

She shook her head. "Never."

I sighed. Just one more thing to add to the long list of

things I wasn't good at. At this rate, I'd be lucky to have one big toe finished by the end of the week.

After a while we paused for tea and scones, which were surprisingly good. Who knew Ella Bellow could bake? Then it was time for more knitting. The evening flew by. Class was just about over when there was a knock at the door.

"Come in!" called Ella.

I looked up to see Coach Maynard in the doorway. Spotting Mackenzie and me, he smiled and sketched a wave. "I'm a few minutes early, honey," he said to his wife. His smile faded as he noticed Mrs. Freeman in the circle of knitters.

"Good evening, Wyatt," said Annie's mother pleasantly.

"You've got some nerve!" Coach Maynard thundered.

Mrs. Freeman looked up in surprise. "Pardon me?"

"Someone cut one of our sap lines, and I have a pretty good notion who it was," my swim coach retorted. "I saw that son of yours out sniffing around my property earlier today, Grace."

Uh-oh, I thought. This didn't sound good.

"Franklin? He would never—"

"I heard all about what happened at your farm last night," Coach Maynard barreled on. "You think we did it, and now you're trying to get even!"

"That's a ridiculous notion!"

"R-I-D-I-C-U-L-O-U-S!" Annie sputtered furiously.

Ella Bellow's head swiveled back and forth, like a

spectator at a tennis match. Her dark eyes gleamed again, and I knew she was filing this information away to be used the minute we all went home. By morning the entire town would know what was going on.

Was Pumpkin Falls facing its very own feud, Hatfield and McCoy style?

CHAPTER 9

"That was more exciting than I expected a sock class to be," said Mackenzie as we were driving home.

"'Exciting' is Pumpkin Falls' middle name!" my mother joked. Then her expression grew serious. "Theft isn't anything to laugh about, though, and I sure hate to see our friends disagreeing. I hope it all gets sorted out quickly."

It will if the Pumpkin Falls Private Eyes have anything to say about it, I thought. Because my mother was right—it wasn't fun to see the Freemans and the Maynards feuding. What if people in town started choosing sides? Things could get seriously out of hand.

"So what do you girls have planned for tomorrow?" my mother asked, glancing in the rearview mirror at us.

"Nothing much," I told her, which wasn't entirely true. Especially if you counted making a field trip to the scene of a crime.

"We might hang out with Scooter and Lucas and Calhoun."

"I thought I'd take Pippa and Lauren out to lunch and a movie over in West Hartfield, if you two want to join us," she offered. "The girls have been begging to see that new cartoon about the robot and the hippopotamus."

Mackenzie and I exchanged a quick smile. My mother clearly thought we were still six.

"Um, no thanks, Aunt Dinah," Mackenzie replied.

"Yeah, that's okay, Mom," I added. "We'll find stuff of our own to do." *Like see if we can catch a sap thief*, I thought.

"Suit yourselves."

Lauren was waiting up for us at home. "Can I see your socks?"

"Later," I told her.

"They're hardly socks at this point, sweetie," my mother explained.

"Hey, guess who was there?" said Mackenzie before I could shush her. "Your friend Annie and her mother."

Lauren shot my mother a wounded look. "Mo-om! If Annie gets to go, how come I can't?"

"Because it's my birthday present, not yours!" I snapped.

"Truly!" My mother gave me a reproachful look.

"Sorry," I mumbled, not feeling sorry at all. It was true, wasn't it? Leaving her to sort things out with my sister, I headed upstairs.

Mackenzie and I changed into our pajamas and brushed our teeth. Grabbing my new bird book, I flopped onto my bed on my stomach and opened it, eager to see if it contained any new information about barred owls.

"So what do you think of Calhoun?" Mackenzie asked casually, picking up her hairbrush.

I froze. "Um, he's okay, I guess."

"He's kind of cute, don't you think?"

The barred owl is most often found in mature forests, I read, keeping my eyes glued to the page. Whatever had prompted this, I was not about to take the bait.

"Of course Cameron's hair is blonder, and he has blue eyes, not brown like Calhoun's, but still, Calhoun is definitely cute," my cousin continued. "And I can't believe his name is Romeo!" She sighed. "That's so romantic."

Clenching my teeth, I read on: *The barred owl's typical call sounds like "Who cooks for you! Who cooks for you-all!"*

"Hey, did you notice the socks Belinda Winchester is knitting?"

This time I looked up. "Huh?"

"Belinda's socks—they're purple. Guess we know who those are for, right?"

Mackenzie clearly had romance on the brain. I shook my head and returned to my book.

Owls can find their prey without even seeing it, thanks to hypersensitive hearing. At certain frequencies, an owl's hearing is ten times more sensitive than that of humans.

Right then I would have been happy not to hear anything at all. Especially not my boy-crazy cousin.

Mackenzie sighed, finally taking the hint. "Fine. I'll read too." Kneeling in front of my bookcase, she ran a finger over the titles that lined its shelves. "Sudoku, birds, sudoku, birds. B-O-R-I-N-G, as Annie Freeman would say."

"S-O-R-R-Y!" I quipped in reply. "Didn't you bring anything from home?"

"Come to think of it, I'm pretty sure my mother stuck something in my suitcase at the last minute in case I wanted to read on the plane. I totally forgot."

She went over to my closet and opened the door. A moment later I heard her rummaging through her luggage, and then "Yes! Thank you, Mom!" This was immediately followed by a loud thud, and then "Whoa!"

"Whoa what?" I asked, looking up again.

"Whoa, as in you'd better come over here and take a look at this!"

There was an urgent note in Mackenzie's voice. I put my book down and crossed the room. My cousin was squatting by her suitcase, holding a fat hardcover book. Looking up at me, she asked, "Do you have a flashlight?"

"Um, maybe with our camping gear out in the garage or something. Why?"

"I need a light."

"Hang on a sec." My cell phone was charging on my desk. Grabbing it, I switched on the torch app and went back to the closet.

"Don't point it at me, you dork, point it at the floor!" my cousin protested, shielding her eyes.

"Sorry." Redirecting the beam, I saw that the corner of one of the wide wooden floorboards was sticking up at an odd angle. "That's weird."

"I know, right?" Mackenzie said. "When I dropped my book, it just popped up like that."

I knelt down beside her and poked at the floorboard's raised edge, trying to work my fingers under it. No luck. Then I pounded on the other end, trying to see if that would jostle it loose, but it still didn't budge.

"Do you have something we can pry it up with?" my cousin asked.

Returning to my desk, I grabbed my letter opener. "Be careful with it, okay? It was a Christmas present."

She spotted the carved owl on the handle and smirked. "You are such a bird nerd!"

I don't mind it when Mackenzie teases me. Most of the time, anyway.

Inserting the point of the letter opener beneath the floorboard's raised corner, she carefully slid the slim blade in all the way to its hilt, then levered down on it gently. The floorboard inched up.

"Do it again," I told her, setting my cell phone down. I poked my fingers underneath the lifted edge as she continued to push. The top of the floorboard was worn smooth from centuries of use, but the underside was rough. I hoped there wasn't anything lurking beneath it. Like spiders, for instance.

This was no time to be squeamish. I redoubled my efforts, and my pulse quickened as I felt the board start to loosen. I told myself not to be silly. I told myself that this wasn't one of Lauren's Nancy Drew books. There weren't any such things as secret compartments.

Mackenzie pressed down again, and I gave one last mighty tug at the floorboard, tumbling back as it suddenly shifted and came loose in my hand. I scrambled up onto my knees and leaned over to peer into the open space that had been concealed underneath. Mackenzie did too, and our heads banged together with an audible crack.

"Ouch!" we both said, sitting back on our heels.

"You go first," Mackenzie told me, rubbing her forehead.

Wincing, I reached for my cell phone again and shined it into the shadowy crevice. There was something tucked into the far corner. A small bundle of some sort, wrapped in a piece of faded fabric and bound with a knotted leather cord.

"What is it?" Mackenzie could hardly contain her excitement.

"I don't know."

Reaching in cautiously, I lifted it out and felt its edges. "A box of some kind, I think?" I shook it, but whatever it was didn't make a sound.

We carried our discovery over to my bed, where there was more light. Mackenzie sat down beside me, bouncing a little on the edge of my mattress. "Open it!" she urged, sounding like Pippa.

"I'm trying!" I replied, working at the age-stiffened knot.

"It's silk, I think," my cousin said, reaching out and brushing the faded fabric with a finger. "Looks like it was a pretty shade of light blue once. Who do you think it belonged to?"

I shrugged. "It's probably Aunt True's. This used to be her room."

The leather knot finally came loose. Unwinding the cord from around the bundle, I peeled back the fabric.

"It's a book," I said, disappointed. When you find a secret compartment in your room, at least a tiny part of you can't help expecting gold and jewels and buried treasure of some sort.

Smallish but thick, the book was bound in dark blue leather worn around the spine and edges. The word "DIARY" was stamped on the cover in faded gold, along with the initials *T. L.* in the bottom right-hand corner.

"See?" I told my cousin, pointing to the letters. "True Lovejoy. It's my aunt's."

"We probably shouldn't open it, then," said Mackenzie. "I mean, since it's her diary and everything."

"Yeah. It could be really personal, or embarrassing."

We sat in silence, staring at it.

"Maybe just a peek?" Mackenzie said finally. She gave me a hopeful glance.

I chewed my lip, considering. "A peek," I agreed, and opened the cover.

CHAPTER 10

"Whoa," whispered Mackenzie. "It's not your Aunt True's."

We stared down at the date on the diary's first page: January 1, 1861. The flesh on my arms prickled. The book I was holding in my hands had been hidden away for over a hundred and fifty years!

I traced the words on the inside front cover: *Property of Truly Lovejoy.*

"This was *hers!*" I told my cousin, my voice rising in excitement. "The original Truly's—the one I was named after!"

"You mean the one in the portrait?" Mackenzie's blue eyes widened. "Are you sure?"

"I can prove it," I told her. "Come on."

She followed me out into the hallway, where I flipped on the light and pointed to the framed document hanging on the wall nearby. "See? That's her passport. Check out the signature at the bottom. It's exactly the same as in her diary."

My cousin compared the two. "But her last name isn't Lovejoy," she said, squinting at the faded writing on the passport. "It's—"

"Becker. I know. She got the passport in Germany, before she came here and met Matthew. And see? Her real name was Trudy, remember I told you that? And about the immigrations officials who misunderstood and wrote it down wrong in her official papers, so she got stuck with Truly?"

Mackenzie smiled at me. "And so did you."

My name has always kind of bugged me, but as I stood there holding the diary in my hands, something changed. *Blue*, I thought, looking down at the faded leather cover and the scrap of fabric it had been wrapped in. Goose bumps again. The original Truly had liked blue too. She was a real living, breathing person, not just a face in an old portrait. For the first time, I felt a flicker of kinship with my ancestor.

"So she arrived here in America in ... let's see"—Mackenzie struggled to make out the faded writing on the framed passport—"September 1860. And by New Year's Day in 1861, just three months later, she was already married to Matthew? Wow, that's what I call a whirlwind romance! It really must have been love at first sight, just like your grandfather told you."

"What are you guys doing?"

We swiveled around. Our voices had drawn my sister Lauren from her room.

"Nothing," I said quickly. Too quickly. Lauren may just be a fourth grader, but she's not stupid.

"Doesn't sound like nothing."

"I was showing Mackenzie the original Truly's passport."

Lauren's gaze fell on my hand. The one holding the diary. She didn't miss a trick.

"And I, uh, thought she might be interested in seeing my life list too," I added quickly. The fib was the only thing I could think of on the spur of the moment. Fortunately, the notebook I kept my list of birds in was about the same shape as the diary, if not the exact same color.

And, fortunately, my sister fell for it.

"Oh," she said, immediately losing interest. Lauren loves animals, but she's not at all into birding. She turned to go.

"Maybe we can all do something tomorrow, like play a board game," said Mackenzie.

Lauren brightened. "That sounds like fun!" And skimming lightly down the hall, she gave my cousin a quick hug. "Night, Mackenzie."

"Night, Lauren."

My sister returned to her room. Her message couldn't have been clearer if she'd spoken it aloud: no hug for the mean big sister. I felt a pang of guilt, followed swiftly by annoyance. The thing was, I wasn't deliberately trying to be mean. I just didn't get to see Mackenzie very often, and I didn't want to have to share her. Was that so awful?

Back in my room, Mackenzie and I sat down on the bed beside each other again and opened the diary.

"Look at her handwriting!" my cousin marveled, carefully turning the pages. Yellowed and brittle, they were covered with elegant cursive. "Nobody writes like that now." She looked up at me. "How about we read it out loud?"

"Okay." I turned back to the first page. Some of the words were in German, but I did the best I could:

> *January 1, 1861*
> *Liebes Tagebuch—Dear Diary,*
> *Mother Lovejoy gave me this diary for Weihnachten—* [this word had been crossed out, and "Christmas" carefully entered in its place]—*in hopes I will use it to practice mein Englisch. I promised her I would write as often as I could. Today begins my new life as Mrs. Matthew Lovejoy. We were married heute Morgen*—[again, the words were crossed out and "this morning" added in their place]—*by Reverend Josiah Bartlett of the First Parish Church.*

"Hey," I told Mackenzie, looking up. "That's the same church my grandparents belong to—the one with the steeple!"

"Cool! Don't forget you promised to take me up there too."

"I won't." I turned my attention back to the diary.

> *How I wish my own Mutti had been here for my wedding! I miss her so. Matthew says I am very brave, traveling so far from home, but this morning I don't feel brave at all. Only full of Heimweh.*

"What's '*Heimweh*'?" my cousin asked, frowning.

"We're going to need a German-English dictionary," I told her. "Maybe we can get one at the bookstore tomorrow, or the library."

> *But I do so love my husband! And I will learn to love Pumpkin Falls, and it will become home too. This Matthew promises me.*
> *Deine Truly*

Yet another cross-out through the final two words, which had been replaced with "*Yours, Truly*."

"Poor thing, she sounds really homesick," said Mackenzie.

"No wonder!" I tried to imagine myself in my ancestor's shoes. She was only a year older than my brother Danny, and she'd left her family and her country and had just gotten married to someone she'd known for only a few months.

Mackenzie sighed dreamily. "Isn't it romantic, though?"

I made a rude noise.

She elbowed me. "Keep reading!"

I looked down at the diary. "We should probably show it to my mom and dad," I said reluctantly. "Since it's a family heirloom and everything."

Mackenzie made a face. "You're probably right. Maybe we could wait until tomorrow, though?"

I was quiet for a moment. For one thing, the minute word got out about the diary, Lauren would be all over it. Something this old—and something she could read, to boot—would be like catnip to my bookworm sister. And if it were valuable, my parents might want to stick it in a museum or a safe deposit box. Mackenzie and I might not ever get another chance to look at it.

There was a knock on the door, and I reflexively stuffed the diary under my pillow.

"Girls?" My mother poked her head in. "I saw the light under your door. Morning's going to come early, and you have swim practice. I think you should call it a night."

Neither my cousin nor I said a word about the diary. We just nodded and climbed into our beds.

"Good night, then." My mother turned off the overhead

light and blew us each a kiss, and we each pretended to catch it. It's a Gifford bedtime ritual.

"Good night, Aunt Dinah," said Mackenzie.

"Good night, Mom," I echoed.

The door closed behind her. The diary stayed where it was.

"Just until tomorrow," I whispered to Mackenzie.

CHAPTER 11

The alarm on my cell phone jangled me awake. I stretched a leg out from under the covers and poked a toe at the nearby air mattress, nudging the lump that was Mackenzie.

"Go away," the lump mumbled.

"Up and at 'em!" I said in my best imitation of Lieutenant Colonel Jericho T. Lovejoy. I sprang briskly out of bed and flipped on the overhead light. "Daily doubles await!"

Mackenzie groaned. "I plead jet lag!"

"Don't you want to wow Mr. Perfect with your new flip turn?"

She cracked open an eyelid. "Who's Mr. Perfect?"

I grinned at her. "Pardon me. I mean Cameron McAllister."

At the sound of her true love's name, Mackenzie sat up and rubbed her eyes. "I was just dreaming about him."

I made a gagging noise, and she threw her pillow at me. I caught it and grinned. "Last one downstairs is a rotten egg!"

Except for that long, scary stretch of months after Black Monday, when my father had a serious case of the doldrums, as he puts it now, I'd rarely known him not to be up before I am. For as long as I could remember, he'd been an early bird, and this particular morning was no exception.

"Morning, ladies," he said, glancing up from his coffee and newspaper as my cousin and I entered the kitchen.

"Morning, Uncle Jericho," Mackenzie replied, yawning.

My father gestured toward the fridge. "Power smoothies await."

"Thanks." I dropped a kiss on top of his head.

My father was big on making sure that the athletes in the family ate right, and that included a little something before early-morning practices. Even when we didn't feel like it, he insisted. Sometimes it was just a banana with a swipe of peanut butter; sometimes it was an energy bar; this morning it was a smoothie.

"How about I drop you off on my way to the bookshop?" my father offered. "It's been a busy few days what with all the tourists, and I want to get a jump on things."

The three of us were quiet on the short ride to town. Neither Mackenzie nor I brought up the subject of the diary, which was still in its hiding place under my pillow. I stared out the window, wondering if Pumpkin Falls had looked much different back when the original Truly had lived here. Probably not.

The last remnants of winter were rapidly melting away, and rivulets of muddy water swirled across the streets. It wouldn't be long now before the migratory warblers returned, along with the chipping sparrows and Baltimore orioles and evening grosbeaks. I made a mental note to work up a list of the spring birds that I should be watching for.

"Work hard, ladies," my father said as we pulled up in front of the pool.

"Always do," I replied as Mackenzie and I got out.

He gave us a thumbs-up and drove off.

I groaned when I saw the workout posted on the white-board. We'd be working hard, all right—Coach Maynard had seen to that.

"I hate speed intervals," Mackenzie grumbled as we started warming up.

"No kidding," I said. "Especially first thing in the morning."

Lucas sidled up to us, his face as red as if he'd just finished a set of sprints. He flashed my cousin a shy smile. "Hey."

"Hey, yourself," said Mackenzie.

I didn't bother replying. What was the point? Lucas wasn't talking to me anyway.

Along with the rest of our teammates—the ones who had remained in Pumpkin Falls for Spring Break, at least—the three of us grunted our way through the required sets of warm-up crunches and planks.

A few minutes later there was a short blast from Coach Maynard's whistle as he emerged from the office. He seemed like his normal self; there was no mention of last night's outburst at A Stitch in Time. I certainly wasn't going to bring it up.

"Let's see how you two do against each other," he said to Mackenzie and me, assigning us to adjoining lanes.

Given our differences in height, you wouldn't think it was fair to pit my cousin and me against each other, but once we're in the water it actually balances out. Mackenzie's so petite she's like a water flea, zipping across the surface of the pool. But my long legs and arms give me an advantage too, and in the end our times are generally really close.

"Good job, girls," he said, checking his stopwatch as we completed our first set. "Truly, you keep turning in these kinds of times, and you'll be going to state championships this year."

While I continued with the posted workout, Coach Maynard turned his attention to honing Mackenzie's flip turn. Lucas spent too much time watching them—well, watching Mackenzie—but at least he wasn't swallowing water like he did yesterday.

"Good workout, people!" Coach Maynard said at the end of our session. "Stay away from the junk food today, and I'll see you this afternoon!"

Lucas was waiting for my cousin and me again when we emerged from the locker room a little while later.

"We're still meeting up after breakfast, right?" he managed to squeak, clearly still awed by my cousin's magnificence.

Mackenzie dazzled him with a smile. "Can't wait!"

Bolstered by this sign of favor, Lucas practically skipped off down the street. What was it about my cousin that boys found so bewitching? I wondered, watching him go. Whatever it was, one thing was for sure—I could use a big dose of it.

Mackenzie and I jogged home, more because breakfast was waiting than because we actually had any energy left.

"I'm starving!" I announced as we burst into the kitchen.

"You're just in time for banana walnut oatmeal," my mother replied, ladling me up a steaming bowlful as I took a seat at the table.

"Hello, thtarving, I'm Pippa," said my little sister, collapsing in giggles at her own wit. She was at the age where stuff like that was still funny.

"Nice to meet you, Pippa, I'm hungry," said Mackenzie, stretching out her hand across the table. Pippa shook it, delighted that at least one of us was joining in on the fun.

Lauren looked up from her book—she'd moved on from *The Westing Game* to *The Sasquatch Escape*—and rolled her eyes. She was at the age where she was eager to distance herself from anything that seemed babyish. Which meant pretty much everything Pippa did.

"So what's on the schedule today over at Camp Belinda?" my mother asked.

"We're going to make muffins," Lauren replied, with a noticeable lack of enthusiasm.

"And we're going to learn how to play cheth," added Pippa.

"That sounds like fun," said my mother. "I didn't know Belinda played chess."

"All of the pieces on her chessboard are cats." Lauren gave her a sidelong glance, adding, "and the pawns are kittens."

"The answer is still no, Lauren," my mother said firmly. "We don't need a kitten."

My sister heaved the deep, dramatic sigh of the misunderstood. Mackenzie's eyes met mine across the table, glinting with amusement.

"We're just going to do boring stuff," I announced to no one in particular. "Hang around here for a while, look at my bird books, that sort of thing."

"Well, I'll be picking Lauren and Pippa up from Belinda's around eleven thirty," my mother told us. "If you change your minds, you're welcome to join us for lunch and the movie."

Pippa scrambled down from her seat and ran around the table. Twining her arms around my cousin's neck, she pleaded, "Come with uth, Mackenthie! Pleathe!"

Mackenzie gave her a hug. "I'd love to, Pipster, but Truly and I have some stuff we want to do. How about we play a board game with you tonight instead?"

Pippa perked up at this. "Candy Land?"

"It's a deal."

As soon as my sisters were safely off to Belinda's, and my mother was settled at her dining room table desk, Mackenzie and I went back upstairs to my room. I drew the diary out of its hiding place. "Should we keep reading?"

"Pleathe!" Mackenzie replied, mimicking Pippa.

I opened to where we'd left off.

January 7, 1861
Today I baked Matthew's favorite Apfelkuchen—
apple cake auf Englisch. Mother Lovejoy says I am
a fine cook.
Yours, Truly

January 23, 1861
Matthew's sister Charity made us a visit today. She
lives in Boston. She brought with her much newspapers.
Matthew reads to us what they say. So much sadness!
So much cruelty! Mother Lovejoy and I both wept.
Yours, Truly

"What's so sad and cruel?" asked Mackenzie.

I shook my head. "She doesn't say."

I skipped over a bunch of shorter entries that just detailed the housework she did and the things she baked. This one caught my eye, though:

February 2, 1861
Mother Lovejoy and Matthew have a secret. I hear
them whispering sometimes late at night. I don't
know what the secret is, and I am afraid to ask.
Yours, Truly

February 5, 1861
I ask. Matthew says the less I know the better. He
tells me it is safer this way. "There is nothing to worry
about," he tells me. But that is all I do, it seems.
Yours, Truly

"More housework, more worrying, more baking," I murmured, running my finger across the next few pages of entries. "Hey, she made pumpkin muffins! Aunt True would love that! And something called '*Zwetschgenkuchen*.'" I sounded the word out, but had no idea if I was pronouncing it properly.

"I'm pretty sure '*kuchen*' means 'cake,'" said Mackenzie, looking over my shoulder. "Go back to where she talked about baking that apple cake."

I flipped back a few pages. From the looks of it, my cousin was right.

"But what the heck is a *Zwetschgen*?" I asked.

Mackenzie shrugged. "Dunno. I'll add it to the list of words we need to look up. Can you spell it for me?"

"Z-w-e-t-s-c-h-g-e-n," I said, feeling like Annie Freeman. Mackenzie wrote it down.

> *March 4, 1861*
> *I have a secret too! Matthew is so happy. I told him I*
> *am sure it will be a fine boy.*

"Wait, does that mean she's going to have a baby?" Mackenzie exclaimed, perking up.

I reread the entry and nodded. "I think so. It's probably their son Booth. He's the one in the portrait at the bottom of the stairs."

I continued reading:

> *I would like to name him for my father. Gerhard*
> *is not very nice for a girl, Matthew said, making*
> *me laugh. I assured him that it will not be a girl.*
> *The firstborns in my family are always boys. I must*
> *write to Mutti with the good news. She will be glad*
> *for me, but also sad. Pumpkin Falls is so far from*
> *Lutterhausen!*
> *Yours, Truly*

"Why do you think she left Germany?" Mackenzie asked.

I shrugged. "No idea. More work here, maybe? We'll have to ask Gramps."

The next few entries all just had the same word: '*Schwangerschaftsübelkeit*.' Mackenzie added it to the growing list.

And then came an entry with another single word. One I could read and easily understand this time:

> *April 12, 1861*
> *War.*

A pleat appeared between my cousin's eyebrows. "Which war?"

I heaved a Lauren-size sigh. "Duh—the *Civil* War, of course! It's 1861! Pay attention!"

Mackenzie made a face at me.

> *April 18, 1861*
> *The war is all that we here in Pumpkin Falls can talk about. President Lincoln has called for volunteers. I am so afraid for Matthew, and for our baby. What will become of us, if Matthew goes to be a soldier?*
> *Yours, Truly*

"Well, we know he did," said Mackenzie. "He's wearing a uniform in the portrait, right?"

I nodded, the flesh on my arms prickling again.

May 3, 1861

This morning I felt the baby kicking for the first time. "See?" I told Matthew. "He doesn't want you to go either." Matthew promises he will not leave before harvest.

August 30, 1861

Matthew left us this morning. He has gone with his friend Booth Harrington to Concord to join the Fifth New Hampshire Volunteer Infantry. Booth's younger brothers will help us with the harvest. Matthew looks splendid in his uniform, but oh, how I wish he did not have to go! Mother Lovejoy and I cannot stop weeping. Yours, Truly

"Booth was Matthew's friend's name, huh?" I said. "I wonder if that's where they got their son's name."

"Guess we'll find out," Mackenzie replied.

September 9, 1861

Mother Lovejoy told me her secret. I have sworn to keep it.

My cousin and I exchanged a glance.

"All this talk about secrets is driving me nuts," Mackenzie drawled, and I nodded in agreement.

September 12, 1861
The wind was from the south tonight. Mother Lovejoy
let me light the lantern. My hands were shaking as I did.
She says with Matthew away, we must be brave together.
Yours, Truly

"What's she talking about?" asked Mackenzie, puzzled.
"What's so scary about lighting a lantern?"

I shrugged. "No idea."

September 13, 1861
Reverend Bartlett spoke with us after church. He says
the package was delayed, but should arrive today.
Tomorrow at the latest. I pray for its safe delivery.
Yours, Truly

I stared at the diary. What was the original Truly up to?
Secrets? Packages? Lanterns? It all sounded so mysterious—
and dangerous.

A knock at the front door interrupted my thoughts.

"Girls!" my mother called up from the dining room.
"Your friends are here!"

Truly and her secrets would have to wait. I shoved the diary
back into its hiding place, and Mackenzie and I went downstairs.

CHAPTER 12

Scooter and Calhoun were waiting on the doorstep. Lucas was squeezed between them, scrubbed within an inch of his life. His hair was slicked back, and he was wearing a shirt I'd never seen before. It looked new. I peered at it more closely. It *was* new—he'd forgotten to take the price tag off. You had to give the kid points for trying, at least.

My trio of friends nearly trampled me in their eagerness to get inside, and apparently closer to where Mackenzie was standing. I might as well have been invisible as far as they were concerned.

"Hey, Truly," said Calhoun, who at least had the grace to acknowledge my presence.

"Hey."

"Are you guys ready to go?" asked Scooter, who only had eyes for my cousin.

"Yeah," I told him, and turned to Mackenzie. "You'd

better borrow a pair of Lauren's boots. It's mud season."

Mackenzie's brow furrowed. "Seriously? That's an official thing?"

"A-yuh," drawled Scooter in an exaggerated New Hampshire accent.

Mackenzie burst out laughing, and Scooter looked pleased.

"You won't laugh when you see where we're going," warned Calhoun. "We're taking the shortcut through the woods, and it's a mess out there."

"Bye, Mom!" I called, stuffing my size-ten-and-a-half feet into a pair of rubber boots and grabbing my jacket. "We're going to show Mackenzie around Freeman Farm!"

My mother waggled her fingers at us, barely looking up from her research project. "Have fun!"

At the top of the hill the five of us left the road and struck out on a path across a field that led into the woods. The sun was fully up now, its light dappling down through the trees. I breathed in the pine-sharp scent of evergreen. Somewhere nearby, an eastern phoebe sang out its raspy, two-note call, and in the distance I heard the brief, lilting trill of a song sparrow. "Heralds of spring," Gramps called them.

I was glad I'd worn my boots. The ground grew increasingly squishy as we approached the flanks of Lovejoy Mountain, and pretty soon we were squelching and sliding with every step.

"See? Mud season!" crowed Scooter. He stamped his

feet, sending up a spray of brown glop as he showed off for Mackenzie.

"Quit it!" I hollered, but my cousin just giggled. I frowned at her. "Don't encourage him."

While it was a relief to have Scooter fixated on something besides me—I wasn't hankering for another lip-lock, that was for sure—I still couldn't help feeling a little overlooked once again.

Fifteen minutes later we emerged onto the road across from Maynard's Maple Barn. Judging by the number of cars in the parking lot, my swim coach was doing a brisk business with the breakfast crowd.

We jogged on down the road to Freeman Farm. The parking lot was not nearly as packed as it was at Coach Maynard's, but then the Freemans didn't serve pancakes and waffles. Annie spotted us from her perch in the Snack Shack and waved.

"Greetings and S-A-L-U-T-A-T-I-O-N-S!" she said, trotting out a championship word borrowed from my Aunt True. "Anybody want a maple donut?"

"My treat," said Lucas, shooting a glance over at Mackenzie as he pulled his wallet from his back pocket.

"They're on the house," said Annie. "My mom heard you were coming."

Crestfallen, Lucas put his wallet back.

"Thanks," I said, helping myself to a donut.

"Hey!"

We turned around to see Franklin trotting over to join

us. "Hi, Mackenzie," he said, flashing my cousin a big smile. Scooter and Lucas both glared at him.

"Hi," she mumbled back, her mouth full of maple donut.

I was beginning to get used to being ignored.

"Do you guys want a tour of the sugarhouse?" Franklin asked Mackenzie. "I'm scheduled to give one right now."

My cousin nodded. The rest of us assumed his invitation meant us, too, and we followed them toward the cabin at the far end of the parking lot. I studiously avoided looking at Scooter as we passed the barn, but I couldn't resist flicking Calhoun a sidelong glance. His face was stony. I sighed and looked away. I still really, really wanted to explain about the kiss.

Woodsmoke drifted from the round metal chimney pipe poking out of the sugarhouse roof, and my cousin sniffed the air happily. "It smells like camping!"

"Yeah," I agreed, suddenly missing Texas again. Some of my happiest memories were of the camping trips that our families had taken together, along with the rest of my Gifford aunts and uncles and cousins.

"Welcome to Freeman Farm, everyone!" said Franklin, offering the handful of tourists waiting by the door a wide smile. "Who wants to see how maple syrup is made?"

From the practiced way in which my classmate kicked into tour guide-mode, I could tell he'd done this before. He herded us efficiently through the front door and into a small entry room. The walls were paneled in rough wood and lined with tools and antique-looking buckets and other implements. We gazed at them curiously as Franklin launched into a history of the maple syrup industry.

"Native Americans were the first to discover the maple tree's sweet gift," he began. "For thousands of years the Abenaki—that means 'people of the dawn'—who lived in this part of New England harvested sap and made it into syrup. They called this time of year 'maple moon.'"

He held up a bowl crudely shaped from bark. "This is a *mokuk*," he continued. "It's made of birch bark and sealed with pine resin, and it's what the Abenaki used to collect sap. Later, the early settlers used wooden buckets." He plucked one from a peg on the wall. "Those evolved into the tin buckets with lids that have become an icon for the industry, and that you often see on syrup jug labels and postcards. Today, buckets are made of galvanized steel or food-grade plastic, although many large operations, like ours, have replaced buckets with plastic tubing that feeds from the trees directly into holding tanks."

As Franklin passed examples of each of these items around, Scooter took the opportunity to smack Lucas playfully on the head with a length of plastic tubing.

"Quit it!" I warned, but once again Mackenzie just laughed.

"So how do you get the sap out of the trees?" someone in the crowd wanted to know.

"I'm so glad you asked!" Franklin replied.

He's really good at this, I thought, impressed.

My classmate held up a small object that looked like a wooden tube or spigot. "This is called a 'spile,' which comes from the Dutch word meaning 'splinter' or 'peg.' This one is made of cedar, but the Abenaki and other tribes also fashioned them out of sumac stems. The spile was inserted into a gash in the trunk of the maple tree, and sap would flow through it into the waiting container, such as a hollowed out branch or a *mokuk*." He held up the birch bark bowl again.

"Do people still use spiles?" asked Mackenzie.

Franklin nodded. "Pretty much, except today they're made of metal, not wood." He pointed to a display board on the wall behind us featuring all different styles and sizes of spiles. "And of course we don't gash the trees with axes these days—we use drills to make the holes."

I fingered the small metal spigot as it came around. A faint memory stirred. The sights and smells in the sugarhouse were giving me a flash of déjà vu, and I was pretty sure that Gramps and Lola had brought me someplace like this when I was little. Maybe even right here to this farm.

"All we need—well, besides maple trees—is for the weather to cooperate," Franklin continued. "Cold nights plus warm days equal a good maple harvest."

"Why is that?" asked another tourist.

"It's simple, really," Franklin told him. "The alternating

temperatures cause pressure changes in the tree, which makes the sap flow. If it's too cold at night, the sap takes longer to warm up during the day. It's a good thing the winter we just had finally decided to call it quits, otherwise we might not have had a sap run at all this year!"

"He sounds like Mr. Bigelow," Calhoun whispered, and I nodded. Mr. Bigelow was our science teacher.

We exchanged a smile, and for a split second I thought maybe this would be the moment to explain about Scooter. Before I could, though, the smile vanished, and Calhoun looked away.

I felt my face flush. I could also feel my cousin watching me. I forced myself to smile at her. If I wasn't careful, she might figure out how I felt about Calhoun, and I didn't need that complication right now.

"So how does the sap get turned into syrup?" asked a gray-haired man in a bright red fleece jacket.

"Early settlers boiled sap in metal cauldrons on tripods they set up over open fires," Franklin explained. "These days, though, we're a little more sophisticated." Crossing the small room to a door on the far side, he paused for dramatic effect. "Which brings me to the next stop on the tour: the evaporation room!"

"He's like Willy Wonka giving a tour of the chocolate factory," said Calhoun, and Mackenzie and I both laughed.

"I'm in heaven," Mackenzie murmured as Franklin flung

open the door and we were suddenly enveloped in a warm, maple-scented cloud of steam. She closed her eyes and inhaled deeply. "Wake me up when Spring Break is over."

"Hello, everyone, I'm Frank Freeman," said Franklin's father, who was waiting for us next to a long piece of gleaming stainless steel equipment. "As you can see, ours is a completely modern processing facility. Our wood-burning evaporator here can process about twenty-five gallons of sap per hour."

We watched as he opened a furnacelike door at the far end of the apparatus and threw in more wood. The coals and half-burned logs inside glowed a brilliant fiery orange. I could feel the heat all the way across the room.

"This is called the firebox," said Mr. Freeman, warming his hands briefly in front of the blaze before shutting the door again. "A storage tank outside feeds the collected sap into this stainless steel evaporator pan." He pointed to the long, low horizontal pan set on top of the evaporator's surface. "As the sap boils, water is released through steam, and the sap becomes more and more concentrated. When it reaches the proper density—a sugar content of sixty-six percent or more—it's officially syrup."

Mr. Freeman looked around the room. "I'm happy to stick around after the tour and answer questions for anyone who wants more technical information, but for the rest of you, I'll conclude by explaining the final step, which is when we filter the syrup to remove any niter, or sugar sand—a sediment of naturally occurring minerals. From there the syrup is bottled and graded and labeled"—he held up a bottle bearing one of Freeman Farm's distinctive orange labels—"and sent next door to our store in the barn, which you fine folks will be visiting next, if memory serves." He winked at the crowd, who all laughed obligingly. "Any questions?"

A hand at the back shot up. "How much sap does a single maple tree typically produce?"

"Good question," said Mr. Freeman. "Usually between ten and twenty gallons, which translates to a quart or two of syrup."

"Wow, that's not much syrup for all that sap," someone else noted, and Franklin's father nodded.

"You are correct. Maple farming is a labor-intensive process, which is one of the reasons that syrup isn't necessarily cheap." He waggled his dark eyebrows. "But every drop is oh so worth it, right?"

The onlookers laughed again.

"Can you put more than one spile in a tree?" asked a woman in a blue cable-knit hat.

"Yes, but you need to be careful not to overtap," Mr. Freeman replied. "The bigger the tree, the more taps you can place. Depending on the circumference of the trunk, you can use one, two, or three spiles."

"So you must have to tap a lot of trees in order to produce a decent amount of syrup," the woman added, and Mr. Freeman nodded again.

"Our farm has one of the biggest and best sugar bushes for miles around," he said proudly. "There are thousands of trees on our property."

"Do the trees mind having their sap taken?" a little kid in the front piped up.

Franklin answered this one. "Not at all. It's kind of like donating blood, in fact. Just as your body replenishes itself, so the tree gets busy producing more sap to replace what's been taken. And, by the way, some maple trees on our property have been tapped for over a hundred and fifty years and are still producing!"

A chorus of oohs and aahs went up at this. I looked over at Mackenzie. I could tell she was enjoying herself. The Freemans put on a good show.

The tour over, Franklin led us out of the sugarhouse and into the barn store next door. It took Mackenzie forever to decide what to buy. I followed her around, keeping an eye on Calhoun as I did. The good thing was, he wasn't hovering around my cousin the way Scooter and Lucas were doing. The bad thing was, he wasn't hovering around me, either. He ignored us both as he leafed through a coffee table book about maple syrup production.

Mackenzie finally settled on maple syrup and maple candy

for her parents. "And Cameron will love this," she said, grabbing a container of maple hot sauce and putting it in her shopping basket.

"Who's Cameron?" asked Scooter, popping up behind us.

"Mr. Perf—" I started to say, but Mackenzie stepped on my foot.

"My, um, friend," she finished, at the same time that I said "Ouch." "We're on the swim team together back in Austin."

I gave her a look. Since when was Cameron McAllister just a "friend"? Apparently my cousin was enjoying all the male attention here in Pumpkin Falls.

"I should be getting back," said Lucas, glancing anxiously at his watch. His outings always came with a time limit. "My mother said she'd treat us all to lunch at Lou's, if you guys want to come with me."

"I never turn down a cheeseburger," said Calhoun, who had rejoined us.

"I thought you were going to show us the scene of the crime?" I murmured to Franklin, glancing around to make sure we weren't overheard.

He nodded. "It'll just take a couple of minutes. We can stop there on our way to Lou's. Let me just ask my mom if I can go first."

As we were leaving the barn store, a car pulled into the lot and a woman in jeans and a down vest got out. I'd seen her before at Lovejoy's Books—she was one of the reporters from the *Pumpkin Falls Patriot-Bugle*.

"There you are, Franklin!" said his mother. "Would you mind showing Janet what we found out in the sugar bush yesterday?"

Franklin flashed us an apologetic look. "Sure," he said. "Can I go to lunch at Lou's afterward, Mom? Mrs. Winthrop's treating."

"*May* I go to lunch," his mother replied automatically. I guess all parents have the grammar reflex. "Make it a short one. We need your help here."

"Okay." Motioning to the reporter to follow, he headed for the woods.

"Why is it called a sugar bush?" asked Mackenzie as we trotted after them. "I thought the sap came from trees, not bushes."

"It does," Franklin replied. "But for some reason a stand of maples—especially sugar maples, which is mostly what we have on our farm—is referred to as a 'sugar bush.' It's tradition, I guess."

"Your family puts a lot of work into managing this operation, doesn't it?" asked the reporter, rapidly scribbling in her notebook.

Franklin nodded. "Yep. The sugar bush has to be constantly monitored and maintained. We clear out underbrush and dead wood in the spring and summer, thin the saplings to make sure there are no more than fifty to sixty trees per acre—lots of stuff like that. Then there's equipment maintenance and repairs, cutting and stacking enough wood to keep the evaporator fire going during the sap run, making sure everything is spotless, ordering supplies, setting up the tubing and vacuum pumps—it kind of never ends. Plus, the barn store is a year-round operation, and we do all our own packing and shipping."

I looked at my classmate with new respect. I'd known he was kind of obsessed with maple syrup, but over the past few days I'd seen firsthand how hardworking he and his family were, and how much pride they all took in their business. It was impressive.

The sun was directly overhead now, and I unzipped my jacket. A light breeze stirred in the branches. I looked up, on the alert for birds. It would be totally cool to see another owl.

"What was it Franklin said the Abenakis called this time of year?" I asked my cousin.

"Maple moon, I think."

We walked along in silence. *Maple moon.* I liked the way that sounded. Maybe the maple moon would bring me luck in spotting an owl of my very own. Or maybe my new silver earrings would. I touched a finger to one of them and glanced over at Calhoun again, wondering if he'd noticed them.

A couple of minutes later Franklin stopped in front of a trio of trees. They looked exactly the same as all the others in the woods to me, but he obviously knew his family's property better than I did.

"This is where the sabotage took place," he told us.

I looked at the network of plastic tubing that linked these trees with all the others in the sugar bush. "How can you tell?"

"See that vertical line?" He pointed to a length of black tubing that connected the spile on the tree in front of us to the fatter horizontal blue tubing below it that led downhill. "When we were doing a routine inspection yesterday, we found that it had been severed. We replaced it, but my dad left the piece that had been cut so that we'd remember the spot."

Leaning over, he picked up a slender piece of black tubing that was lying on the ground. The reporter took out her camera, and Mackenzie and I both snapped a few photos as well.

The reporter made us all pose for a picture, and then my friends and I all milled around inspecting the evidence. Suddenly, there was a crashing noise in the underbrush behind us. We turned around to see someone striding toward us through the woods.

It was Coach Maynard, and he did not look happy. Not one bit.

"So this is the way you Freemans want to play it, is it?" he said, shaking something at Franklin. It was a piece of black plastic tubing, identical to the one we'd just photographed. "You want to ambush me *again*? Well, two can play at that game. Where's your father?"

CHAPTER 13

Word travels fast in a small town.

Ella Bellow helped it along, of course. How she found out about the showdown in the sugar bush was a mystery, but I suspected that Janet-the-reporter had something to do with it. Whoever or whatever fed the flame, by the end of the day Pumpkin Falls definitely had a full-blown feud on its hands, and people had started taking sides.

After our photo session at the scene of the crime with the *Pumpkin Falls Patriot-Bugle*, my friends and I had continued into town to Lou's, where we'd discussed what we'd seen over burgers and fries.

"If Coach Maynard's place was hit a second time, do you think it might happen again at your farm too?" I asked Franklin.

"I don't know," he replied, his expression troubled. He dipped a French fry into the puddle of ketchup on his plate. "I hope not."

"It seems like kind of a stupid thing to steal," said Mackenzie. "They'd have to take a ton of sap to even make a single gallon of syrup, right?"

Franklin nodded. "Yup. Forty gallons or so. My dad thinks it might just be vandals. You know, teenagers blowing off steam."

"From Pumpkin Falls?" Scooter looked doubtful.

Franklin shook his head. "He's thinking West Hartfield, maybe. Remember last fall, when some guys from their football team spray-painted their stupid bobcat mascot on the side of one of the Farnsworths' cows?"

Scooter and Lucas and Calhoun started to laugh.

"I'll never forget the look on their faces when Mr. Farnsworth drove up to their next home game with his trailer and unloaded the cow right onto the field during halftime," crowed Scooter. "He said, 'This belongs to you, apparently,' and then let it loose."

"It was epic," Calhoun told Mackenzie, grinning. "That cow chased their football team and marching band into the gym."

"Seriously?" My cousin's voice shot up in disbelief. "People actually do stuff like that here? Pranks with cows?" She paused, gave my classmates a mischievous grin, then trotted out her fake radio announcer voice. "Pumpkin Falls: the town that time forgot."

"Yeah, it's a hopping place," Calhoun replied. Then his

expression grew serious. "I hope your dad's right, Franklin, and it's vandalism. Because if it's sabotage, that means someone deliberately wants someone else's business to fail."

Lucas looked down at his plate. "Wow, I hadn't thought about that."

We were all quiet for a moment, considering this possibility.

"I just wish there was a way to find out for sure who's responsible," said Franklin finally.

Scooter got a funny look on his face. At first, I thought maybe he'd accidentally bitten his tongue or something, but then I realized he'd just had an idea.

"I have to go check something out," he told us, sliding off his counter stool. "I'll text you guys later, okay?"

"That was weird," I said, watching as Scooter sprinted out of the restaurant.

"Uh-huh," Mackenzie agreed.

We finished our lunch, thanked Mrs. Winthrop for treating, and then went our separate ways, agreeing to be in touch again later after we heard back from Scooter.

"So what else do you feel like doing today?" I asked my cousin when we were back outside.

"Weren't we going to try and find a German-English dictionary?"

"Oh yeah, I totally forgot."

I steered her down the street toward Lovejoy's Books,

pausing by the antiques store so she could gawk at the moth-eaten moose head in the display window. It was sporting a pair of sunglasses today, along with a "Maple Madness!" sign around its neck. The Mahoneys had jazzed things up for the celebration.

My cousin pulled out her cell phone and snapped a picture. "Cameron is crazy about—"

"Taxidermy?"

"Shut up. Vintage sunglasses. Those are really cool."

"Vintage sunglasses. I'll be sure and make a note of that," I said drily, and she made a face at me, then laughed.

"Greetings and salutations!" said Aunt True, looking up from the shipment of books she was unpacking as we came through the bookshop door. "You girls are just in time for afternoon treats."

I'd been hoping that was the case.

"Don't touch the ones on the red tray," she added. "I need to drop those off at the General Store later for the Bake-Off."

"I'll bet you win," Mackenzie told her, grabbing two Bookshop Blondies from the other tray on the counter. She took a bite out of one of them. "These are fantastic!"

My aunt looked pleased. "Why, thank you, ma'am."

Miss Marple, who'd heard the word "treats," roused herself from her nap and trotted over. She sat obediently before anyone could say a word—"the preemptive sit," my father has dubbed it—and looked at us expectantly.

"Yes, Miss Marple, you can have a treat too," Mackenzie told her, taking a dog biscuit from the cookie jar on the counter. My grandparents always kept it there for four-legged visitors.

"Dog people are book people," Gramps liked to tell customers. When Lola pointed out that cat people were book people too, my grandfather would wink and add, "But cats don't bring their owners into bookshops on a leash."

"Any chance there's a German-English dictionary somewhere around here?" I asked.

Aunt True's eyebrows shot up. "I didn't know you were taking German."

"I'm not."

"Oh?" She gave me a quizzical look.

"Um, actually, it's for me," Mackenzie said. "It's for this, uh, project I have to do." Out of the corner of my eye, I saw her slip one hand behind her back and cross her fingers.

"Really? Interesting." My aunt disappeared into the travel section, returning a moment later with a thick paperback. "Will this do?"

Mackenzie and I nodded, and my cousin reached for her purse.

"Absolutely not," said Aunt True, waving it away. "What's the point of having a family business if you can't do something nice for your family now and then?" She handed the dictionary to my cousin and smiled. "Good luck with your project."

Mackenzie's face flushed. She was obviously feeling guilty about the fib. Not too obviously, I hoped. "Thanks."

"So I was showing Mackenzie the original Truly's passport," I said quickly, changing the subject. "You know, the one that's hanging on the wall outside my bedroom door? Anyway, we were wondering if you knew what Matthew Lovejoy did for a living. Besides being a soldier in the Civil War, I mean."

"Farming, I think," Aunt True replied absently, turning her attention back to the box of books she was unloading. "I'm pretty sure most of our ancestors were farmers. When they weren't founding colleges and naming lakes and mountains after themselves, that is."

Mackenzie and I exchanged a glance. Whatever it was that the original Truly was so worked up about in her diary sure didn't sound like farming.

"Oh good!" cried my aunt. "The new Inspector Mistlethwaite mystery is here!"

I smiled at her. "You thound like Pippa."

She smiled back and passed me a stack of books. "I thuppothe I do. Stick two copies on the new releases table by the front door, would you? And put one with Miss Marple's Picks. The other three can go in the mystery section."

I nodded and took them from her. "Um, did Matthew maybe have another business on the side?"

Aunt True peered at me over the top of her zebra-striped reading glasses. "What makes you ask?"

I shrugged. "No particular reason."

"Your grandfather would probably know. He's the family historian."

I glanced up at the clock on the wall and frowned. "What time is it in Namibia?"

Aunt True made a quick mental calculation. "Let's see, they're six hours ahead of us this time of year, so early evening, I think."

I turned to Mackenzie. "Dang! We won't have time to call them before swim practice, and by the time we get home, it will be too late." We'd have to wait and try first thing in the morning.

"Sounds urgent." My aunt gave me a thoughtful look, her curiosity definitely piqued.

"Uh, no, not really," I said hastily, and grabbing my cousin, I scurried off to distribute the new mystery books.

The rest of the afternoon was uneventful, aside from the fact that Coach Maynard was uncharacteristically quiet during afternoon swim practice. I just figured he was embarrassed about losing his temper in front of Mackenzie and Lucas and me earlier at Freeman Farm. I wanted to tell him it was okay, and that I'd seen far worse from Lieutenant Colonel Jericho T. Lovejoy, but I didn't want to embarrass him. Plus, he didn't look like he was in the mood to chat, so I just kept my head down and focused on the workout.

By dinnertime, there'd been no further word from

Scooter, and we were no closer to solving the sabotage mystery. Since it was Hatcher's and Danny's turn to do the dishes, after second helpings of my mom's awesome mac and cheese, Mackenzie and I went up to my room and got out the German-English dictionary. We looked up *"Heimweh"* and *"Zwetschgen"* and *"Schwangerschaftsübelkeit"*—they meant "homesick" and "plum" and "morning sickness"—and then I sent off an e-mail to Gramps. It was the middle of the night now in Namibia, but he'd get it first thing in the morning.

"Want me to read some more?" I asked my cousin when I was done. She was lounging on her air mattress, texting Cameron.

"Sure."

As I pulled the blue-bound diary out from under my pillow, there was a scrabbling noise in my closet. I froze. Had my sister's hamster gotten out of his cage again? The scrabbling didn't sound Nibbles-size, though. It sounded bigger. Bilbo-size, maybe. If Lauren had snuck that ferret into our house, she was in big trouble. Setting the diary down, I got up and crossed the room to check. When I opened the closet door, however, it wasn't Bilbo I discovered, but my sister herself.

"You little sneak!" I said furiously. "You're spying on us!"

"I am not!" Lauren protested.

"You are too!" Grabbing her arm, I yanked her from the closet and pointed to my bedroom door. "Out! Now!"

"But I just—"

"I am sick and tired of your stupid Nancy Drew stuff! We all are. Just quit it, would you?"

Mackenzie shot me a warning glance. "How about we play that board game I promised you and Pippa, Lauren?"

My sister gave her a grateful look. "That sounds good."

"Don't let me catch you spying on us again!" I snapped, still seething. "Ever!"

My cousin frowned at me as the two of them left, but I didn't care. Lauren deserved it—she was really getting under my skin.

I stayed in my room and fumed until it was time to head downtown to our knitting class.

Which was when the real fireworks started.

CHAPTER 14

The first hint we had that something was wrong was that Coach Maynard's wife didn't show up for class.

"That's odd," said Ella, frowning at the clock on the wall. We'd all been at A Stitch in Time for nearly half an hour, which unfortunately wasn't long enough to miraculously transform my project. My so-called sock still looked like a droopy dishcloth. "I ran into Alice this morning at the post office, and she said she was looking forward to our gathering tonight."

"Her car was parked in front of the General Store when I left the library earlier," Mr. Henry reported. "I figured she was dropping off her entry for the Bake-Off."

The other thing that Pumpkin Falls was all abuzz about, besides the string of sap thefts, was the Maple Madness Bake-Off. The General Store traditionally hosted the presentation table, where people could ogle the entries before the judges made their decision. Mackenzie and I had offered to drop off

Aunt True's Bookshop Blondies on our way home earlier, so we could scout the competition.

"She's definitely going to win," Mackenzie had said, eyeing the assortment of muffins, bars, cookies, candy, cakes, and other assorted treats on display.

"I don't know," I'd replied, my mouth starting to water. "I've had Mrs. Freeman's Maple Fudge, and it's awesome. And Mr. Henry's Maple Walnut Cupcakes look pretty great too."

Everything had looked pretty great, actually. I had no idea how the judges were going to decide.

Now, back at A Stitch in Time, the phone on Ella's sales counter rang. She got up to answer it. And then Mrs. Freeman's cell phone rang, and so did my mother's, and so did just about everybody else's in the knitting class.

"She said what?" said Ella.

"They're doing what?" said my mother.

"You've got to be kidding me!" said Mrs. Freeman, and sprang to her feet.

Ella ran for the door, and my mother shoved her knitting into the bag of books about the Underground Railroad that Mr. Henry had brought for her and got up to follow her.

My cousin and I looked at each other, mystified.

"What's H-A-P-P-E-N-I-N-G?" asked Annie.

My mother looked over at my cousin and me. "Come on, girls. That was your father. Your aunt needs reinforcements over at the General Store. It sounds like a riot's about to break out."

By the time our entire sock class arrived, the General Store was in an uproar.

"Absolutely no way!" I heard Mrs. Farnsworth shouting, as I peered over the crowd to try and see the cause of the commotion. Sometimes it really helps to be six feet tall.

Mackenzie tugged on my sleeve. "What's going on?"

I glanced down at her, grateful for once that I wasn't petite. The only thing my poor cousin could see was Bud Jefferson's back. "Mrs. Farnsworth—she and her husband run the store, remember?"

"I thought they raised cows."

"They do that, too," I replied. "She's upset about something, but I'm not sure what yet."

"This is ridiculous!" Aunt True was shouting back. "We can't let this divide our town!"

I edged my way through the crowd. My mother and Mackenzie followed, using me as a battering ram. The General Store owner was squared off against my aunt. Behind them were two long tables covered with maple leaf–printed fabric. The plates piled high with Bake-Off entries were evenly divided between the two.

"We've never had two tables before—just one," Aunt True continued. "What kind of a message does this send to our community?"

"The message that some of us don't agree with what's going on," Mrs. Farnsworth said stubbornly.

"Surely we're bigger than this!" my aunt protested.

That's when I saw the signs. One table was marked TEAM FREEMAN, and the other TEAM MAYNARD. My swim coach's wife was standing behind the Team Maynard table with her arms folded across her chest.

"Uh-oh," I said.

"What?" asked Mackenzie, tugging my sleeve again. "Uh-oh," she said, when I pointed to the signs.

"Hatfields and McCoys," said my mother grimly.

Just then my father stepped forward. "I'd like to offer a solution," he said, his deep voice booming.

One thing about having a father who's ex-military, he knows how to command respect. The crowd quieted down as he turned to face them. "The Farnsworths have generously hosted the Maple Madness Bake-Off here at their store for many years—since I was a boy, in fact!"

"Last week, you mean?" someone called. That got a laugh.

"We all owe them our thanks," my father continued, smiling. He clapped his good hand against his prosthetic one and a ripple of applause and nods of agreement ran through the gathered throng as people followed suit. "Perhaps it's unfair to ask Ethel to go against what she feels is her right, since it's her store. And so, if it's amenable to everyone—Joyce, are you here to count the vote?" He looked around for the town clerk, who raised her hand from the back of the crowd. "If you all agree, I'd like to offer Lovejoy's Books as host for this year's Bake-Off."

You'd have thought he'd just suggested removing Paul Revere's bell from the steeple of the church. People looked that shocked. His offer completely took the wind out of Mrs. Farnsworth's sails. From the expression on her face it was clear that she didn't know what to say.

"What an excellent idea!" The crowd parted as Ella Bellow swept forward. "Jericho, I heartily agree."

Ella Bellow may be many things, including gossip central, but she's also one of our town's oldest residents, and people respect her.

"I think it's a good idea too," said Mrs. Freeman. "And, Alice, I want to assure you again that my family had absolutely nothing to do with what has been happening on both of our farms. Can't we rise to the occasion here, together, for the good of Pumpkin Falls?"

Mrs. Maynard didn't look convinced.

"This will just be a temporary change of venue, of course," my father hastened to explain. "I'm not trying to steal the spotlight or undermine town tradition in any way. I'm simply offering a solution during what seems to have become a stressful time for our town. Think of Lovejoy's Books as Switzerland—neutral territory. No choosing sides, no swirl of rumors or counter rumors, just delicious baked goods being judged on their own merits."

"Switzerland? Are you kidding me?" murmured Mackenzie, who was having trouble keeping her face straight.

"Don't say it," I warned, but it was too late.

"The town that time forgot," she whispered in her radio announcer voice, grinning at me. I pretended I didn't hear her.

The vote was taken, and everyone agreed. Well, almost everyone. Coach Maynard's wife took her Maple Coffeecake from the Team Maynard table and swept past us without a glance. A couple of her close friends followed suit. The rest of the crowd formed a procession down Main Street as the baked goods were gathered up and transferred to our bookstore. My aunt and I ran ahead to grab a long folding table from the basement.

"We'll set it up back in the Annex," Aunt True said as we wrestled the table into place. In short order it was covered with a tablecloth and the baked goods and their entry cards arranged—all mingled together, this time, with no TEAM MAYNARD and TEAM FREEMAN signs. Then everybody stood around awkwardly for a few minutes trying to pretend nothing had happened. And then they went home.

"Well done, J. T.," said Ella Bellow, patting my father's good arm as the last of the crowd left.

"That was brilliant, honey!" My mother beamed at him. "I was worried for a moment there that a few people might grab pitchforks."

Mrs. Freeman looked tired but relieved. "This really has been a stressful couple of days."

"Let's just hope the truce holds until the judging," said my father.

My aunt looked up from where she was busy covering all the Bake-Off entries with plastic wrap. "It will hold for you, J. T.," she said, smiling at him. "You're a hero in this town."

My father gave her an uncharacteristically shy smile in return. He doesn't like to think of himself as a hero, just a soldier who did his duty for his country.

As I watched the two of them, I thought about what Aunt True had told me, back when I'd asked why she'd given up her travels to work at the bookshop. "Family is everything," she'd said. Maybe she was right.

"Small-town life can be tricky sometimes, but when it works, there's nothing like it," my mother observed.

"Pumpkin Falls," whispered Mackenzie in her radio announcer voice, quietly so nobody but me could hear her. This time I didn't pretend to ignore her. Instead, I slipped my arm through hers and whispered back, "The town that time forgot."

CHAPTER 15

"You keep telling me that this town is boring," said Mackenzie, looking up from the *Pumpkin Falls Patriot-Bugle*. She was seated at the kitchen table, eating a bowl of cereal. "It's not boring at all."

Of course it's not boring when you're the center of attention all the time, I thought, glancing over at the front page. My cousin had been glued to it ever since we came downstairs for breakfast.

SABOTAGE IN PUMPKIN FALLS? blazed the headline. SAP RUSTLERS STAGE BRAZEN HEIST!

Prominently featured beneath the headline was the picture taken yesterday of my friends and me at Freeman Farm. We were standing in front of one of the maple trees at the scene of the crime, and Mackenzie was front and center, her trademark Gifford sunflower smile on full display. I was barely visible, just a part of my head poking up behind Franklin, Scooter,

Lucas, and Calhoun. Franklin and Scooter and Lucas were supposed to be examining the evidence, but the camera had caught them gawking at Mackenzie. It was hard to tell which way Calhoun was looking. Not at me, though. That much I could tell.

Mackenzie was my cousin and my best friend. It wasn't as if she were doing something on purpose to make me feel like I was in stealth mode. She was just being, well, Mackenzie. But I didn't like feeling this way either. Left out. Overlooked. Ignored.

And what she'd said about Calhoun the other day—that he was cute—bothered me too. I couldn't figure out what she'd meant by it. Was it just a casual observation, or was she interested in him? And, more important, was he interested in her?

I pushed back abruptly from the table. My mother held up her coffee cup wordlessly. She was engrossed in a picture book she must have pulled out of Mr. Henry's library bag—*Moses* was its title, and it looked like it was about Harriet Tubman. Apparently, she'd finally settled on a topic for her term paper. I poured her a refill, then grabbed my jacket from its hook by the back door and went outside to feed the birds.

A light breeze danced through the row of evergreens that marked the edge of my grandparents' property. The branches swayed like swimmers' arms. Closing my eyes, I leaned back against the door for a moment and inhaled deeply. I held my breath for a count of three, then exhaled.

"I hear you," I said, opening my eyes again. Judging by the excited chatter of chickadees in the trees, they knew breakfast was coming. "Be patient."

I took my time filling the feeders and checking the water level in my grandfather's prized heated birdbath, pausing to listen to the twitter and jabber of the juncos, jays, and—wait, was that a song sparrow? I cocked my head. It was! Spring had definitely sprung.

My spirits rising, I headed back to the house. I'd find a way to talk to Calhoun about Scooter and Freeman Farm, and this thing with Mackenzie would sort itself out too. One thing I knew about my cousin for sure—she was loyal. She might tease me if I confided to her that I liked Calhoun, but if her interest in him was more than casual and she knew that I liked him, she'd back right off.

It was all so ridiculous, really—the surprise kiss, the way the boys were falling all over themselves to get Mackenzie's attention, the showdown last night at the General Store—even the whole notion of sabotage in pokey Pumpkin Falls. Sap rustlers? Seriously? The whole idea made me want to laugh.

The problem was, though, that people I knew and cared about were involved, which didn't make it funny at all. The Freemans depended on a good sap run each year to help earn income for their farm, and even though Maynard's Maple Barn was more of a hobby than a livelihood for my swim coach, he was my friend too. That scene at the General Store last night had been ugly. I really didn't want to have to choose sides.

The only solution to the whole mess was to get to the bottom of it quickly, before things got out of hand. Pulling my phone from my back pocket, I scrolled back through the pictures I'd taken at the scene of the crime. Nothing had changed since I'd puzzled over them last night. A bunch of trees in a forest; muddy footprints around the base of several trunks; a length of severed plastic tubing. Something had happened, that much was obvious. But exactly what was anybody's guess.

I scraped the mud off my boots by the back door and went inside. There was no sign of my mother or Lauren, but Mackenzie was still dawdling over the newspaper. And I could hear Pippa in the family room, singing along to *Chicken Parade*, her favorite morning cartoon show.

"I'm going to check my e-mail," I told Mackenzie. "Maybe Gramps has gotten back to us."

"I'll come with you." Dumping her empty cereal bowl in the sink, she followed me upstairs.

My grandfather had indeed e-mailed back. I read his response aloud: *Sorry I missed you last night. Can we connect at nine a.m. your time?*

I glanced at the clock. We had fifteen minutes.

Sure, I wrote back. *Talk to you soon!*

My cell phone vibrated just then. "It's Scooter," I said, frowning at his text message.

PFPE STAKEOUT TONIGHT!

"'PFPE' means Pumpkin Falls Private Eyes, right?" said my cousin, reading over my shoulder.

I nodded.

"But what does he mean by 'stakeout'?"

WHAT DO YOU MEAN, STAKEOUT? I texted back.

SURVEILLANCE, DUH. AT FREEMAN FARM.

Scooter was such a pain.

YOU MEAN US? I texted.

DOUBLE DUH.

I sighed, and rolled my eyes at my cousin. WHAT TIME? I texted back.

NINE THIRTY.

I groaned. Besides the fact that Scooter was infuriating, the last thing I wanted to do was spend Spring Break hiding in the woods, freezing my socks off while we tried to catch a sap rustler.

FORGET IT, I texted back.

My cell phone rang instantly. It was Scooter, of course. I put him on speaker.

"C'mon, Truly," he coaxed. "Calhoun's in, and even Lucas said he'd go with us."

Of course he did. Lucas was hardly going to miss out on an opportunity to spend an evening with the new love of his life.

"I borrowed some stuff from one of my dad's colleagues," Scooter continued.

"What kind of stuff?" I asked suspiciously.

"Video surveillance equipment."

"Seriously?" said Mackenzie. "Cool!"

I could practically hear Scooter's ego inflating. "Yeah, this guy's a private eye—a real one," he boasted. "My dad's law firm hires him sometimes. Anyway, this is sophisticated stuff. We just need to set it up, turn on the camera, and it will relay video to my phone."

"Wow!" Mackenzie sounded impressed. I was too, but I wasn't about to tell Scooter that.

"Why can't we set it up in the daytime, if it's all automatic?" I asked.

"I can't pick it up until later this afternoon. And after that, Calhoun's father is taking us to the Burger Barn over in West Hartfield."

"You just had burgers yesterday."

Scooter's grin was audible. "Calhoun's not the only one who never turns down a burger."

I wasn't sure I liked this idea at all. Sneaking out of the house at night was not only way up on the list of things that I wasn't any good at, but it was also guaranteed to get me a permanent spot in Lieutenant Colonel Jericho T. Lovejoy's doghouse if I were to get caught.

"Oh, come on, Truly!" said Mackenzie, her eyes alight with excitement. "All we're trying to do is help the Freemans—and Coach Maynard."

I hesitated. "I guess."

"Trust me on this one," my cousin said. "I'm older and wiser, after all."

I shot her a look. "By a *week*."

"Kidding! Sheesh."

"We'll meet by the entrance to the shortcut off Hill Street," Scooter told us. "I'll see you at nine thirty sharp. Bring flashlights." He hung up.

I shook my head. "I hope we're doing the right thing."

My cousin shrugged. "If not, at least I'll go home to Austin with an exciting story to tell."

"Yeah, about how I got grounded for life! You're not the one who'll have to face the music with my father if we get caught."

"We won't get caught."

I looked over at the clock again. "Gramps should be calling any minute."

Grabbing the diary from its hiding place under my pillow, I crossed to my desk and sat down in front of my laptop. I didn't have to wait long. A moment later I heard the alert tone that signaled an incoming call.

"Truly!" cried my grandfather as his face flashed onscreen.

"Gramps!" I cried back.

We beamed at each other.

"Your grandmother sends her love," he said. "She's sorry she couldn't be here to talk to you, but she started a crafts class in the village, and today's the first meeting."

I laughed. "Sounds like Pumpkin Falls," I told him, and explained about Ella's knitting class.

"I'll be sure and tell her that you're with her in needle-work solidarity." Peering closer at the screen, Gramps added, "My goodness, is that Miss Mackenzie I spy?"

My cousin leaned over my shoulder and waved. "Hi, Mr. Lovejoy!"

He waved back. "Are you girls having a fun Spring Break?"

We both nodded.

"How's that life list of yours coming along, Truly?"

I told him about hearing the eastern phoebe and the song sparrow. "And guess what? I finally saw an owl!" I left out the fact that Mackenzie spotted it first.

"Huzzah and wahoo!" Gramps gave me two big thumbs-up. "Congratulations, sweetheart! I remember my first owl like it was yesterday. What kind?"

"Barred," I replied.

"Lovely. One of my favorites. Those beautiful dark eyes!"

"I know! I could have watched him forever."

We beamed at each other again. My grandfather and I speak the same language.

"So I e-mailed you because we found something," I told him finally.

"What kind of something?"

I held up the diary.

He looked puzzled. "A book?"

"Not exactly." I explained about the diary, and how and where Mackenzie and I had discovered it.

"How extraordinary!" he exclaimed when I was done. "To think that it was hidden there all these years. Have you read it?"

"Some of it. It's kind of confusing, though, which is why I wanted to talk to you. Can I read you a bit?"

"By all means." He leaned closer to the computer screen, tilting his head in concentration as I read him the passages in question.

"Wind is from the south, she says?"

I nodded.

"And she definitely mentioned a package?"

I nodded again.

"You need to show the diary to your parents right away!" The excitement in my grandfather's voice crackled over the computer screen. "It sounds to me like Truly and Matthew were involved with the Underground Railroad!"

CHAPTER 16

"Where's Mom?" I cried, bounding downstairs to the kitchen. Mackenzie was right behind me.

"She must have gone out while I was feeding Bilbo," said Lauren, coming through the back door.

I pulled my cell phone out of my pocket and shot off a text to my mother: WHERE R U?

HEADING TO CAMPUS, she texted back a moment later. STOPPED BY BOOKSTORE TO SEE DAD.

STAY THERE! HAVE TO SHOW YOU SOMETHING!

NOT GOING ANYWHERE—CUSTOMERS COMING OUT OF THE WOODWORK. COULD USE YOUR HELP.

"Come on, Mackenzie," I said. "We're going into town."

Hearing this, Pippa detached herself from the TV in the family room. "But Mom thaid you have to walk uth to Belinda'th!"

I frowned at her. "Can't you and Lauren go by yourselves?"

Lauren shot me a dirty look. "Of course."

"But Mom thaid you'd do it," Pippa whined, clinging to Mackenzie's hand.

"I'd like to see Belinda's anyway," my cousin said. "You've told me so much about it."

I sighed. "Fine." And tucking the diary into my jacket pocket, I hustled everyone out the door.

Belinda's house was at the very end of Maple Street. A sprawling Victorian with a wrap-around porch, it was nearly as big as my grandparents' house. Belinda was outside, bundled in her favorite old army coat and sweeping the front path in time to a melody we couldn't hear. Seeing us approach, she paused and leaned on her broom.

"Good morning, ladies!" she called, pulling out her earbuds. "You're right on time."

I glanced down at her feet. The fuzzy slippers she was wearing were improbably pink. Belinda didn't seem like someone who'd wear pink. Maybe this was a new look for her, now that she had a "gentleman caller."

Inside, we followed her down the hall to the kitchen, which smelled of something cinnamony baking in the oven. A trio of plates and mugs were set out on the counter, ready for a midmorning snack at Camp Belinda. Mackenzie drifted over to the wood stove. Half a dozen cardboard boxes were clustered around it in a semicircle. She peeked inside the closest one and squealed in delight.

"Kittens!"

"You were expecting maybe lizards?" I murmured, and she swatted my arm.

"You could take one home with you," said Belinda, who never gave up. "That little gray one, maybe? I have an extra airline carrier. It fits right under the seat."

Mackenzie gazing longingly at the contents of the nearest box.

"Feel free to pick one out—I mean up," Belinda added, tossing my sisters and me a wink.

I had to get my cousin out of here, fast, or she'd be a goner. I grabbed her by the arm and steered her toward the door. "Sorry, but we can't stay," I told Belinda. "Mom says the bookstore is getting slammed, and she needs our help."

"I could come along too," Lauren offered.

I glared at her. I was still pretty angry about yesterday's little spying episode. "No way. You need to stay here with Pippa."

"But—"

"I need your help too, missy," Belinda added hastily, noting Lauren's mutinous expression. "And so do the kittens. Now that the Bake-Off has moved to the bookstore, Ethel Farnsworth said we could use the General Store to set up a kitten display. Cash in on all the tourists, you know." She turned to me. "Tell True I'll just be down the street if she needs an extra pair of hands. No reason Lauren and Pippa can't handle Kitten Central on their own for a bit if need be."

The minute we were out of the house, I broke into a run. Mackenzie and I were breathless by the time we reached the bookshop. It was jammed, just like my mother had said.

"I haven't seen this many customers since our grand reopening during Winter Festival," I told my cousin, scanning the crowd for my mother. Spotting her back in the children's section, I made my way through the crowded aisles.

"Can I show you something?" I asked.

"Not now, honey," she said. "Your aunt needs you up front."

She shooed us off, and Mackenzie and I maneuvered our way back through the throng to the sales counter.

"Girls!" said my aunt, looking uncharacteristically frazzled. "Thanks for coming—it's all hands on deck today."

She passed a tray of Bookshop Blondies to Mackenzie. "You're on treat patrol—just walk around the store and pass these out, okay?" Turning to me, she said, "And if you could take over the cash register for these lovely customers, that will free me up for—well, for everything else." She glanced around, frowning.

The diary could wait. Taking off my jacket, I stuffed it under the counter and turned to the first person in line. "May I help you?"

For the next hour, I did nothing but ring up sales. Tour bus after tour bus pulled up in front of the store, disgorging customers. Apparently, half the senior centers in Boston were offering midweek "sugaring off" tours, and Maple Madness in Pumpkin Falls was a priority destination.

"Want to swap assignments?" asked my father, leaving his station at the front door and coming over to the sales counter. He added in a whisper that only I could hear, "I've had about enough of charm detail."

My father was in charge of ferrying the new purchases— and their delighted owners, most of whom were elderly ladies—back to the buses. He wasn't the most sociable person on the planet, but he'd sucked it up and put his Lieutenant Colonel Jericho T. Lovejoy game face on today.

"I'll take over for you, J. T." Aunt True emerged from the back office. "You can take the cash register. I need Truly to do some restocking." She handed me a hastily scribbled list. "Everything maple themed is selling like hotcakes, if you'll pardon the pun. Grab as many of these titles as you can find and put them on the table near the door."

"Got it."

"Oh, and give Grace Franklin a call, would you? We can't keep their merchandise on the shelves this week. See if they can bring over more of whatever surplus they've got in the barn store."

I hurried off to do her bidding. After I made the call to Freeman Farm, I gathered up cookbooks, coffee table books, travel guides, children's picture books—whatever we had with even a vaguely maple theme—and stacked them on the big table with the new releases where they could easily be seen, and hopefully purchased.

"Do you have a copy of *Maple Country Mufflers*?" asked a petite woman in a bright red sweatshirt. Emblazoned on it was a picture of a crown and the words KEEP CALM AND KNIT ON.

I shook my head. "We sold the last one just a few minutes ago. Sorry. You could check across the street at A Stitch in Time, though. They had a few copies when I was there last night. Be sure and tell Mrs. Bellow, the owner, that I sent you!"

Maybe that would win me a brownie point or two with Ella.

"Aren't you a helpful young lady!" the woman told me, reaching up and pinching my cheek. I stared after her in astonishment as she headed for the door.

Mackenzie, who'd come by with a nearly empty treat tray just in time to witness this scene, burst out laughing. "The last time anybody did that to me, I was, like, six."

"No kidding."

"Is that all that's left of the Bookshop Blondies?" said Aunt True in dismay. "Truly, could you see if maybe there are more in the freezer up in my apartment? I may need to bake another batch." She lowered her voice. "These tourists are like locusts. It's all I can do to keep them away from the Bake-Off table in the Annex. They keep lifting the plastic wrap and sneaking bites—I'm worried there won't be anything left for the judges!"

I dashed upstairs, making sure that Memphis was locked securely inside when I left Aunt True's apartment. Today was not a good day for him to escape.

A few minutes later I returned with the frozen Bookshop Blondies to find half the customers lining up to pose for pictures with Miss Marple, and the other half clustered around Augustus Wilde.

"He came in looking for Belinda, and someone recognized him," Mackenzie muttered. "Or maybe he told someone who he was."

I grinned. "That sounds more like Augustus."

"Either way, you missed a lot of fangirling."

"Believe me, I've seen it before."

Augustus had a very devoted group of readers, especially older ladies, among whom his colorful capes and shoulder-length silver hair were cause for heart palpitations.

Aunt True flew into high gear arranging an impromptu book signing. I brought up another folding table and chair from the basement while she sat Augustus down with a pen and the half-thawed Bookshop Blondies. My mother herded the eager customers into a line, and Mackenzie and I scooped everything by Augusta Savage off the shelves in the romance section (and from Miss Marple's Picks, where a couple of Augustus's paperbacks had mysteriously appeared) and stacked them in front of our visiting celebrity. The books were snapped up nearly as fast as we set them down.

Forty-five minutes later, the tour buses finally rolled out of town.

"Whew!" said Aunt True, collapsing onto the old church pew that served as a bench by the door. "That was intense."

My mother turned to Mackenzie and smiled. "And here y'all thought Pumpkin Falls was a sleepy little town, didn't you, sweetheart?"

"Too bad it isn't like this every day," said my father. "We'd be gazillionaires."

The bell over the door jangled, and we looked over to see Erastus Peckinpaugh come in. He smiled at my aunt. "Ready for our lunch date?"

Aunt True's cheeks turned pink. "Ready," she replied primly.

"Wait," I told her. "Before you go, Mackenzie and I have something you all need to see."

CHAPTER 17

"Shhhhhh!"

"Shhhhhh yourself!" I hissed back.

Scooter was driving me nuts. He was in full show-off mode again tonight, swaggering around in an attempt to impress Mackenzie.

Who seems to be in the mood to be impressed, I thought sourly, casting a sidelong glance at my cousin. Her pent-up excitement had found an outlet in giggling over Scooter's antics.

Mackenzie had been wound up ever since the two of us had managed to sneak out of the house. Not an easy trick, given the fact that my father had radar that didn't quit. Fortunately, he'd been worn out after the Maple Madness rush at the bookstore and had fallen asleep in front of the TV. As for my mother, the house could have burned down and she wouldn't have noticed. When we left, she was still totally absorbed in another book about the Underground Railroad.

My cousin and I had reached the rendezvous at nine thirty sharp, just as we'd all planned. Scooter and Calhoun were waiting for us, but there'd been no sign of Lucas, who was just now straggling into sight.

"Sorry, guys," he panted. "I wasn't sure how I was going to get past my mom. I ended up climbing out my bedroom window."

"Whatever," said Scooter. "Let's go."

We followed him into the woods, using our cell phone torch apps to illuminate the muddy path.

All of a sudden, a voice boomed out of nowhere: "WHAT ARE YOU KIDS DOING?"

I jumped and let out a shriek. Mackenzie and Lucas did too. Scooter dropped his cell phone, along with a word that's at the very top of Lieutenant Colonel Jericho T. Lovejoy's Ultimate No-No List.

"Scooter!" I said, shocked, then turned around and shined my cell phone at—"Hatcher?"

My brother grinned at me.

"I thought you were Dad!" I said, smacking his arm. "You nearly gave us all heart attacks!"

"I spotted you and Mackenzie sneaking out. What's going on?"

My friends and I looked at one another. What choice did we have? We were going to have to let him in on our secret.

"Um, Operation Sugar Bush," I said reluctantly, knowing even as I said the words that I was in for it.

Which I was.

"Operation *Sugar Bush?*" Hatcher's voice shot up an octave. "What are you guys, the marines?"

Squirming, I opened my mouth to retort, but before I could say anything, he continued, "Oh, wait—this is one of your 'Pumpkin Falls Private Eyes' things, right?" He smirked, clearly enjoying my discomfort. He'd teased me endlessly about my "dorky little club," as he called it, back around Valentine's Day when he'd found out about it.

"If you must know," I said hotly, "we're going on a stakeout."

Scooter held up his camera bag. "We have surveillance equipment and everything."

Hatcher eyed the bag doubtfully. "Real surveillance equipment?"

Scooter nodded.

Calhoun did too. "I've seen it," he assured my brother. "It's legit."

That got my brother's attention. His cocky grin faded. "So what's the plan?"

I explained about how we wanted to help the Freemans— and Coach Maynard—by seeing if we could get to the bottom of the sap thefts. "Franklin's meeting us in the woods by their farm at twenty-two hundred hours," I told him. "He's going to help us set up the video camera near the scene of the crime."

"That's not a bad idea," said Hatcher. "It might actually work."

"You're not going to tell Dad, are you?"

"Not if you let me come along."

"I want to come too!"

I whirled around to see my sister Lauren emerge from behind a tree. I gaped at her. "What are *you* doing here!"

She shrugged. "I saw you and Mackenzie sneak out, and then Hatcher did too. I wanted to see where you all were going."

"You need to go home on the double!"

She scowled. "No."

"Lauren!"

"I'll tell Mom and Dad."

"You, you—*weasel*!" I sputtered. "If you do, I swear I'll—"

Mackenzie placed a hand on my arm. "It's okay, Truly. I'll keep an eye on her."

Hatcher and I exchanged a glance over Lauren's head. He lifted an eyebrow. I knew exactly what he was thinking. He was thinking that if our parents got wind of this—if Lieutenant Colonel Jericho T. Lovejoy got wind of this, to be exact—we'd be grounded until we were thirty. Lauren had us over a barrel, and she knew it.

"Fine," I snapped at my sister. "You can come along. But

I don't want to hear a word out of you, understand? Not a single word."

She held up a finger to her lips and nodded.

Making a big show of turning my back on her, I looked at my friends. "Let's go."

My brother took over the lead as we continued up the trail. Dad said Hatcher was a natural leader, and it was true. I hadn't spent much time with him lately, and it was nice to have him along. My brother and I used to be inseparable, but ever since the move to Pumpkin Falls, things had been different, especially now that wrestling season and swim team were in full swing. Practically the only time I got to see Hatcher anymore was at the dinner table.

Fifteen minutes later he held up a closed fist. I stopped abruptly, and my friends all piled into me.

"What's the *matter* with you, Truly Drooly?" Scooter demanded.

"Don't call me that!" I shot back. "And what's the matter with *you*—don't you ever watch movies?" We Lovejoy kids had known the military hand signals since we were still being pushed around in strollers. I held up a closed fist. "It means 'stop,' duh."

Scooter reddened and opened his mouth to retort. Before he could, though, my brother shushed him.

"Zip it," he said. "We're about to pass Coach Maynard's place, and he's got a dog."

I'd forgotten about that. We all fell silent as we snuck past Maynard's Maple Barn. A few minutes later we reached the edge of the Freeman family's property.

Franklin must have been watching for us, because he stepped out of the shadows almost immediately. "Hey, guys," he whispered, motioning us over. "Thanks for coming. My dad and I found more evidence of tampering today. It looks like the sap rustler is still at large."

As quietly as we could, we followed him single file to the spot where we'd been photographed yesterday morning by the *Pumpkin Falls Patriot-Bugle*.

"This is where we'll set up, then," said Scooter, putting his camera bag down. He unzipped it and rummaged inside, pulling out a video camera, a funny-looking tripod, and several attachments.

"It's freezing out here!" Mackenzie complained, hopping from one foot to the other.

"Cold nights plus warm days equal a good sap run, remember?" Franklin told her, moving closer and rubbing her nearest arm briskly.

Leaving his camera bag, Scooter sprang into action too, and began rubbing Mackenzie's other arm.

"Thanks, y'all," said my cousin, as a beet-faced Lucas shifted from one foot to another, looking for an opening. Only Calhoun was oblivious; he was too busy examining the surveillance equipment.

The corner of my brother's mouth quirked up as he watched my friends. He looked over at me, and I stifled a giggle. I might not be seeing a lot of Hatcher these days, but at least our sibling shorthand was still working loud and clear. One of the things I liked best about my brother was that the same things strike us funny. That and the fact that we rarely even had to say a word to know what the other was thinking. And right now, we were both thinking that my classmates were completely twitterpated.

"How does this thing work?" asked Calhoun, who was still fiddling with the camera equipment.

Scooter pried himself reluctantly away from Mackenzie and picked up the tripod.

"See these flexible legs? You can wrap them around just about anything," he told us, demonstrating on a nearby branch. Once the tripod was secure, he attached the camera and angled it so that it pointed directly at the maple tree in question. "I've already programmed in my cell phone number." He glanced over to check and see if Mackenzie was impressed, and she smiled at him in encouragement. "Let's give it a test." He pressed a button on the camera, and a second later his cell phone vibrated. "Check it out!" he crowed. We clustered around him, and he showed us the image that had just been sent.

"That's really awesome," said my brother.

"How long will it record for?" I asked.

"For as long as it senses activity," Scooter said.

"What if the battery wears out?" Mackenzie wanted to know.

"It won't. The camera only comes on when something's actually moving." Scooter pointed to a small attachment that perched on top of the camera. "See? That's a motion detector."

"So now what?" asked Lucas.

"Now we wait," Scooter replied.

"Here?"

"Weren't you paying attention, Winthrop? The camera will send the video feed directly to my cell phone, so we can all go home. I'll let you know the minute it alerts me to any activity."

Franklin dropped us off at the edge of the path leading back to town, and we said good night and squelched off into the forest. The walk home seemed longer. We were all tired and cold. Lauren had kept her promise and hadn't said a word, but her teeth were chattering audibly. I glanced back at her. The little moron had run out of the house with only a sweat-shirt on. I felt a prickle of guilt. *I should probably give her my jacket*, I thought. She was my sister, after all.

Before I could do it, though, Calhoun beat me to it.

I looked at him in surprise. His eyes met mine, and he shrugged and looked away. *Cool on the outside, marshmallow on the inside*, I thought. That was part of the mysterious equation that was Romeo Calhoun.

"I am so not looking forward to swim practice tomorrow

morning," said Mackenzie, who was shivering despite all of the arm rubbing earlier.

"Me neither," said Lucas.

Mackenzie looked over at me, a hopeful expression on her face. "Maybe we could skip it?"

"You could get away with it, but not me," I told her. "Dad would never let me skip."

"What if you told him you were sick?"

Hatcher snorted. "He knows every trick in the book."

"We'll just have to power through," I said, and Mackenzie made a face. I could see my brother grinning at us in the darkness.

"Gotta think like a wrestler," he said. "No pain, no gain."

Mackenzie groaned.

A few minutes later we reached the corner of Maple and Hill Streets.

"Don't forget to text us if the camera picks anything up," I whispered to Scooter.

"I won't."

My classmates vanished into the darkness. Hatcher and Mackenzie and Lauren and I turned down Maple Street and headed for home.

"Uh-oh," I said as we drew closer. The lights in the kitchen were on, and I could clearly see my parents sitting at the table. Aunt True and Professor Rusty were with them. "Do you think they noticed we were gone?"

"I hope not," said Hatcher.

"There's no way we're going to be able to sneak past them!" Mackenzie had a panicked look on her face. "Uncle Jericho will probably put me on the first plane home."

"Don't worry, I've got your six," my brother assured me, using Dad's military-speak for "I've got your back." "You guys go wait in the bushes by the front door. Give me a minute or two, and I'll let you in."

"You're going to get caught!" I protested.

He flashed me one of his sunflower smiles. "I'll just tell them I went for a run."

Mackenzie and Lauren and I did as Hatcher told us to. Sure enough, a minute later the front door opened a crack and he motioned us inside.

"Piece of cake," he whispered.

There was a burst of laughter from the kitchen. The three of us darted past him and started upstairs. Lauren and I automatically remembered to avoid the creaky step, but it let out a screech as Mackenzie stepped on it. We all froze.

"Hatcher?" my mother called.

"Yes, Mom?"

"Hurry up and get to bed—you need your rest for wrestling tomorrow."

"Just heading up now!" Hatcher called back.

"And don't wake the girls."

Hatcher grinned at us. "Too late," he whispered, and we grinned back at him.

The four of us tiptoed the rest of the way up as quickly and as quietly as we could.

"Let me know if you hear anything from Scooter," Hatcher murmured, and I nodded as he disappeared down the hall toward the third-floor stairs.

I took Calhoun's coat from Lauren and made sure she went directly to her room. I didn't want her sneaking back downstairs and double-crossing us. Back in my room, Mackenzie and I changed into our pajamas. My cousin flopped down onto the air mattress with a contented sigh.

"I'm exhausted!" she said. "That was fun, though."

"Yeah," I replied, crawling under the covers. "I hope Scooter's scheme works."

"Do you think Professor Rusty brought the diary back?"

At the bookshop earlier today, he'd about jumped out of his skin when we showed everyone the diary and told them what Gramps had said. He'd begged us to let him take it over to the college so his colleagues in the history department could examine it. My parents agreed only after he promised to bring it right back.

"Want to go downstairs and check?" I asked.

"I'm too tired," my cousin said, her eyes already shut.

I threw off the covers. "I'll go. Back in a flash."

I yawned and rubbed my eyes as I entered the kitchen, feigning sleepiness. "I heard voices," I said in my best you-just-woke-me-up voice. "What's going on?"

"Sorry, honey. We didn't meant to wake you," my mother replied. She glanced over my shoulder. "Or you, Lauren."

I turned to see that Little Miss Tagalong had followed me downstairs. She gave me a smug look, then pretended to yawn too. I glared at her.

"Just too much excitement around here today!" said Aunt True, smiling at us both.

"Is that the diary?" Lauren's gaze was riveted to the small blue leather-bound book that lay open on the kitchen table in front of my aunt. "The one Truly told us about at dinner?"

"It is indeed!" said Professor Rusty. His wild halo of hair was wilder than usual, as if he'd been running his hands through it a lot in excitement today. Which he probably had.

"Professor Rusty and his colleagues think your ancestor's diary is credible evidence of an Underground Railroad operation here in Pumpkin Falls!" my mother told us. "Isn't that thrilling, girls?" Her eyes were shining. Her professor's love of history was clearly contagious.

"'Packages' is definitely Underground Railroad code for runaway slaves," Professor Rusty had told us back at the bookshop, after I'd read a couple of the passages Gramps had told me to share. "This is amazing!"

Aunt True had immediately put the CLOSED sign up on the door.

"I don't know about you all, but I have goose bumps," she'd announced. "I need to see where you found the diary right this minute."

"No need to close the shop, True," my father had told her. "I'll man the fort."

"You will not! This is a Big Moment in Lovejoy History, and you need to be there too, J. T."

My mother nodded and linked her arm through my father's good one. "True is right. We're all going home."

Outnumbered, my father had shrugged, placed a sticky note on the door that said *Back in an hour*—"just so we don't miss out on too many customers"—and followed us to the minivan, where we all piled in for the short drive back to Gramps and Lola's house.

"I just can't believe it," Aunt True kept saying as Mackenzie and I showed off the loose floorboard in my closet and the crevice beneath it where the diary had been hidden. "All those years when this was my bedroom—it was right here waiting!"

Now, standing in the kitchen, I was glad that Professor Rusty had kept his promise. I very much wanted to find out what happened to the original Truly. I reached out to pick the diary up.

Lauren beat me to it.

"I want a turn too," she said, snatching it away.

"Lauren! I was the one who found it!" I tried to tug it away from her, but she gripped it tighter.

"Girls!" said my mother, sounding shocked. "Be careful!"

"Put the diary down this minute." The warning note in my father's voice meant business.

"Historical artifacts require special handling," Professor Rusty added anxiously as I let go, and Lauren reluctantly set the small blue book back on the table. Professor Rusty slanted a disapproving glance at the two of us, then turned to my parents. "I highly recommend that the diary remain at the college for safekeeping. There are professionals on staff who will know how best to preserve the fragile pages. Plus, our curator has offered to have it transcribed. That way, scholars and researchers can read it too. This is a find of major historical significance, and deserves a wide audience."

Aunt True must have seen the crestfallen expression on my face, because she said, "It's an important historical artifact, Rusty, true, but it's also a family heirloom, and one with a direct connection to me, and to my niece and namesake. We'd like a chance to read it first. All of us."

"True, you don't under—"

"Erastus Peckinpaugh," said my aunt, pulling herself up to her full height. Which is the same as me—six feet tall—and impressive, at least when she does it. "You can wait another day or two."

"Yes, ma'am," Professor Rusty replied meekly.

I smothered a smile. Lieutenant Colonel Jericho T. Lovejoy himself had nothing on my aunt when she was in full boss mode.

Aunt True looked over at me again. "If you want access to the diary, Truly, there's a condition."

"Fine. What?"

"Lauren gets to read it with you."

I groaned. "Aunt True! No! She'll ruin everything."

"Truly!" said my mother, shocked. She gave me that look she always gives me when I disappoint her.

I hurtled on, oblivious. "It's true, Mom! Ever since Mackenzie got here, all Lauren's done is get in the way. She never leaves us alone! She's a total pest."

"I am not!" my sister protested. "You're the mean one— you don't want to let me do anything with you! Mackenzie is my cousin too!"

"Maybe she doesn't want you around either—did you ever think of that?" The words came flying out of my mouth before I could stop them.

Lauren's brown eyes filled with tears. "I *hate* you!" she shouted. "Cross my heart and hope to fly! And I'm going to tell—"

"That's enough!" said my father severely.

We Lovejoys know an order when we hear one. The room fell silent. I clenched my jaw so hard my teeth hurt. If Lauren spilled the beans about what the Pumpkin Falls Private Eyes had done tonight, I'd—I'd—I didn't know what I would do.

"So," I said after a long moment, "can I take the diary back upstairs with me?"

"*May* I take it," said my mother automatically, "and not a chance. Not after that outburst."

"But—"

"No buts," said my father firmly. "It remains to be seen whether you get to read any more of it at all. We should probably just give it to Rusty and be done with it." He pointed toward the hall. "To bed. Both of you. Now."

Lauren heaved one of her dramatic sighs, shot me a murderous look, and stomped out of the room. I was tempted to do the same, but figured if I wanted a chance at the diary again I'd better watch my step.

"Yes, sir," I said meekly, and went back upstairs.

CHAPTER 18

I awoke to the sound of rain.

Rolling over, I gazed at the droplets spattering the nearest window and saw that Mackenzie was awake too.

"You're up early," I told her.

"Yeah," she replied. "I think I'm finally getting over the jet lag." She sat up. "So what was going on downstairs last night? I was too tired to come see."

I filled her in on my argument with Lauren—leaving out the part I still regretted saying—and Aunt True's ultimatum about reading the diary with my sister. "If we even get to read it, that is," I finished glumly. "My dad was pretty steamed at Lauren and me. He may have given it back to Professor Rusty already."

But when we went downstairs a few minutes later, the diary was still on the kitchen table.

"Power bar?" my father said nonchalantly, as if nothing had happened.

"Thanks," I replied, taking one. I looked at the diary. I wondered if I should mention it or just wait for my father to bring it up.

He didn't, though. He just grabbed his keys and headed out to the car.

"Calhoun's jacket!" Mackenzie exclaimed as we started to follow. "Weren't we going to return it after swim practice? Hang on, I'll go back upstairs and get it."

When we got to the pool, we found Coach Maynard in a grumpy mood again. He didn't greet us in his usual cheerful manner, but just paced up and down silently on the pool deck, arms folded across his chest as we completed the warm-up.

"Coach stopped by Lou's this morning for coffee," Lucas whispered to Mackenzie and me between sets of crunches. "The Farnsworths were there, and I overheard them talking. I guess he found more sap lines cut. Mom said the Freemans did too."

"Did you hear anything from Scooter?" I asked.

He shook his head. "Nope. You?"

I shook my head too.

"Pipe down over there!" hollered Coach Maynard. "Save your breath for the workout."

It was a punishing one, almost as if our swim coach was taking out his frustration by making us practice extra hard.

I trudged my way through the sets of intervals and sprints. Up and back, up and back, I churned down my lane in one unending, uninspired slog. Most days swimming cleared my thoughts, but this morning they stayed a stubborn jumble: Truly and Matthew. Scooter's ambush. Calhoun. Mackenzie. The severed sap lines. My pest of a sister.

I'd never been so glad in my life for swim practice to be over.

"Do you guys want to hang out today?" Lucas asked hopefully, as Coach Maynard blew the "all clear" signal on his whistle and we got out of the pool. "My mom said she'd drive us to the bowling alley over in West Hartfield if everybody wants to go."

"Sorry, Lucas," I told him. "We've got plans."

I watched as he drooped off toward the men's locker room. I couldn't help feeling a little guilty. But for some reason I wasn't ready for him or for any of my other friends to know about the diary just yet. It was bad enough that Mackenzie and I had to share it with Lauren.

Hatcher texted me while I was changing: ANY NEWS FROM SCOOTER?

NOTHING YET, I texted him back.

"Almost ready," Mackenzie told me, as I pulled on a pair of jeans and a clean sweatshirt. "I've just gotta dry my hair."

She headed for the mirrors on the far side of the locker room. My hair was still wet. I just couldn't see the point of using a blow dryer. It wasn't like I had a hairstyle, after all— just hair. It would dry on its own soon enough. Tucking it up under my Longhorns baseball cap, I pulled on my clothes, then stuffed my wet swimsuit and towel in my pool bag. I reached for Calhoun's jacket, which had fallen on the floor. As I did, something fluttered out of one of the pockets. It was a piece of paper.

I bent down to pick it up, and froze.

The handwriting on it was Mackenzie's.

Call me! I have something to tell you! she'd written, along with her name and cell phone number.

I stared at the note, numb. *So much for loyalty.*

"Almost done!" sang my cousin, and I crumpled the note in my fist and shoved it into the pocket of my jeans.

Mackenzie was her usual chatty self as we left the pool. We stopped briefly at Calhoun's house to drop off the jacket, but he and his dad had gone out for breakfast, so we left it with his sister.

"I still can't believe that Calhoun has a sister named *Juliet*," Mackenzie said as we splashed our way home.

I just grunted.

"Who wants omelets and bacon?" my mother asked as we came through the back door.

"Me!" Mackenzie replied, peeling off her raincoat and hanging it up in the mudroom. "I'm starving. Thanks, Aunt Dinah!" She slid into a seat at the table.

I hung up my raincoat and sat down too—at the opposite end of the table. The diary had moved, I noticed. It was now directly in front of Lauren.

"Did you remember to feed Bilbo this morning?" my mother asked my sister.

"Yes, ma'am," Lauren replied virtuously. "And I cleaned out his cage, too."

"Good girl." My mother set plates down in front of Mackenzie and me. My cousin dove into her breakfast, but I didn't even pick up my fork. My appetite had evaporated.

"Truly, I'm expecting you to keep your word and let Lauren read the diary with you and Mackenzie," my mother said.

I nodded.

"I'm heading down to the bookstore for a bit this morning. Aunt True has a new marketing idea she wants to run by me."

I nodded again, and she gave me a sidelong glance. "You girls promise me you'll try and get along—and remember what Professor Rusty said about the diary. It's very old and very fragile."

"Yes, ma'am," Lauren repeated.

"I'm putting Truly in charge of it," my mother warned her, and my sister made a face.

"Fine," she mumbled.

My mother placed two more strips of bacon on my cousin's plate, then glanced over at mine. "Truly? Aren't you going to eat your breakfast?"

"I'm not hungry," I said shortly. How could I possibly be

hungry after what I'd discovered in the locker room?

She gave me another look, then turned to Pippa. "How about you, Pipster? Would you like Truly's extra bacon?"

My little sister nodded vigorously.

"And do you want to go to Belinda's, or would you rather stay here with the big girls?"

My heart sank. It was bad enough that I was stuck with Lauren—the last thing I wanted to do was babysit Pippa, too.

But Pippa shook her head. "It'th kitten delivery day," she informed us, smiling her gap-toothed smile. "Belinda thaid I could ride along in her truck and help."

I could tell by the expression on Lauren's face that she was feeling torn. Kittens—all animals—were way up on her list of favorite things, and I was guessing that riding around the Pumpkin River Valley delivering kittens sounded like sheer catnip to her. At the same time, though, I knew how much she wanted to read the diary, especially after she'd made such a big stink last night about feeling left out.

Staying put won out.

"Great. It's settled," said my mother. "I'll see y'all later, then."

As she and Pippa left for Camp Belinda, Lauren got up from the table. I frowned at her. "Where are you going?"

She paused. "Aren't we going to read upstairs in your room?"

I shook my head. "Family room," I said firmly. I might

have to share the diary with her, but I wasn't about to share my room, too.

"Hang on a second," said Mackenzie. "I'm going to go grab my knitting. Want me to bring yours down too?"

"Whatever."

She gave me a funny look. I ignored her.

"Don't touch the diary," I told Lauren as Mackenzie went upstairs. "I've got to feed the birds."

I put the diary on the coffee table in the family room, then grabbed my rain jacket and rubber boots again. It was still pouring outside, and the backyard was a dreary, muddy mess. Pulling my hood up, I picked my way across the soggy lawn to the nearest feeder. There was no excited chatter from the birds this morning. I knew they were out there, though, huddled in the shelter of the tree branches, feathers fluffed as they tried to stay dry. Eventually, hunger would cause them to venture out, and the food would be waiting for them.

Not the owls, though, even if there were any in the neighborhood. Owls and rain didn't mix at all.

There was a price to be paid for that gift of silent flight—owl feathers weren't waterproof. Grounded by soggy feathers, an owl couldn't hunt, and an especially loud, driving rain made it hard for them to hear their prey even if they could. They had to wait it out, and prolonged bad weather could mean hypothermia and starvation.

Talk about kryptonite!

Was Mackenzie my kryptonite? I wondered, swiping angrily at my eyes. Here I thought Lauren was my biggest problem—who knew that it was actually my cousin? I couldn't believe she was writing notes to Calhoun behind my back.

After I was finished filling the bird feeders, I went back inside. Lauren was sitting on the family room sofa next to Mackenzie, who was almost done with her first sock. It looked pretty good—much more like a real sock than the hot mess hanging from my knitting needles, that was for sure.

"So, are you going to read to us?" Mackenzie asked.

"Whatever." As I took a seat in the armchair across from them, my cell phone vibrated.

My cousin looked up sharply. "Is it Scooter?"

I pulled my phone out of my pocket, looked at the screen, and shook my head. "Cha Cha." I read the text message aloud: JASMINE AND I WILL BE BACK TOMORROW! TELL MACKENZIE WE CAN'T WAIT TO MEET HER!

Mackenzie smiled. "Tell them I can't wait to meet them, too."

I grunted, tapped out the message, then shoved the phone back into my pocket and picked up the diary.

"Why don't you tell Lauren what's happened so far," Mackenzie suggested, and I grudgingly explained how the original Truly had received the diary as a gift, then described some of the entries that she'd written.

"Can I see it?" Lauren asked.

"Sure," said Mackenzie.

I didn't move.

"Truly! Let her see it!"

I heaved a sigh and passed the diary to my sister. "Remember what mom said about being careful, okay?"

"Duh." She opened it, took one look at the handwriting, and frowned. "It's in cursive."

"What did you expect?" The words came out sharper than I'd intended, and Lauren flushed.

"Isn't it beautiful?" gushed Mackenzie, moving closer to my sister and putting her arm around her. She glared at me. "I wish I could write that neatly."

Lauren examined the pages. "It's hard to read," she said, disappointed.

"Yeah," I told her, taking the diary back. "That's why I'm in charge."

She shot me a look. I pretended not to notice and began to read aloud:

> October 15, 1861
> My little angel arrived early yesterday morning. I have named him Booth, as Matthew wished. But Matthew honors my wish as well, and his middle name is Gerhard, after my dear departed father. Little Booth is the light of my life already, and Mother Lovejoy says he is just the tonic she needed

for missing her son. We have written to Matthew,
sharing the happy news.
Yours, Truly

October 20, 1861
Another package arrived last night. I was not able to
help this time, being still abed. Mother Lovejoy hid it
safely, and tonight it will be shipped to its destination
in Maple Grove, Maine.
Yours, Truly

"Professor Rusty said that 'package' was a code word for 'runaway slave,' right?" said Mackenzie.

I nodded.

"I'll bet they had Maple Madness in Maple Grove," said Lauren, snickering at her own dumb joke.

My cousin laughed obligingly. I didn't, and Mackenzie shot me another look. "It is kind of a funny name, isn't it, Lauren? But why Maple Grove, I wonder?"

"What do you mean?" I asked.

"I mean I wonder why they sent the slaves there."

I shrugged.

"We should find out," Mackenzie continued. "Maybe the Lovejoys had a family connection there or something. We could ask Professor Rusty, or your mother—she's been studying this stuff, so she might know, right?"

"I thought you didn't like history," I said.

"But this really happened!"

"So did history, duh."

"You know what I mean!" she retorted, stung. "This was real people—people who are related to us. Well, to you."

I knew what she meant. And actually, I was just as curious as she was, especially about the original Truly. Eighteen years old, living in a foreign country—a country at war, at that—newly married, and now a new mother, plus she was involved in this supersecret, dangerous work. How could I possibly not want to know more?

"Mr. Henry at the library could help," suggested Lauren. "He knows everything. You could ask him tonight—he's in your knitting class, right?"

"Good idea, Lauren," said Mackenzie. "Let's start a list of questions for him." She scrabbled around in the drawer of the end table for a pen and some paper as I continued reading:

> *November 2, 1861*
> *I pray daily to our heavenly Vater to keep Booth's papa safe. We have not heard from Matthew in many weeks. I am glad I have our boy to keep my mind occupied. He is growing splendidly fat, like a little Ferkel.*
> *Yours, Truly*

Lauren snickered again. "Splendidly fat!" she repeated in delight.

Mackenzie reached for the German-English dictionary. "'*Vater*' is 'father,'" she reported.

"I could have told you that," I muttered.

"And '*Ferkel*' means 'piglet!'" she added a moment later with glee, and she and Lauren both shrieked with laughter. Suddenly, my cousin got a stricken look on her face. "Do you know if something happened to Matthew? In the war, I mean. I don't know if I could stand it if it did!"

I shook my head, wishing I knew more about my family's history. "We'll find out one way or another, I guess."

November 10, 1861
Reverend Bartlett came to see us today. He says Booth is a fine boy, and he looks forward to the christening. Then our talk grew serious. There are slave hunters in the Pumpkin River Valley, he says. We must be very careful. Our work grows increasingly dangerous. We are always to wait for the sign of the owl before receiving a package, and we are not to trust anyone. There are whispers of money changing hands in exchange for information—yes, even here in Pumpkin Falls. I am much troubled by this news.
Yours, Truly

I paused for a moment, wondering about the sign of the owl that she'd mentioned. Was it a physical sign, like a drawing perhaps? Or was it a sound—a fugitive hooting from the nearby woods, the owl's call a request for help? I wondered too, if Truly knew anything about owls, or was interested in them the way I was. She was feeling more real to me with every page I read in her diary.

> *November 17, 1861*
> *We have had a letter from Matthew! He has been ill,*
> *but is now recovered and has rejoined his regiment.*
> *He sends his dearest love to little Booth and me and*
> *says he cannot wait until our family is together again.*
> *Until that time, he begs me to write often and tell him*
> *of our baby, and of home.*
> *Winter is coming. I fear for my dear husband, sleep-*
> *ing in a tent out in the cold. Mother Lovejoy and I*
> *busy ourselves knitting. At least we can be sure our*
> *Matthew has warm socks.*
> *Yours, Truly*

I stared at the page. *No way*, I thought. Truly was knitting socks too? This was almost eerie.

My cell phone buzzed again. I glanced at the screen. "It's Scooter."

Mackenzie looked up from her knitting. "Any news?"

I read his text aloud: "APB to PFPE!"

"What does 'APB' mean?" asked Lauren.

"All points bulletin," Mackenzie explained. "He's alerting the Pumpkin Falls Private Eyes."

WHAT'S UP? I texted back.

GOT SOMETHING TO SHOW YOU, Scooter replied.

CAN U COME OVER? I'M BABYSITTING LAUREN.

"What's he saying?" Mackenzie begged.

"Hang on, hang on," I replied irritably.

BE THERE IN A FLASH, Scooter texted.

BRING LUCAS AND CALHOUN, I texted back. LOLA'S STUDIO.

K.

I put my cell phone back in my pocket and closed the diary. "They're coming over," I told my cousin and my sister. "I told them to meet us in Lola's studio."

My sister's face lit up. "An official meeting of the Pumpkin Falls Private Eyes!"

"You're *not* one of us," I warned her. "You're only allowed to come today because I'm stuck babysitting you."

"You're not babysitting me!" she protested. "I don't need a babysitter!"

I gave a short laugh. "Right."

"What is *wrong* with you, Truly?" Mackenzie demanded. "You're in such a bad mood today!"

I looked at her. What was wrong with *me*? I thought about the crumpled note that was still in my pocket. How about the fact that I had a double-crosser for a cousin?

I knew I was being unfair—Mackenzie didn't know that I'd found her note, and I'd never told her how I felt about Calhoun. I knew that the two of us needed to talk, but right now I was still too upset, plus I didn't want to say anything in front of Lauren. I had enough problems without her knowing about Calhoun too. Talking would have to wait.

"Nothing is wrong with me," I snapped back.

Mackenzie threw down her knitting. "Fine. Have it your way. Let's go up to the studio."

Earlier this winter my grandmother's art studio in the barn ended up being the unofficial hangout for the Pumpkin Falls Private Eyes. I really hadn't expected we'd be using it again—Pumpkin Falls was such a small town, after all, that I couldn't imagine there would be any more mysteries for us to solve. But life was full of surprises.

We went out to the barn-turned-garage and up the stairs to the studio. I slipped the key from its hiding place behind one of Lola's paintings on the landing and unlocked the door.

"It's cold in here," said Mackenzie, shivering.

"It used to be a barn—what did you expect?" I switched on

the space heater. "It warms up pretty quickly, though."

Lauren prowled around the room, inspecting our grandmother's art supplies and books and knickknacks.

"Don't touch anything," I warned.

"Truly!" Mackenzie glared at me.

"What?"

"Quit it!"

"Quit what?"

"Quit being so mean to Lauren."

"I'm not being mean. She's a *pest*."

"You're hopeless." My cousin retreated to the sofa.

A few minutes later I heard footsteps pounding up the stairs. The studio door flew open, and Scooter and Calhoun and Lucas crowded in.

"She's not part of the, uh, PFPE now, is she?" Scooter asked, looking over at my sister Lauren.

"No," I said at the same time that Lauren said, "Yes."

Mackenzie put her arm around my sister's shoulders and shot me a look. "We'll talk about it later. What do y'all have to show us?"

"We're not sure," said Scooter. "We've watched it a few times, and we need you guys to take a look."

We all crowded around his cell phone. Somehow Calhoun ended up beside me, and I was suddenly very conscious of my cousin's note for him in my pocket.

"See the time stamp?" Scooter paused the surveillance video almost as soon as he started playing it, and pointed to a corner of the small screen. "It's just after midnight. That's when something tripped the motion detector and the camera started filming."

He clicked the PLAY button again and the video continued. Nothing was visible at first, just a lot of darkness and the vague outline of tree branches. Then two pinpricks of light swam into focus in the underbrush.

"What's that?" asked Lauren.

"Eyes," Scooter told her.

"Whose eyes?" asked Mackenzie, peering closer.

"Wait and see," said Scooter.

The pinpricks drew closer, glowing green in the reflected light of the camera. Suddenly, they vanished.

"Wait for it," said Scooter.

The picture wobbled. A second later it wobbled again, then began rocking wildly from side to side.

"What's happening?" I asked.

"Something's shaking the camera," said Calhoun.

The final few seconds of the video were a confusing blur of tree branches and dark sky and what looked like fingers and a lot of hair—or was it fur? Mackenzie gave a little shriek and Lauren and I both jumped, startled, as a set of very sharp teeth loomed large, and the hairy something snarled ferociously before the screen went blank.

"Did that . . . that *thing* just try and eat the camera?" I asked. "What the heck was it?"

Scooter shook his head. "Beats me. Calhoun and Lucas and I have watched it about a zillion times, trying to figure it out. Those teeth are huge."

"I think it's a wolf," said Lucas.

"Are there wolves in Pumpkin Falls?" Mackenzie looked genuinely freaked out.

Scooter grinned. "Don't listen to Lucas. He doesn't know what he's talking about."

"Could it be a bear?" I asked. I vaguely remembered Gramps telling Hatcher and Danny and me something about bears once.

"It's possible," said Calhoun. "There are black bears in New Hampshire."

"I think it's Sasquatch," Lauren announced, and five heads swiveled in her direction as we all turned and stared at her. "You know, Bigfoot?"

"There is no such thing as Bigfoot," I scoffed. "You read too much."

She scowled at me. "Nobody knows for sure. It might be for real—people have taken pictures and stuff."

"Those are fake."

She shrugged. "What if they're not?"

My friends and I looked at one another. I thought of those fingers and sharp teeth we'd just seen on the video, and my skin prickled.

But there was no such thing as Bigfoot, right?

CHAPTER 19

"So what do we do now?" Lucas asked.

"Reset the camera and try again, I guess," said Scooter reluctantly. I could tell that Lauren's theory had gotten to him, too. "What else can we do?"

"No way am I going back out there, not if this place is crawling with bears and Bigfoot." Mackenzie crossed her arms over her chest. "Y'all are nuts to even think about it."

"I'll go," offered Calhoun.

If he thought he was going to impress my cousin by volunteering, he was wrong. She just looked at him like he'd lost his mind.

"It's not like it's dark out or anything," Calhoun told her. "It's broad daylight."

My cell phone rang just then. "It's Aunt True. I've gotta take this."

"Truly?" my aunt said when I answered. "We have a

situation here, and I could use your help. Your dad's at physical therapy, and I tried your mother but she didn't answer."

"I think she's over at Belinda's," I told her. "She probably can't hear her phone over all that meowing."

Aunt True didn't laugh at my joke, which was a lame one, admittedly, but still. She usually laughed at my jokes. "Could you come down here and help cover the cash register for a bit?"

"Sure. Is everything okay?"

"Uh, yeah. Mostly. Sort of. We're getting set up for tonight's Maple Madness Bake-Off finals, and we seem to have hit a, uh, road block."

That didn't sound good.

"I'll be right there." I hung up and turned to my cousin. "Something's going on at the bookshop," I told her. "I need to go."

"I'll go with you."

"Me too," Scooter said quickly.

"Dude, you need to come with me," Calhoun protested. "You're the one who knows how the camera works, after all."

Scooter didn't look too enthusiastic about that idea. *Wait a minute*, I thought, watching him. Was Scooter *scared*? Not that I blamed him—I wasn't eager to go back to Freeman Farm, either, after seeing that video—but this was a very un-Scooter-like reaction. Especially in front of Mackenzie.

"The sooner we get this thing fixed, the sooner we can

figure out who the thief is," Calhoun reasoned. "Lucas, we'll need your help too."

Lucas looked about as thrilled as Scooter did to hear this.

Scooter sighed. "Fine." His gaze drifted over to to my cousin. "We'll meet you guys at the bookstore afterward, okay?"

The three of them left, and Lauren and Mackenzie and I closed up the studio, then got our jackets and headed downtown.

Lovejoy's Books was in an uproar.

"What the heck is going on?" my cousin asked.

"I have absolutely no idea," I replied.

A tourist bus was parked outside, and its occupants were milling around inside the bookshop, craning their necks to try and see the cause of the commotion in the Annex. My cousin and my sister and I made our way back to where Aunt True was standing helplessly by the Bake-Off table.

"My Maple Snickerdoodles will *not* be sitting next to her Maple Banana Bread," we could hear someone insisting. It was Augustus Wilde, looking mad enough to spit, squared off against Mrs. Mahoney from the antiques store next door. Our celebrity author swept by in a blur of purple, grabbing his plate of cookies from one end of the table and marching it down to the other.

In a flash, plates of goodies started whizzing back and forth along the long table as the Bake-Off contestants separated back into the two camps. My father hadn't solved the problem at all—Pumpkin Falls was still feuding, and with or without signs on the table, the dividing line was Team Freeman and Team Maynard.

Bud Jefferson shouldered his way through the crowd just then holding a platter labeled BUD'S BODACIOUS MAPLE WALNUT MUFFINS. Spotting Lucas's mother at the far end of the table, where all the Freeman family supporters had gathered their baked goods, he stopped in his tracks. Mrs. Winthrop was hovering protectively over a plate of Maple Caramel Popcorn. She watched Mr. Jefferson hesitate, then slowly head for the opposite end of the table to join Team Maynard. Her face fell. *Uh-oh*, I thought, glancing from one of them to the other. *So much for winding wool together.* Was their budding romance doomed?

There was a crash as a plate fell to the floor. Aunt True leapt forward. "People, please!" she cried. Catching sight of me, she mouthed a single word: "Help!"

"This is unreal," said Mackenzie. I could tell she was preparing to launch into her radio announcer voice and offer a commentary on small-town living.

"Don't," I snapped. "Not now."

One good thing about being six feet tall—people tend to get out of your way. I elbowed my way through the crowd like Moses parting the Red Sea, and a moment later I was at my aunt's side.

"We need to get this under control, and fast," she whispered frantically, making a dive for a platter of Maple Oat Scones teetering on the edge of the table. "Rusty's in class, and I still haven't been able to get ahold of your mother. See if you can reach Mr. Henry, maybe. Or Reverend Quinn. Somebody—anybody!"

I nodded. As she returned to her refereeing, I grabbed Lauren by the shoulders. "Go. Library. Now. Get Mr. Henry and bring him back here on the double."

I turned to Mackenzie. "Keep trying my mother. Tell her it's an emergency. I'll . . ."

My voice trailed off as the bell over the door jangled and Ella Bellow swept in. *Oh no!* I thought. Ella was the last thing we needed at a time like this.

"Have you no decency?" she cried as I elbowed my way back through the crowd toward her. "I can hear the ruckus from across the street—you're driving my customers away!"

And right into our bookshop, I thought. That was the real reason for Ella's outrage. The last thing we needed right now was her interference.

"Sorry, Mrs. Bellow." I tried to sound contrite. "We're dealing with the Hatfields and the McCoys again."

"I don't care if the lost heir to the Romanov throne is making a personal appearance!" she barreled on. "You people need to take control of the situation." Her mouth pruned up indignantly.

"Unless we can calm everybody down, none of us will have any customers today," I pointed out.

That got her attention. Ella's eyes narrowed as she considered her options. Stepping gingerly onto a nearby armchair—my aunt had comfy reading nooks set up all around the bookshop—she braced herself against a bookshelf and cupped her hands around her mouth. "Attention, everyone!" she announced. "This is neutral territory, remember? If this doesn't stop, we're going to have to cancel the Maple Madness Bake-Off finals tonight!"

The angry buzz died down as the crowd looked over at her.

"Well, if it isn't our own Ella Bellow, bellowing orders," said Augustus snidely. "Who put you in charge?"

I wanted to smack him over the head with his plate of Maple Snickerdoodles. If Belinda were here right now, she'd make mincemeat out of her "gentleman caller," who wasn't being much of a gentleman, if you asked me, which nobody ever did.

As Ella climbed down from her perch and marched over to deal with Augustus, the bell over the door jangled again, and Calhoun, Scooter, and Lucas rushed in.

"We did it!" panted Scooter. "The video camera is up and running again!"

Mackenzie glanced around to see if anyone was listening. They weren't—the tourists were still completely transfixed by the squabble in the Annex. "Any sign of Bigfoot?" she whispered to my classmates.

"You should have seen the huge footprints out there!" said Lucas, his eyes wide.

"They could have been Mr. Freeman's," Calhoun noted cautiously.

"But it was probably Bigfoot," boasted Scooter.

Mackenzie shivered. "I think y'all are incredibly brave."

Scooter preened, and Lucas puffed out his skinny chest too. "Yeah, it was probably Bigfoot," he echoed.

I looked at my classmates. Could this really be true? Was Bigfoot on the loose here in Pumpkin Falls?

Behind us, the bell over the door jangled again, and this time Mr. Henry came in. Lauren was right behind him. Spotting the boys, she made a beeline for us. Mr. Henry headed directly to the back of the store, meanwhile, where Ella was wrangling with Augustus Wilde and my beleaguered aunt was trying to convince the owner of the Suds 'n Duds, who was Coach Maynard's brother-in-law, to put his pan of Maple Gingerbread beside Mrs. Freeman's Maple Fudge.

"Did you find signs of Bigfoot?" my sister asked breathlessly.

Scooter gave her a solemn nod. "It's almost a hundred percent certain."

I glanced over at Calhoun, who was fiddling with the

zipper of his jacket. I wanted to hear what he had to say, but before I could ask, Mackenzie put her hand on his arm and whispered something in his ear. He smiled down at her, and she laughed her perky little laugh.

I turned away. As usual, I might as well be invisible.

CHAPTER 20

I stared in the mirror, turning my head from one side to the other. I frowned. I was almost positive that I looked the same as I always had—same brown eyes, same freckles, same stick-straight Lovejoy brown hair. I didn't have the Lovejoy proboscis, as far as I could tell, and I had a nice enough smile. So why was it that I seemed to be in complete stealth mode these days, at least as far as boys were concerned?

Since when had I started worrying about boys, anyway?

Since Calhoun, of course.

I told myself to quit stewing about it. I told myself I didn't really care, and that it was silly to wish that things were different. Wishing wouldn't shrink my size-ten-and-a-half feet. Wishing wouldn't make me petite, or blond, or perky. Wishing wouldn't turn me into Mackenzie. I was stuck just being me, Truly.

Down the hall, I could hear laughter coming from Lauren's room. My cousin and my sisters were playing with

Nibbles, Lauren's hamster. A series of crashes told me that his little plastic hamster ball was currently rocketing around her room. Closing my bathroom door behind me, I crossed the hall to my bedroom and flopped facedown on my bed.

I hated feeling so out of sorts, and I hated feeling jealous of Mackenzie. I could tell she was puzzled and hurt by the way I was acting. I wanted things to go back to the way they'd always been between us, but I didn't see how they could.

I buried my head under my pillow. This whole thing was just a big tangled mess. An even worse mess than the stupid pathetic socks I was trying—and failing miserably—to knit.

There was a soft knock at my door. I lifted the edge of my pillow and peeked out to see my mother standing in the doorway.

"Is everything okay?" She came over and sat down on the edge of my bed beside me.

To my horror, I burst into tears. "I don't know, Mom!" I sobbed. "One minute I'm fine, and the next I'm—"

"Thirteen?" My mother laughed softly. "Oh, honey, I remember only too well being your age!" She leaned down and put her cheek next to mine. "It's not easy being a teenager," she murmured. "Give yourself some time to adjust. There are physical changes, of course—"

"Yeah, Mom, I know all about that," I said hastily. The one thing I did not need right now was a lecture on *Your Changing Body and You!*

"—and emotional changes too. It's all part of growing up." She hesitated, then added, "Are things okay between you and Mackenzie? Y'all seem a little . . . I don't know, tense."

I lifted a shoulder, too ashamed and embarrassed to admit what I'd been thinking. "Yeah, we're good." I was quiet for a moment, then added in a low voice, "Mom, do you think I'm pretty?"

She laughed. "Pretty? Sweetheart, I think you're beautiful, inside and out!"

I scowled. "You're just saying that because you're my mother."

"I am not!" She ruffled my hair. "Cross my heart and hope to fly. Why, just the other day at the bookshop your aunt True was saying how pretty you are! Ella was there, and she agreed too."

Ella Bellow thinks I'm pretty? Great. Not exactly the target audience I was shooting for.

My mother stood up. "Pull yourself together and come keep me company in the kitchen. Professor Rusty's bringing his research assistant to dinner tonight, and I'm making Tex-Mex."

"Chicken enchiladas?" I sat up. Chicken enchiladas were one of my mother's specialties. My mouth watered just hearing the words.

She nodded, passing me a tissue. "Now, dry your eyes and blow your nose."

I did as she told me. Downstairs, I set the dining room table for eleven, then settled in at the kitchen counter to help prepare the enchilada toppings.

"You've been reading about the Underground Railroad for your term paper, right?" I asked.

My mother nodded. "Uh-huh."

"So have you ever heard of a place called Maple Grove, Maine?"

"Not that I can remember. Why?"

I told her what we'd read in Truly's diary, about the "packages" being shipped to Maple Grove.

"Interesting. You should ask Professor Rusty tonight at dinner. He's an expert." She gave me a sidelong glance. "This diary is getting under your skin, isn't it?"

I nodded. "Yeah, I guess. It's just that reading it makes it all feel so real, you know?"

The door behind us burst open. My mother didn't even wait for my brothers to greet us. She just pointed her spatula toward the ceiling. "Upstairs! Shower! Now!"

Hatcher and Danny grinned and loped off.

"Whew, those boys get stinky." My mother wrinkled her nose and waved her spatula in front of her face as if to clear the air, and I laughed.

A few minutes later the back door opened again. It was my father this time. He crossed the kitchen and gave my mother a kiss. "Mmmm," he said, wrapping his arms around her waist from behind and resting his chin on top of her head. "Could that be chicken enchiladas I smell?"

"Might could," she replied.

"What's the occasion?"

"Dinner guests." She explained about Professor Rusty and his research assistant.

"So is it okay if I keep the Terminator on, or should I accessorize with Ken?" My father raised his prosthetic arm. We called it "the Terminator" because it was made of black titanium and polymer, and it was super high-tech. He controlled it with electrical impulses from his brain, and it had a wrist that swiveled like a real one and metal fingers that could grasp even the smallest things. Ken was made of flesh-colored silicone and looked more like a real arm, but Dad said it was useless. He named it Ken after Barbie's boyfriend, because even though it was good-looking, all it did was hang around.

My mother tapped his prosthesis lightly with her spatula. "I think the Terminator is just fine. Very macho and handsome."

Dad laughed and kissed her again. "Glad to know it has the Dinah Lovejoy Seal of Approval."

I'm relieved my father can joke about these kinds of things now. For a long time after Black Monday, we were really worried about him. But he was adjusting to the loss of his arm, just like he was adjusting to life in Pumpkin Falls.

Hatcher materialized, his hair still wet from the shower. He'd changed into jeans and a clean T-shirt.

"You smell almost as good as my chicken enchiladas," my mother said, sniffing him appreciatively.

My brother grinned. "Operative word being 'almost.' *Nothing* smells as good as your chicken enchiladas."

"A charmer, just like your father," she replied, mirroring his sunflower smile back at him.

The doorbell rang.

"Would you kids get that?" she said to my brother and me. "It must be True and Rusty."

It was. Hatcher took everyone's coats as they came inside, and Professor Rusty introduced the girl he'd brought with him.

"This is Felicia Grunewald, my research assistant."

"Nice to meet you," I murmured, trying not to stare at her hair. It was braided into twin coils that perched on her ears like a pair of blond cinnamon buns.

"Looks like someone raided Captain Romance's closet," Hatcher whispered as the cinnamon buns and their owner followed my aunt down the hall to the kitchen. My brother held up Felicia's navy blue cape, and I stifled a giggle. He was right—it looked exactly like something Augustus Wilde would wear.

"And what's up with that hair?" I asked.

"Princess Leia just called—she wants her earmuffs back,"

my brother quipped, and this time I laughed out loud. I love Hatcher.

A few minutes later my mother called everyone to dinner. We took our seats, and my father went around the dining room table, introducing each of us. Then he turned to Professor Rusty. "I'll let you do the honors with your guest."

"Felicia Grunewald is my research assistant, and a history major at the college," Professor Rusty told us. "Her field is medieval studies, but she's also quite knowledgeable about the Civil War. She's working for me over Spring Break." He looked over at Aunt True. "True, you might remember her parents, Bridget and Hans Grunewald? They own the Edelweiss Inn."

"The place near Mount Washington that looks like a Bavarian chalet?" cried my aunt, delighted. "We used to go there for birthday dinners when we were kids! Remember, J. T.?"

Felicia inclined her head, like royalty accepting a peasant's compliment. "I'm gratified to know that our alpine retreat inspires such fond memories."

Across the table, Hatcher flicked me a glance. I flared my nostrils at him, and he smirked. I knew exactly what he was thinking: *Who is this girl, and why is she sitting at our table?*

"So," said Professor Rusty, looking over at me, "have you finished reading the diary? I'd love for Felicia to take a look at it after dinner."

"Almost," I told him.

"I hear congratulations are in order, by the way," he continued. "The Pumpkin Falls Private Eyes are working on another case!"

My fork, which had been in the process of conveying my first bite of chicken enchilada to my mouth, froze in midair. The table fell quiet as everyone looked at me.

"The Pumpkin Falls Private Eyes?" Felicia snorted. "Who made up that cretinous name?"

I had no idea what "cretinous" meant, but I could guess. I felt the blood rush to my face, staining it the same shade as the enchilada sauce dripping from my fork.

How on earth had Professor Rusty found out?

"Trying to snare the sap thief, are you?" asked Aunt True. "Not a moment too soon, in my opinion. I don't want a repeat of today's scene at the bookstore, that's for sure."

Across the table, my sister Lauren seemed way too fascinated with her place mat. *Busted*, I thought, my glance frosting into a glare. Lauren was the only one who could possibly have leaked the news. This was her revenge for our argument over the diary, and all the other stuff that had happened between us these past few days.

I needed a distraction to change the subject.

"Hey, Professor Rusty," I began, "I was wondering—"

"Hay is for horses," my mother corrected me, and I sighed. Living with an aspiring English teacher was like living with the grammar police.

"Sorry. Professor Rusty, I was wondering if you've ever heard of a place called Maple Grove, Maine?" Glancing at my mother, I added "sir" for extra credit.

He furrowed his brow, considering. "Can't say that I have. Why?"

"We were reading about it in the original Truly's diary earlier—she talks about 'packages' being shipped there, so I guess that's where some of the slaves she was hiding were sent."

"Is that so? Fascinating! I'll look into it right away. Remind me tomorrow, would you, Felicia?"

Her mouth full of chicken enchilada, Felicia nodded, sending her Princess Leia muffins bobbing.

"Also, how come Truly sounds so scared all the time?" I continued. "Everything's all so hush-hush."

"It was incredibly dangerous work she was involved in," Professor Rusty replied. "That they were all involved in, really. For the slaves themselves, it took an extraordinary act of courage—not to mention a huge leap of faith—to run. Remember, they had no maps, few if any supplies, and in most cases no knowledge of the landscape outside their plantation. Running meant being ripped away from everything that was familiar, and leaving everything behind, including family and friends. There was danger at every turn: hunger, exhaustion, possible injury or illness, and relentless pursuit by their owners. A runaway never knew if those offering to help were friend or foe. What he or she did know was that if they were caught, the consequences would be dire. Many lost their lives. But none of that mattered one speck, compared to their burning desire for freedom."

I could see why my mother liked Professor Rusty's classes. He had a way of bringing things to life, even if he was a bit long-winded.

Down at the end of the table, my sister Pippa shuddered. "I wouldn't want to be a thlave," she announced as she set her glass of milk down, nearly spilling it.

Aunt True's hand flashed out just in time.

"Nice save!" My father smiled at his sister, then reached over and patted Pippa's hand. "No one wants to be a slave, honey."

"I understand why it was dangerous for the runaways," I said, "but I guess I don't understand why it was dangerous for the people—the conductors, right?—who worked on the Underground Railroad helping them."

"Ah," said Professor Rusty. "That would be on account of the Fugitive Slave Act."

I dimly remembered reading something about that at school.

"The Fugitive Slave Act was enacted by Congress on September 18, 1850," Felicia suddenly spouted, making me jump in my chair. "It made it the federal government's job to capture and return runaways."

Professor Rusty nodded. "That's exactly right, Felicia.

The law meant U.S. marshals could force local authorities in the Northern states—including New Hampshire—to help them round up suspected fugitives. In fact, all citizens were obliged to aid in the recapture of runaways, or face imprisonment and fines."

"But that's so unfair!" I cried.

"The abolitionists thought so too," my mother added, passing me a plate piled with the avocado I'd sliced earlier. "They called it the 'Bloodhound Law,' because of the dogs that were used to track down runaways. I read that some of the fugitive slaves would rub themselves with things like onion and pine pitch, hoping the hounds wouldn't pick up their scent." She shook her head sadly. "Can you imagine it? Here in this country?"

Professor Rusty reached over and speared a slice of avocado. "The law also made helping fugitive slaves a more serious federal crime. The marshals had the legal right to search anyone's home for runaways at any time, and arrest anyone caught harboring or aiding them."

"What happened if they got caught?" asked Mackenzie, her blue eyes round with concern. I knew she was thinking of the original Truly. I sure was.

"There were stiff penalties," Professor Rusty told her, taking a bite of his dinner. "Oh my goodness, Dinah, these enchiladas are amazing!"

"Thank you," said my mother.

"While the consequences weren't as dire, of course, as those facing the slaves if they were caught," he continued, "still, your ancestors could have been sent to prison for six months and had to pay a big fine. It was a very brave thing your Truly did."

No wonder she'd been so scared! I thought. Prison? What would have happened to little Booth?

"How big a fine?" asked my brother Danny from the far end of the table.

"A thousand dollars," Felicia told him. "Which doesn't sound like that much, but it translates to almost thirty thousand dollars today."

Danny gave a low whistle. "That's a lot of money!"

"No kidding," said my father. "A fine like that could have meant financial ruin."

I wondered if he was thinking of the bank loan that nearly put our bookshop out of business this past winter, before Belinda Winchester stepped in to help.

I turned to Professor Rusty. "So do you think that's why Truly hid her diary? Just in case the house was searched?"

He nodded. "Most likely. Others did. There was a famous African American abolitionist by the name of William Still, who lived in Philadelphia and was a conductor on the Underground Railroad there. He kept meticulous records of the hundreds of runaways that he helped, hoping it would help reunite them with their families later. He hid his journal every night in a crypt in a nearby cemetery."

"A crypt?" Lauren looked puzzled.

"A grave," he told her.

My sister shivered. "Eew! I guess he figured no one would look for it there."

Professor Rusty nodded again. "Exactly."

I digested this information, wondering if I'd have had the kind of courage that my namesake did. One thing still bothered me, though.

"How would anyone have even found out that Truly was involved with the Underground Railroad?" I asked. "New Hampshire is a Northern state. Wasn't everybody in favor of freeing the slaves?"

Professor Rusty shook his head. "New Hampshire abolished slavery in 1783, but some people still felt strongly that the Southern states had a right to determine their own laws. Whole towns were split over the issue of abolition. It pitted neighbor against neighbor in some instances, and even split families. Pumpkin Falls experienced some of that."

"Plus, slave catchers and bounty hunters offered rewards for those who turned in fugitives and those aiding them," my mother added. "Greed has always been a part of human nature, unfortunately, and some people succumbed to the temptation."

"Weasels," muttered Hatcher.

I thought of the diary entry I'd read earlier: *There are whispers of money changing hands in exchange for information*, Truly had written. Weasels indeed.

"The Fugitive Slave Act brought everything to a head," said Professor Rusty, warming to his theme. I'd wanted a distraction, and I was getting my money's worth. No one was thinking about the Pumpkin Falls Private Eyes now. "Harriet Jacobs, a fugitive slave living in New York at the time, called the law 'the beginning of a reign of terror.' The Northern states were no longer a safe haven. Slaves who had fled the South and who had been living freely in cities like Boston and Philadelphia were forced to leave the new lives they'd forged for themselves and flee even farther north to Canada."

"So they were safe from the slave catchers there?" Hatcher asked.

"Yes."

"Canada was part of the British Empire at that time, which abolished slavery in 1834," Felicia spouted again. The girl sure knew her dates. "Some forty thousand blacks took refuge there after the Fugitive Slave Act was passed, and before the Civil War and the passage of the Thirteenth Amendment."

"What amendment was that?" Mackenzie whispered to me.

"The amendment to the Constitution abolishing slavery, duh," I whispered back, and she reddened. "Don't you pay attention in social studies?"

"The Underground Railroad's code word for Canada pretty much says it all," Professor Rusty told us. "They called it 'heaven.' Former slaves weren't entirely free from racism in Canada, but they had the right to vote, and they could become citizens and own property—things that were denied them in the United States."

"It was a bad time here," my mother said. "I can hardly bear to read about it! Not only were runaway slaves captured and returned to the South, but many free blacks were also taken, and forced into slavery."

"But that's awful!" I cried. "Couldn't they do something about it?"

Professor Rusty shook his head. "Slaves had no legal rights. They were completely defenseless."

No wonder my ancestors had been so on fire to help! I thought, feeling a sudden rush of pride in their actions. I was beginning to wish that I could travel back in time and give them a hand. I glanced down the table at my brother Danny. Truly had been only a year older than he was when she started keeping her diary. She had a new baby to care for, a husband off fighting a war, and a farm to run. Getting caught could have meant prison and financial ruin. And yet she'd risked it all to help others to freedom.

Professor Rusty served himself another enchilada. "If there was any good thing that came from the passage of that inhumane bill," he said, "it was the fact that it steeled this country's resolve to put an end to slavery. The Fugitive Slave Act reenergized the Underground Railroad and got Northern folks thinking more about and caring more about the issue of slavery. Many who'd been on the fence about abolition joined the movement."

"It was the beginning of end, in other words?" asked Aunt True.

He smiled at her. "You might say that."

Felicia dabbed her mouth with her napkin and turned to me. "So from your perusal of the primary source document, have you been able to ascertain where the fugitives may have been concealed?"

Hatcher kicked me under the table. I didn't dare look at him; I wouldn't be able to contain my laughter. I knew exactly what he was thinking, because I was thinking the same thing: Was this girl for real? Who talked like that?

"Um," I said, uncertain how to reply. I didn't want to be called "cretinous" again, whatever that was.

"What I think Felicia is trying to say," said Professor Rusty, "is that thanks to the diary we now know that your family was definitely involved in harboring runaway slaves. But the question remains, where did they hide them?"

CHAPTER 21

We didn't have time to look just then. Not with the finals for the Maple Madness Bake-Off about to start down at the bookshop.

My thoughts swirled as I piled into the minivan with my parents and brothers and sisters. Between everything that Professor Rusty had just told us, worries about Bigfoot, the town feud, and Mackenzie's apparent interest in Calhoun, it had been a confusing day.

And it was about to get more confusing.

"I insist that Reverend Quinn be disqualified as head judge," announced Ella Bellow, who was lying in wait for us on the bookstore's doorstep.

"Really, Ella?" said Aunt True calmly, taking her keys from her pocket and unlocking the front door. "It's his turn this year, remember?"

"I don't care," Ella continued, following her inside. Hatcher raised an eyebrow at me as the rest of us went in too.

The bookshop looked great. My aunt had gone to a lot of trouble this afternoon decorating for the contest, after she and Ella and Mr. Henry finally managed to quell the rebellion. There were big fake orange and red maple leaves hanging from the ceiling, and signs pointing to the Annex that read THIS WAY TO THE FAMOUS PUMPKIN FALLS MAPLE MADNESS BAKE-OFF! The long table that held the baked goods showed no sign of the earlier skirmishes. Plates and platters were lined up in an orderly fashion, with no regard to Team Freeman or Team Maynard.

"Reverend Quinn is one of the only people in town without an entry in the contest," my aunt said mildly. "If anyone's going to be an impartial head judge, it's him."

"Ha!" said Ella. "Explain to me, then, why he was spotted talking to Grace Freeman this morning on the village green."

My aunt gave her a look. "She goes to his *church*, Ella. So do the Maynards."

Ella Bellow sniffed. "That's beside the point. He shouldn't be seen consorting with the finalists on the very day of the judging!"

"You think she was maybe trying to bribe him with some fudge?" My aunt laughed. "Come on!"

From the look on her face, our former postmistress clearly

felt this was a possibility. Hatcher elbowed me. He was getting a kick out of this. I could only imagine what Mackenzie thought, but the two of us weren't exactly on speaking terms at the moment.

"Ella, how about you dial it back just a whisker?" asked my father, stepping forward. "I've had your Maple Bread Pudding, and it's wonderful. A strong contestant, I'd say."

My aunt, who had bent down to open a large box containing what looked like the new espresso machine, looked up sharply. "Maple *Bread* Pudding? This wouldn't have anything to do with the fact that everyone knows Reverend Quinn is on a gluten-free diet, would it?"

"The idea!" Ella sputtered, but her face reddened.

Hatcher elbowed me again. "Busted," he whispered, grinning from ear to ear.

"You have two choices, Ella," my aunt informed her, straightening up and putting her hands on her hips. "You and your pudding can stay in the contest, but I don't want to hear any more on this subject."

"And if I refuse?" Ella bridled.

Aunt True pointed to the door. "There's the door. Don't let it hit you on the way out."

An awkward silence descended on the bookshop. I'd never seen my aunt like this. The feud must have really gotten to her.

"Well, I never!" Ella suddenly seemed aware that we were

all looking at her. She scowled at us. "You Lovejoys think you're—"

It was Pippa who saved the day.

"I like your bread pudding too, Mithith Bellow," she said, stepping forward and taking Ella by the hand. "Belinda gave Lauren and me thome of your tetht batch yethterday. I think it dethervth a blue ribbon."

"You do, do you?" Ella replied, some of the wind going out of her sails.

Pippa nodded vigorously.

"Maybe we should ask Pippa to judge," my father joked. "Would that satisfy you, Ella?"

"Pleathe, Daddy?" begged Pippa, jumping up and down. "I want to hand out ribbonth!"

In the end, that's exactly what happened. My parents and my aunt decided that Pippa's presence might help defuse the tension, so she stepped in as last-minute assistant to Reverend Quinn. My little sister's irresistible charm once again worked its magic—at least for the hour that the finals lasted—and Pumpkin Falls managed to pull itself together and be civil while Reverend Quinn and the other two judges considered the entries.

Which was more than could be said for Mackenzie and me. Or at least for me. When Calhoun and his family came into the bookshop—Calhoun's sister Juliet had entered her

Maple Macaroons—my cousin started over toward him.

"Can't you just leave him alone for once?" I growled, grabbing her arm.

Mackenzie turned and looked at me, shocked. "What are you talking about?"

"I'm talking about how you already have a boyfriend!" I said hotly. "Stop being so boy crazy!"

She pulled her arm out of my grasp. "And you stop being just plain crazy!" she shot back.

Ella Bellow's Maple Bread Pudding didn't win, but neither did Mrs. Freeman's Maple Fudge or Coach Maynard's Maple Cream Pie. It was Mr. Henry who won, coming from behind with his Maple Walnut Cupcakes and scooping up the blue ribbon.

"Let's go home and see if we can salvage what's left of the evening, shall we?" my father said to us when it was all over and the last picture of the winner and his entry had been taken and the bookshop was empty again.

Fat chance, I thought, my eyes sliding over to Mackenzie. She'd been ignoring me ever since our blowup earlier.

"And how exactly do you plan to do that, J. T.?" asked my aunt.

"For starters, with some of your Bookshop Blondies, which are a winner in my book," my father said gallantly.

"Mine too," echoed Professor Rusty. "How about I swing

by the General Store and pick up some vanilla ice cream to go with them?"

"You said 'for starters,' J. T.," my mother said. "What else do you have in mind?"

My father looked around at all of us. He smiled. "Anyone interested in searching for the Underground Railroad's hiding spot?"

CHAPTER 22

"Team Lovejoy will scour the main part of the house, top to bottom, while Team, uh, History Department tackles the family room and the garage," ordered my father. We were back at Gramps and Lola's house, where he'd slipped effortlessly into command mode. "Hatcher and Danny, you two start in the basement."

My brothers exchanged a glance. "Can we maybe be in charge of the attic instead?" ventured Hatcher. He feels the same way I do about spiders.

"Show some team spirit, boys," said my father, pointing to the cellar door. "Downstairs, on the double."

Resigned to their fate, my brothers slouched off. The rest of us fanned out to search every nook and cranny we could think of, including closets, pantries, fireplaces—even bookshelves.

"Remember when we were stationed in Germany and

went to Amsterdam to see the Anne Frank house?" my mother said as the two of us began to explore the living room. While I rooted around in the window seats—nothing but blankets and board games there—she ran her fingertips around the edges of the built-in bookcases that flanked the fireplace.

I nodded. Hatcher had read *The Diary of Anne Frank* as a school assignment that year, and he'd been the one who'd begged to go.

"Yeah," I said, recalling the hinged bookcase that had concealed the Frank family's hiding spot from the Nazis. "Do you think there's something like that in our house?"

My mother shrugged. "You never know."

In the end, though, we came up empty-handed. So did everyone else.

"Perhaps they just stashed the fugitives in one of the attic rooms until the coast was clear," said Professor Rusty, running a hand through his hair. Aunt True, who was seated next to him on the front stairs, reached over and patted it back into place. Or tried to. Professor Rusty's hair was pretty U-N-R-U-L-Y, as Annie Freeman would say.

"I thought for sure the fireplace in the family room held the key," he continued morosely. "That was likely a summer kitchen back in the day, and I've read about a number of those big old fireplaces concealing secret chambers and passageways and trapdoors leading to tunnels."

I could tell he was disappointed. So was I, actually. It

would have been really cool to find the hiding place.

Lauren was the only one who refused to give up. While Mackenzie and I were showing Felicia the original Truly's diary, my younger sister wandered around, knocking on walls and stairwells. She was still at it when bedtime rolled around.

"Good heavens, Lauren, let's give it a rest, shall we?" said my mother. "Go get ready for bed."

My sister's gaze slid over to me. "We were supposed to finish reading the diary tonight."

"I'm not reading anything with a double-crosser like you," I told her. "Not after what you did."

"I didn't do anything!"

"You told Professor Rusty about the Pumpkin Falls Private Eyes!"

Lauren's eyes widened in feigned innocence. "I did not!"

"You are such a bad liar!"

"So what if I did, anyway? Who cares about your stupid club!"

My mother put her hands on her hips, exasperated. "Girls! Just stop, would you? Between you two and the Bake-Off feud, I've had enough squabbling to last a lifetime. Lauren, get to bed. You can finish reading the diary in the morning. And, Truly, I don't want to hear another word about any of this, do you understand?"

"Yes, ma'am," I muttered.

Maybe she was feeling sorry for me because of my tears

earlier in the evening, or maybe she was just tired and forgot, but my mother didn't ask for the diary back. And I didn't bring it up.

"I'm too tired to read any more tonight," Mackenzie told me when we were back in my room. She'd been uncharacteristically quiet all evening, and I felt a pang of guilt. The two of us hadn't talked since I'd lashed out at her earlier at the bookstore.

"Mind if I read ahead?"

"Nope." She got into bed and rolled over, turning her back on me.

I gazed at her ruefully for a moment, then opened the diary to where we'd left off:

> *February 9, 1862*
> *F arrived just before midnight. We have been waiting for weeks for this special delivery. Reverend Bartlett sent a note with one of the Harrington boys after breakfast, letting us know the shipment was finally on its way, and the reason for its delay. Mother Lovejoy and I were busy all day preparing.*
> *Yours, Truly*

> *February 11, 1862*
> *Our single package is now two! F is terribly ill, however, with a rattling cough and fever. This was the reason for the delay. I am on duty as nurse, and doing*

*the best I can, but with my own wee Booth to care
for, and the threat of house search hanging over our
heads, it is not easy.
Yours, Truly*

Wait a minute, I thought, going back and rereading the
entry. What did she mean by *our single package is now two?* I
frowned, wondering if I'd missed something.

The next entry was very brief:

*February 15, 1862
I have grown fond of this package. F and I have much
in common, and much to talk about.*

And then a few days later, this:

*February 20, 1862
We heard the bloodhounds in the woods on Lovejoy
Mountain tonight. Strangers are going door to door
in town, with promises of fat payments for informa-
tion, and neighbor looks at neighbor with suspicion.
The owner is determined to get this package back,
Reverend Bartlett tells us. No one is to be trusted. I
must find a way to ensure safe passage—but F is too
weak to be moved.
Yours, Truly*

February 23, 1862
No word from Matthew in weeks. And worse, Mother
Lovejoy has fallen ill too.
Yours, Truly

This did not sound good. I read on:

February 28, 1862
I have been awake for three days and am nearly at
my wits' end. Last night there was a knock at the
door. Men I did not recognize were on the doorstep.
Mother Lovejoy was taken by the fever, I told them.
We are a house of death, I told them. They didn't
believe me, even when I showed them her coffin in the
parlor, where it rests awaiting burial tomorrow. One
man wanted to pry it open and see if I was telling
the truth, but after I pleaded with him he relented. I
am pale and hollow-eyed from lack of sleep, and they
finally took pity on me and left, Gott sei dank.

I looked this one up in the German-English dictionary.
"*Gott sei Dank*" meant "thank God."

But they will be back. This I know. So tonight, whether
the packages are ready or not, and no matter how dear F
has become to me, I must send them on to a safer place.

Yours, Truly

Mother Lovejoy *died*? I scanned the entry again, trying to understand. What safer place was Truly talking about? Maple Grove? Canada? How would the packages—the runaways— get there? Who was F? Could Truly manage it, right under the noses of the dogs and bounty hunters?

There were so many unanswered questions.

My eyelids were heavy by the time I finally closed the diary and switched off the light. Sleep didn't come easily, though. I lay there for what felt like forever, thinking about what I'd just read. I couldn't stop thinking about what I'd read. And when I did finally manage to drift off, my restless dreams were filled with baying bloodhounds and men with torches chasing desperate men and women on the run.

CHAPTER 23

"Knock it OFF, Lauren!"

I stuffed my head under my pillow, trying to block out the noise. Spurred on by last night's fruitless basement-to-rafters search, my sister had redoubled her efforts to find the Underground Railroad's secret hiding spot.

Sleep was impossible. I gave an exasperated sigh and threw my pillow over at Mackenzie. No response. Pushing myself up on my forearms, I glanced over at the air mattress. It was empty; my cousin was already up.

I found her downstairs, eating a banana with peanut butter and talking to my father. She was pleasant to me, but distant. Neither of us mentioned my outburst at the bookshop last night.

I yawned all the way to swim practice—never a good sign. This was the final morning of daily doubles. After today, regular once-a-day practice was going to be a breeze. I leaned my head back and closed my eyes, savoring the prospect of sleeping in.

At the pool, Coach Maynard barely said a word to anyone. He just wrote down our workout on the whiteboard and motioned us into the pool.

"More sap lines were cut last night, after the Bake-Off," Lucas reported in a whisper. "At the Freemans, too. I overheard people talking at Lou's."

Maybe Felicia Grunewald, Professor Rusty's know-it-all research assistant, was right, I thought as I carved my way up and down my lane. Maybe the Pumpkin Falls Private Eyes wasn't only a cretinous name, but also a totally cretinous idea.

I'd looked up "cretinous." It meant "extremely stupid," which we probably were. How on earth were a bunch of seventh graders supposed to solve a crime like this? Could even hope to end the feud?

Swimming usually helped clear my mind and cheer me up, but I was still feeling discouraged by the time practice finished. My cell phone buzzed as Mackenzie and I were in the locker room changing.

"It's a text from Cha Cha," I said. "She and Jasmine want to come over after breakfast."

"Whatever."

"Cha Cha says we can take you to see the steeple."

"Fine." Mackenzie's voice was still cool; she wasn't giving an inch.

The steeple on the First Parish Church is one of our town's claims to fame, thanks to its bell, which was made by Paul Revere. I got to see it up close and way too personal earlier this winter. Mackenzie knew all about that fiasco, of course, and she'd been pestering me all week for a tour of the steeple. Now it didn't seem like she cared.

"I can't believe you're only here for two more days!" my mother lamented to Mackenzie a little while later, when the two of us sat down to breakfast—French toast, my favorite. "This week has just flown by, darlin'."

"Yep." My cousin picked up her fork and started to eat, while I just stared at my plate.

My mother regarded the two of us thoughtfully. "Y'all better make the most of it," she continued lightly. "You won't get to see one another again until summer vacation."

I glanced over at Mackenzie, struck by another pang of guilt. The day after tomorrow she'd be on the plane back to Texas. I needed to patch things up somehow—if that was even possible at this point.

"How did the kitten deliveries go yesterday?" my mother asked, setting a plate in front of Pippa.

"We gave away thix," my little sister told her proudly.

"Six? That is impressive," my mother replied, leaning

down to kiss the top of her head. She turned to Lauren. "Did you feed Bilbo this morning?"

My sister looked up from her book—*The House of Dies Drear*, one of the ones from the stack that Mr. Henry had given to my mother—and nodded.

"I remember that book!" I told her, figuring I'd better start extending olive branches if I really wanted to patch things up with my cousin. "It totally creeped me out. All those secret tunnels and that weird guy who lived in that cave—"

"Annie wants me to spend the night," Lauren interrupted, ignoring me. Mackenzie didn't even look up from her French toast. So much for olive branches.

My mother frowned. "This is an awfully busy week for the Freemans. The last thing they probably need is a house guest."

"I told them I'd help on the farm," Lauren assured her.

"Why don't I call Annie's mother and see if Annie can have a sleepover here instead?"

My sister's face lit up. "Thanks, Mom!"

After breakfast, Mackenzie and I walked Lauren and Pippa down the street to Belinda's, where we found the former lunch lady grooving to the Beach Boys again as she vacuumed. Her house might be stuffed with cats, but it was spotless. Belinda loved to clean.

"Morning!" she shouted after we banged on the door

about a hundred times. Pulling out an earbud, she flipped a switch on the vacuum cleaner, and it whined to a stop. I could hear the faint strains of "Help Me, Rhonda" coming from her dangling earbud.

"Any more kittens need delivering?" asked Lauren hopefully.

Belinda shook her head. "Sorry, sweetheart, that train has left the station. There'll be more soon enough, though, never fear." She looked over at Mackenzie. "I'm still counting on you to take one home with you."

My cousin laughed. "I'll ask my mother, but I'm pretty sure the answer is 'no.'"

Cha Cha and Jasmine were already at my house by the time Mackenzie and I got back.

"I wish you could have come with us, Truly," said Cha Cha. "We had a blast!"

"We had a very good reason for keeping her here in Pumpkin Falls," my mother told her, and placing her hands on my cousin's shoulders, she nudged her toward my friends. "Cha Cha, Jasmine, I'd like you to meet Mackenzie Gifford, my niece and Truly's cousin."

My friends smiled at Mackenzie, and she smiled back.

Bunting meets raven, I thought, glancing from my cousin to Jasmine, whose glossy dark hair was a constant source of envy. I would kill for hair like that.

"Hey, we got you something," Cha Cha said, handing us each a gift bag. My friend Cha Cha isn't like any bird I've ever seen—she's more of a feline. Her hair is dark, too, but short, and as fluffy as one of Belinda's kittens. I opened my present to find a T-shirt with a picture of a chicken roosting on top of the logo I CHICKENED OUT IN KEY WEST!

"There are these wild chickens all over the place that roam around on the streets," Jasmine told us. "It's kind of hilarious."

"I love it!" I said.

"Me too," said Mackenzie. "I'm going to put mine right on."

She chattered away to my friends as the four of us went upstairs to my room, sounding so much like her usual self that my heart gave a hopeful lift. Maybe things would be okay between us after all.

But the tendril of hope quickly shriveled.

Mackenzie paused at the top of the stairs and turned to me as Cha Cha and Jasmine went on ahead down the hall to my room. "Don't wear your T-shirt today," she whispered. "I'm not into being twins."

Hurt, I mumbled, "Okay." The message couldn't have been clearer: I was not forgiven.

"Hey, I brought something for you guys too," Mackenzie said to Cha Cha and Jasmine, all smiles again as she went into my bedroom and crossed to the closet. I knew what she was getting; she'd brought one for me, too, and she'd given one each to Lauren and Pippa as well.

"Super cute!" said Jasmine, when my cousin handed her a small ceramic cowboy boot with a big Texas Lone Star on it.

"Thanks, Mackenzie!" echoed Cha Cha. She plunked down cross-legged on my rug. "Now, tell us everything."

CHAPTER 24

I left out the part about Scooter's surprise birthday kiss, of course. No need to publicize that disaster, plus Jasmine was Scooter's twin and would be seriously creeped out at the thought of her brother crushing on one of her friends. Not that he was crushing on me anymore. Mackenzie's arrival had taken care of that.

I also didn't bring up the fact that my cousin had bewitched every middle school male in Pumpkin Falls. Cha Cha and Jasmine would find that out for themselves soon enough.

I filled them in on the sap heist, and Jasmine's eyes widened when I told them about the stakeout. "You seriously think it could be Bigfoot?"

I shrugged.

"The guys think so," said Mackenzie, and Cha Cha shivered.

After that, my cousin showed them the loose floorboard

in the closet where we'd found the original Truly's diary. My friends listened openmouthed as I read aloud a few entries.

"That is the coolest thing *ever!*" said Jasmine. "I can't believe you have a secret compartment in your room!"

"I know, right?"

Cha Cha reached for the diary. I passed it to her, and she ran her hands over the smooth, worn leather. "This is amazing," she said. "When you read the stuff she wrote, it's like she's right here in the room with us. The person you were named after and everything!"

"I wish I could talk to her," I said. "There's so much I want to know." Before I could continue, though, my mother called to us from the front hall.

"Girls! That was Reverend Quinn on the phone—he says he's got time to give Mackenzie a tour of the steeple, if you head over to the church right now!"

Leaving the diary safely tucked under my pillow, the four of us went back downstairs.

"Lunch is on me, ladies," said my mother, handing me some money. "And take your swim things with you," she reminded Mackenzie and me. "You'll save yourselves a trip that way."

Mackenzie and I grabbed our swim bags—last practice!—and we all headed for town. The rain had cleared up, and everything smelled of freshly washed earth. Jasmine and Cha Cha rattled on about their vacation as we walked, but while Mackenzie hung on their every word, I listened with only one ear. Beaches, boys, bikinis—been there, heard all about that.

I scanned the trees for owls. Was it a barred owl call that the Underground Railroad used, I wondered? Or another one? A great horned owl, perhaps—now, that was a distinctive call. *Hoo-h'Hoo-hoo-hoo.* They sounded just like what you'd expect an owl to sound like.

Reverend Quinn was waiting for us at the church.

"Hello, girls," he said with a welcoming smile. "You must be Truly's cousin Mackenzie."

Mackenzie nodded.

"I'm sure you've heard all about our steeple from Truly."

I blushed. The last time I'd been up in the steeple, disaster had struck. Disaster in the name of Scooter Sanchez, who had accidentally on purpose rung the bell while I was in the belfry. I'd been deaf for days.

But Reverend Quinn didn't know about that. I'd managed to make a clean getaway while he was bawling out Scooter.

"This is so awesome!" Mackenzie said happily as we climbed the ladder leading to the steeple. "I can't believe I'm actually getting to go up here! With a bell made by Paul Revere and everything! Wait until I tell—"

"Mr. Perfect?" I said, the words popping out before I could stop myself.

Mackenzie's happy smile faded. Once again I'd put my size-ten-and-a-half foot into my mouth. Felicia was right—I really was cretinous.

I hung back while Cha Cha and Jasmine explained the history of the steeple to my cousin and showed her the view. I was feeling worse by the minute. What was *wrong* with me? Could I never do anything right?

When Reverend Quinn offered to take a group picture of us after the tour, Mackenzie made a point of making sure she stood as far away from me as possible.

"What's up with you two?" Cha Cha murmured, watching her.

"Nothing," I lied.

"Doesn't seem like nothing."

I sighed. "It's just—you know, kind of hard to explain."

"She seems really nice," said Cha Cha.

I nodded. "She is." I blinked rapidly, fighting back tears. I really wanted things to be okay again between my cousin and me.

At Lou's, Mackenzie took a seat at the opposite end of the counter from me. I ended up with Jasmine on one side and Ella Bellow, of all people, on the other.

"How are those socks coming?" Ella asked just as I bit into my grilled cheese.

"Mmmph mmmph," I replied.

"That bad, huh?" Her dark eyes glinted with amusement. She seemed to have gotten over her snit at the bookshop last night. "We'll have to see if we can do something to remedy that."

After lunch Cha Cha took us across the street to the Starlite and showed Mackenzie around. One of the dance studios was empty, and she made my cousin laugh as she grabbed Jasmine and mimicked how Scooter and I looked together at first at Cotillion.

"It's amazing you have any toes left at all, Truly," Jasmine joked. "My brother really flattened them."

"The two of them got better, though," said Cha Cha. "Competition will do that."

"And you should have seen how Cha Cha transformed Calhoun!" Jasmine crowed. "She's a genius—he looked like someone on one of those dance competition shows by the time she was done with him."

I looked away, remembering how Calhoun had asked me to dance. Now, if he had the chance, he'd probably ask Mackenzie. I wasn't so cretinous that I didn't know that.

Glancing down at my watch, I frowned. "Gotta go," I told my friends, shouldering my swim bag. "Last swim practice of Spring Break awaits."

As I turned to leave, my cell phone buzzed. It was Scooter.

"What's up?" asked Jasmine.

I frowned at his text message. "Um, I'm not sure. It's from your brother. He says 'Big foot brigade reporting in.'"

Mackenzie gasped. "Did he get *footage*?" She and Cha Cha and Jasmine all crowded around.

WHAT ARE YOU TALKING ABOUT? I texted back.

GOTTA SEE IT TO BELIEVE IT, Scooter replied.

My cousin squealed. "He got Bigfoot on camera!"

My fingers flew over my cell phone keyboard. WHERE R U GUYS?

MY HOUSE, Scooter texted back. YOU?

DANCE STUDIO. MEET US AT THE BOOKSTORE?

I looked over at my cousin and my friends. "Wow, you guys! This could be huge. If we got Bigfoot on film, we're going to be famous!"

"You should tell Lauren too," said Mackenzie. "It was her theory, after all."

I made a face. Just what I needed. Little Miss Tagalong, tagging along again. *Olive branch*, I thought. "Fine," I replied, and sent my sister a quick text too.

The four of us left the dance studio and ran back across the street.

"What do you think of the name 'Cup and Chaucer'?" Aunt True asked as we came through the front door.

"Cup and what?" I looked around for the boys. They weren't here yet.

"Chaucer."

"Um, as a name for what?"

"For the mini café I'm thinking of adding over there," my aunt replied, waving a hand at the space to the left of the cash register. "We could serve tea and coffee to go with our signature treats. As another income stream."

Aunt True is always thinking up new ways for our bookstore to make money.

"There's room at the end of the counter for an espresso machine," she continued, "and I think we could squeeze in two or three little tables and chairs."

"Cool, Ms. Lovejoy," said Jasmine. "I'd totally hang out here if you do that."

"You already totally hang out here," Cha Cha reminded her with a grin.

"Cup and Chaucer." My mother nodded slowly. "That's cute, True."

"Who's Chaucer?" my father asked, emerging from the back office.

My mother and my aunt gave him a look.

He grinned. "Kidding! I'm not a complete philistine." And striking a pose, he began to recite aloud in what sounded like a foreign language:

> *Whan that Aprille with his shoures soote*
> *The droghte of Marche hath perced to the roote,*
> *And bathed every veyne in swich licour,*
> *Of which vertu engendred is the flour . . .*

We all stared at him, speechless.

"Um, what was that?" Mackenzie asked.

"Unless I'm mistaken, that was your uncle Jericho spouting

Middle English." There was a note of awe in my mother's voice.

"Middle English?" I asked. "Isn't that something out of *The Hobbit*?"

"That's Middle-*earth*," scoffed Lauren, the bell over the door jangling as she came in to join us. "Duh. Everybody knows that."

I glared at her.

"Middle English was the dialect spoken and written in the British Isles in medieval times," Aunt True explained hastily, spotting the look on my face. "I have to say, J. T., I'm impressed."

"Contrary to popular opinion, I didn't just wrestle at the University of Texas—I actually received an education," my father told her smugly. "My freshman English professor happened to be a Chaucer nut, and one of the requirements for passing his course was memorizing the opening stanzas of *Canterbury Tales*."

"Will wonders never cease," said Aunt True, shaking her head.

"Apparently not," my mother agreed.

The bell jangled again, and we all turned to see Mr. Sanchez stride into the bookshop. He had Scooter firmly in his grip. Calhoun and Lucas slunk in behind them.

"Was your daughter in on this too?" Mr. Sanchez demanded, his face like thunder.

My father frowned. "In on what?"

"This!" Mr. Sanchez shook the video camera at him.

Uh-oh, I slid a glance at Scooter.

He gave Mackenzie and me a hangdog look. "I kind of borrowed it without asking," he muttered.

My father pinned me with one of his signature Lieutenant Colonel Jericho T. Lovejoy glares. "Truly? Were you involved in taking this camera without permission?"

I squirmed, hoping that someone would jump in and help me out. But I was on my own. Nobody wanted to face the wrath of Lieutenant Colonel Jericho T. Lovejoy when he was in full commanding officer mode.

Lying wasn't an option. Not to my father. It was time to face the music. "Yeah," I admitted. "I mean, yes, sir."

Before either my father or Mr. Sanchez could say anything more, Scooter held up his phone.

"Here's the thing, though," he told us. "It worked."

CHAPTER 25

"What worked?" demanded Mr. Sanchez.

"The surveillance feed," Scooter explained. "We set up a stakeout at Freeman Farm to try and catch the sap rustler."

My father and Mr. Sanchez exchanged a glance.

"And you're telling us you caught the thief on film?" said my father.

Scooter nodded.

"This still doesn't excuse what you did," Mr. Sanchez told him sternly. "My colleague is hopping mad. He left his equipment at my office earlier this week, planning to pick it up first thing this morning for an assignment. He was worried that it had been stolen."

Scooter hung his head. "I know. I'm sorry. It's just that Franklin is my friend, and with all the stuff going on between his family and the Maynards, I thought—"

"The problem is that you didn't think!" Mr. Sanchez retorted.

"Let's see what you've got, son," said my father.

We crowded around and watched over Scooter's shoulder as he tapped on his cell phone screen to pull up the video feed.

At first there was nothing to see but a lot of dark. Then, some sort of movement must have triggered the motion detector, because all of a sudden the camera's flash kicked on, illuminating the sugar bush. A cluster of maple trees was clearly visible straight ahead, along with the network of plastic tubing strung between them. A moment later, a dark shape skulked into view.

Mackenzie and Lauren both gasped. I clutched my cousin's arm involuntarily. *Here it comes*, I thought. Bigfoot! Life as we knew it would never be the same. There would be magazine covers and movie offers. We should probably think about scheduling a press conference.

"Keep watching," said Scooter, slanting us a glance. Behind him, Calhoun and Lucas had the oddest expressions on their faces. As if they were trying not to—

"Are you kidding me?" I blurted, dropping Mackenzie's arm.

Behind me, Aunt True started to giggle.

"Oh my goodness," exclaimed my mother. "That's the funniest thing I've ever seen!"

The video camera had caught the sap rustler red-handed, all right. Or red-pawed, in this case. Out of the undergrowth waddled not Bigfoot—not even close—but rather a fat mama raccoon, followed by a trio of roly-poly babies. The mother raccoon climbed up one of the trees and ventured gingerly out onto a branch. Reaching down with her paws, she grabbed a section of the tubing that was attached to the spile and severed it neatly with her sharp teeth. On the ground below, one of her babies grabbed the dangling end and began sucking vigorously on it.

"Man, I can't believe we thought it was Big—" I stopped short as I realized that everyone had turned to look at me. Scooter and Calhoun were drawing their fingers across their throats, desperately trying to get me to shut up. So were Cha Cha and Jasmine.

"Big what, honey?" my mother asked.

"Uh, nothing," I mumbled, embarrassed. "Some big, uh, kids. You know, from West Hartfield."

So much for a press conference, I thought glumly.

We continued to watch as the mother raccoon repeated the crime for each of her babies. By the end, we were all howling.

"I love the way she keeps looking around!" my mother said, wiping her eyes. "As if she knows she's doing something wrong and might get caught!"

"You are so busted, Mama!" crowed Aunt True.

"So much for 'sabotage in Pumpkin Falls,'" said my father, shaking his head.

"You have to take this down to the *Pumpkin Falls Patriot-Bugle* right away," my mother told Scooter. "They can post the video on their website and get the word out. This will put a stop to any feuding. I'm going to call Grace Freeman and tell her the good news."

"And I'll call Coach Maynard," my father said. He turned to me. "You're not off the hook, young lady. I'll speak with you later."

My heart sank. I'd be lucky if I got to set foot outside the house before the Fourth of July.

"I'll let Ella Bellow know, and the rest of the town will hear within the hour," said Aunt True as my parents disappeared into the back office. "Thank goodness this is settled. Pumpkin Falls is too small a community for a full-blown feud."

Mr. Sanchez blew out his breath. He looked at Scooter for a long moment, considering. "Well, I guess your heart was in the right place," he said finally. "I'll go see if I can patch things up with my colleague."

"Thanks, Dad," Scooter replied. "I really am sorry."

"I'm still planning to take it out of your hide, though," his father warned. "I seem to recall that the garage could use cleaning."

Scooter's face fell when he heard this.

"Next time you get a bright idea that involves someone else's property, run it by me first, would you, buddy?" His father took the video camera and left.

As the adults scattered on their various missions, my friends and I were left standing alone in the middle of the bookshop.

"So I guess we can chalk up another win for the Pumpkin Falls Private Eyes, right?" said Scooter.

"Some win," said Calhoun. "Talk about the biggest anticlimax ever. Even I can write tomorrow's headline: *Masked bandits unmasked!*"

Mackenzie giggled, and Calhoun grinned at her. I looked away.

"So, what's next?" Scooter asked. "You guys want to hang out or something?"

"Can't," said Cha Cha. "It's Shabbat." The Abramowitzes are Jewish, and Friday nights are special for their family.

I shook my head. "We can't, either. It's the last day of swim practice."

"After that, maybe?" Scooter gave Mackenzie a hopeful look.

"We're kind of in the middle of a project," I told him before my cousin could say anything.

He frowned. "What sort of project?"

"Knitting, mostly. We have our last sock class tonight."

Hearing this, Lauren looked over at me sharply. Before she could spill the beans about the diary, I added quickly, "Plus, we were going to head over to the library."

That quickly extinguished any spark of interest on Scooter's part. The library was not at the top of his list of Fun Things to Do in Pumpkin Falls.

"Okay." His eyes slid over to my cousin again. "Maybe we can all hang out tomorrow?"

"Sounds good to me," said Mackenzie.

"See you guys then!" Scooter said, beaming. Calhoun and Lucas both waved—at Mackenzie—and followed him out the door. Cha Cha and Jasmine went with them.

"Can you believe that video? It was so funny!" Lauren said to Mackenzie.

"I know!" Mackenzie replied. "I can't wait to send a link to Cameron!"

"So now you remember Cameron," I muttered.

She turned to me. "What?"

"Nothing. Forget it."

"No! I will not forget it! I'm sick of your snide remarks, and I'm sick of your attitude. You've been a total pain this week, Truly!"

"I've been a pain? You're the one who's boy crazy!"

Mackenzie's mouth dropped open. Lauren's head whipped back and forth as she watched us. Ignoring them both, I grabbed my swim bag and stomped off to the rec center.

"Pool party!" Coach Maynard announced as I came out onto the deck a little while later. Mackenzie was still in the locker room. Neither of us had said a word to each other while we were changing.

There was a smile on my swim coach's face and a spring in his step that definitely hadn't been there this morning. Word must have gotten out about the surveillance video. Ella

Bellow's doing, most likely. Ella worked fast. "We have cause for celebration."

I knew that Coach Maynard was talking about a lot more than just the effort we'd put into daily doubles this week. He was clearly just as relieved as we all were that the mystery was solved and the feud was over.

My teammates and I jumped in the pool and played water polo for a while, then just horsed around, happy we didn't have to swim laps. There was cake and ice cream on the deck when we'd finished swimming, and Coach Maynard praised Mackenzie for her hard work and told her that she was bound to be a success, if she kept it up. He even gave her this goofy certificate he'd printed up, crowning her with the title "Flip Turn Ninja."

As we headed up the front walk to my grandparents' house a while later, I heard loud hammering coming from inside.

"What's going on?" I asked, opening the door and tossing my jacket and swim bag onto the bench in the front hall. I poked my head into the dining room. My mother was seated at the table as usual, working on her research paper.

"Your father's finally tackling the honey-do list," she said absently. "He's working on replacing the garbage disposal in the kitchen, and after that he promised he'd fix the squeaky step on the front stairs. Pizza should be here soon."

Fridays are always pizza nights for our family.

"So where is everybody?"

"Hatcher and Danny just got back from wrestling. They're showering, I think. And Lauren and Pippa are upstairs somewhere," my mother said, flapping her hand vaguely toward the ceiling. "Annie's with them." She finally looked up. "How was your last practice?"

"Good," I replied, and Mackenzie nodded.

"What are you two going to do now?"

"I want to finish my socks," my cousin told her, without so much as a glance in my direction. She was almost done with them and would be heading home with a completed pair, just as Ella had promised. I, on the other hand, was far from done. Probably because I'd had to unravel mine twice and start over.

"I'm going upstairs to read," I said. I didn't care if I was forging ahead without everybody else—I had to know what happened to Truly and the fugitives.

Mackenzie followed me just long enough to grab her knitting, then disappeared back downstairs. I flopped onto my bed and opened the diary.

March 2, 1862

Disaster! The packages were mailed tonight, but something went terribly wrong. I had to leave Booth alone in his cradle and run for Reverend Bartlett. He told me to go home and keep the door closed and not let anyone in, no matter what.

Yours, Truly

March 3, 1862
Much activity on Maple Street today, and on into the
night. I stay hidden behind the curtains with my son
and pray.
Yours, Truly

March 4, 1862
A letter from Matthew! But it brought sad news:
Booth Harrington, his friend for whom our son is
named, was killed by a sniper on reconnaissance at
Manassas. I must go to his family as soon as it is safe
and comfort them. We all have to drink from the cup
of sorrow in life, but this is a hard, hard loss.
My letter telling Matthew of his mother's death must
not yet have been received, for he did not mention it. I
can only imagine how difficult this news will be.
No word yet on whether the delivery arrived safely.
I am on pins and needles, as Mother Lovejoy used
to say.
Is there more darkness ahead, or will we finally see
some light?
Yours, Truly

March 5, 1862
Light! Reverend Bartlett reported that the packages
were miraculously unharmed, though shaken from the

*ordeal. They have gone on their way undetected. Next
stop, Maple Grove. And then, God willing, heaven.
Yours, Truly*

Heaven. That meant Canada, right?

Only three more entries. My eyes fairly flew over the
pages:

*May 15, 1862
I have had a letter from F! Both packages arrived
safely. F promises to return someday. A love token
was enclosed—a beautiful bracelet of intricately
braided hair, black and brown so close in hue I almost
cannot tell them apart. There are two bracelets, I am
told. F has kept one. Our hearts are forever entwined
by our ordeal. I will write back and promise again
that the secret will be kept for always.
Yours, Truly*

Wait a minute, I thought. Special friendship bracelets?
Had Truly fallen in love with someone else? Was it the fugitive slave she'd harbored? The mysterious F? Was that the
secret she had vowed to keep? What about Matthew?

*October 7, 1862
These past months have been an agony. No further*

*word from F, and now this! Matthew has been cap-
tured by the enemy. I am closing up the house, which
echoes with sadness and loss. Booth and I must travel
to Washington, where I will try and arrange for his
father's release. We will be back, God willing, and
together again as a family. I pray for my beloved
husband, and for F, and for an end to all pain and
suffering. I pray for peace.*

Yours, Truly

*October 10, 1862
We leave Pumpkin Falls today, Booth and I, but our
hearts are here in this home, always.*

Yours, Truly

And then, nothing. That was it. The rest of the pages were
empty. I flipped through to the end twice to be sure.

I lay there on my bed, trying to make sense of what I'd
read. A few minutes later, my cell phone buzzed.

Probably Mom letting me know the pizza's arrived, I thought.
But a split second later the buzz turned into a familiar tune:
"The Magnificent Seven."

A moment after that, I heard cell phones ringing all over
the house.

I sat up. It wasn't pizza—it was Dad's special signal,
the one he'd programmed into all of our phones in case of

an emergency. The one that meant RED ALERT! DEFON 1! ALL HANDS ON DECK!

In a flash, Lovejoys came out of the woodwork. I dashed out of my room as Hatcher and Danny thundered down from the attic. Pippa and Lauren popped out from wherever they'd been playing, trailing a puzzled Annie Freeman. Downstairs, my mother emerged from the dining room. Mackenzie was right behind her, clutching her knitting.

"What's going on?" my cousin asked, bewildered, as we all converged on the front staircase.

My father was standing just below the portrait of the original Truly. In his left hand he was holding a hammer, and in his right, firmly clamped in the titanium grip of the Terminator, was one of the wooden stair treads.

He smiled at us. "I found the Underground Railroad's hiding place."

CHAPTER 26

I couldn't see a thing.

Opening my eyes as wide as possible, I stared into the darkness.

Nothing.

Not even a glimmer of light.

It was pitch-black inside, and airless. It smelled of moldy newspapers and dust and time that had slowed to a crawl and then stopped altogether. It smelled of something else, too, something that I really, really hoped was the decaying rag rug beneath me and not spiders.

I tried to shift position, and smacked into the wall. It was unbelievably cramped, especially for someone my size. I couldn't stand, I couldn't stretch out, I could only sit or lie down curled up on my side. I couldn't even begin to imagine how anyone had spent more than a few minutes in here.

I was tempted to use the torch app on my cell phone, but I

resisted the urge. Instead, I held my breath, trying to envision what it would have felt like to be hidden away, terrified that you'd be discovered and returned to a life you'd risked everything to leave.

A minute later, a crack of light appeared above my head. My father peered in. "Had enough?"

I nodded, and he lifted the stair tread away, then reached down and gave me his good hand as I clambered out.

"My turn! My turn!" shrieked Pippa.

"Only Truly and Mackenzie get to go in tonight," my mother told her.

"No fair!" Lauren protested. "How come?"

"Because they were the ones who found the diary, and without it we wouldn't have known what this space was, even if we'd ever managed to find it," my mother told her calmly.

"Someone would have discovered it eventually," Lauren muttered. She was resentful about the fact that she hadn't been the one to find the hiding spot. *So much for all that tapping, Nancy Drew*, I thought spitefully.

"Chin up, Lauren," said Aunt True. "Good things come to those who wait."

My mother had called my aunt the minute Dad showed us his discovery, and she and Professor Rusty were here practically before my mother hung up the phone. Professor Rusty looked like he'd just won the lottery. He'd taken a zillion pictures already, and he kept shaking his head and saying things like "Amazing!" and "Incredible!" and "Extraordinary!"

Watching him, I suddenly realized something: This was his owl. This was the thing Professor Rusty had been waiting his whole life to see.

He'd been super anxious about us touching anything. "It's vital to preserve the integrity of a historical find of this magnitude," he'd said, shining a flashlight into the secret room and leaning in. "Look at the dates on these newspapers lining the walls!" he'd cried, his voice muffled. "1848! 1853! 1860! What a treasure trove! They prove this is the real deal."

"Why are the walls lined with newspaper?" Mackenzie had asked.

"For warmth," he'd explained, standing up again.

Hatcher and I snickered. Professor Rusty really looked like Albert Einstein now, what with all the dust in his hair. Aunt True reached over and swatted at it, sending up a small cloud.

Professor Rusty coughed. "It would have been drafty in there in the wintertime, and the newspaper would have helped with that. It also probably helped absorb sound, making it safer. Same thing with that rug on the floor." He grinned at us. "Isn't it just marvelous, to think that this secret has been here all these years, completely undisturbed? It's like finding Tutankhamen's tomb!"

"You do have a tendency to exaggerate, dear," said Aunt True drily.

I swiveled around and stared at her. This was the first time I'd heard her call him a pet name. Did this mean he was really her boyfriend?

We'd all taken turns peering inside, and then I'd managed to persuade Professor Rusty to let me climb in.

"I'll be careful," I said. "I promise not to touch anything."

He'd finally agreed, although reluctantly. "Once the team from the museum has examined and photographed everything, it won't be such a big deal," he'd explained. "You can spend all the time in the world in there if you want to."

"Just for a minute," I'd begged. "Seriously, I won't touch anything."

And I didn't, but I sure looked, at least until my father replaced the stair tread, plunging me into darkness.

Did you leave me a clue, Truly? I wondered. But no artifacts had been left behind, from what I could see. No initials were written on the walls or on the floor. If I'd been hoping for a message, there wasn't one. Or else it had been cleared away long ago.

"I can't believe nobody noticed this spot before," my father said after I climbed out and Mackenzie climbed in. "It's as plain as the nose on your face once you know it's there."

"Not really," said my mother. Opening the telephone closet, she turned on the light and pointed to where the sloping ceiling angled to the floor. "Whoever built it did a very clever job. This space doesn't extend all the way to the foot of the stairs—they built a false wall to conceal the hiding place."

Professor Rusty and my father got a tape measure to see if she was right.

"Extraordinary," said Professor Rusty when it turned out that she was.

"I wonder who built it?" said my father, helping Mackenzie climb out. She was clutching her camera and looking smug, which I was pretty sure meant she'd been taking pictures and texting Cameron. Or maybe Calhoun? I scowled.

"Matthew, perhaps," said Aunt True. "If he was the first one in his family to get involved with the Underground Railroad. Or maybe his father or grandfather."

"We might be able to figure that out, based on the dates of the earliest newspapers, once we've made a thorough examination," Professor Rusty told her.

"I'm still mystified why no one else in the family seemed to know about this," said my father.

"Gramps might be able to answer that," I pointed out. "We should call him."

"Not in the middle of the night, we shouldn't," said Aunt True, glancing at her watch. "We'll try him in the morning."

The doorbell rang. It was the pizza delivery guy. We must have looked like complete nuts, what with three of us covered in dust and all of us buzzing with excitement. Pippa was hopping up and down the stairs nonstop, squealing. Danny had come straight from the shower and was still wrapped in his bath towel. Lauren had temporarily abandoned her bad mood and was playing ring-around-the-rosy in the living room with Annie, who was spelling words at the top of her lungs. The pizza delivery guy arrived just as she'd gotten to A-B-O-L-I-T-I-O-N! I noticed that he left as quickly as he could.

We ate on paper plates, right there in the front hall. None of us wanted to peel ourselves away from our discovery.

"I don't suppose you girls feel much like going to knitting class tonight, what with all this excitement," my mother said as we finished up.

"No way, mom," I said. "Sorry."

Mackenzie shook her head too.

"I know how you feel because I feel the same way," my mother told us. "I'll call Ella and let her know we're not coming."

In the end, everybody skipped sock class, as it turned out. The minute Ella heard why we weren't coming, she invited herself—and our fellow students—over to view the secret room for themselves.

"I brought currant scones!" she announced breathlessly, barreling through our front door. Right behind her were Mrs. Winthrop, Bud Jefferson, Belinda, Augustus Wilde—who wasn't in our sock class, but seeing a flash of purple at his ankles, I figured Belinda had probably brought him along to model the socks she'd made—Mrs. Maynard, Annie's mother, and Mr. Henry.

"I ordered pizza," said Mr. Jefferson.

"Uh, how kind," my mother replied.

My brothers looked pleased to hear this. But then, they were bottomless pits.

The rest of the Pumpkin Falls Private Eyes arrived just as the pizza truck pulled into the driveway again.

"How did they find out?" I wondered when I spotted my friends.

"I texted them." Mackenzie avoided my gaze—which probably meant she'd texted Calhoun.

"I won't even begin to try and explain," my mother said to the bewildered pizza guy, taking the stack of boxes from him and handing him a huge tip. Turning to my brothers and sisters and me, she added in a low voice, "FHB," which is Lovejoy family shorthand for "family hold back."

Like I wanted any more pizza. My brothers, on the other hand, waited until she wasn't looking and helped themselves to two more slices each.

We all crowded into the living room, and the sofas and chairs and window seats and even the big stone hearth in front of the fireplace quickly filled up. I started to take a seat on the floor next to Cha Cha, but my mother placed her hand on my arm.

"Truly, why don't you tell everyone about what you found, and maybe read us a little from the diary," she suggested. "That will provide a little background to tonight's discovery."

"Okay." I went upstairs to get it. When I came back

down, I couldn't help noticing that Calhoun had taken a seat by my cousin. I tried not to look at them as I explained how Mackenzie and I had found the loose floorboard and the package that had been hidden underneath it.

"A secret compartment? How come you didn't tell us?" Scooter looked hurt.

"We, uh, wanted to keep it a surprise," I replied lamely. "But you can see it now, if you want to."

Of course everyone wanted to. I led them all upstairs. My room wasn't at its tidiest, but at least I'd made my bed.

I studiously avoided looking at Calhoun, but out of the corner of my eye I saw him gazing around curiously. At one point he leaned over to Mackenzie, then pointed at the framed woodcut of the snowy owl that hung on the wall above my bed. It was one of my prized possessions. She said something to him, and he laughed.

My stomach lurched. *She probably called me a bird nerd*, I thought bitterly.

Back downstairs, everyone took turns looking at the hiding place while I skimmed through the diary, picking out some of the better entries to read aloud.

There were audible oohs and aahs of excitement as I read about the bloodhounds on Lovejoy Mountain, and sighs when my audience learned of Mother Lovejoy's death.

"It's all so mysterious!" cried Mrs. Winthrop when I

got to the part about the original Truly's unnamed visitor. "Packages! A disastrous ordeal! Something that went terribly wrong!"

"And a bracelet made of hair, did you say?" Mrs. Freeman asked sharply.

I nodded.

"Interesting."

"It all ends so abruptly," sighed Aunt True. "What a cliffhanger! Any insights for us, Rusty?"

He cleared his throat. "About the ending, and what happened afterward? Alas, no. We'll have to wait for the call to Namibia." He turned to me. "I did find an answer to your question about Maple Grove, however. It turns out there was quite an astonishing discovery made there several years ago at a small Quaker church. The town is just two miles from the Canadian border, and it had long been rumored to be one of the final stops on the Underground Railroad. A married couple who founded the church were conductors. But there was little hard evidence to go on."

Coach Maynard's wife leaned forward in her chair. "Why is that?"

"Lack of documentation has proven difficult for historians," Professor Rusty explained. "So much of what we know has been passed down through oral history—through stories," he added, seeing Pippa's puckered forehead. "It makes sense, really, when you think about it—the people who helped were otherwise law-abiding citizens, and they didn't want to be discovered breaking the law. So their activities weren't openly discussed, and in most cases never recorded. A diary like the original Truly Lovejoy's is a rare thing indeed."

"So what was this astonishing discovery you started to tell us about?" asked Bud Jefferson.

"Ah yes. Twenty years ago or so, some renovations were being made to the church in Maple Grove, and a layer of wood was stripped away from the raised platform in the main meeting area. Beneath it was a trapdoor leading to what was clearly a hiding place. And so it would seem that the rails from Pumpkin Falls indeed led to Maple Grove, Maine, and from there on to Canada."

"To heaven," I whispered.

Professor Rusty smiled at me. "Exactly."

"Well," said my mother, "I know this has been an incredibly exciting evening—"

"E-X-C-I-T-I-N-G!" shouted Annie, who was still wound up like a top.

"Shhh, honey," said Mrs. Freeman. "Settle down or I'm taking you home."

"—but I think it's time we called it a day," my mother finished.

As coats and jackets—and one purple cape—were rounded up and distributed, everyone took a last look at the hiding place. Everyone except Mackenzie and Calhoun, that was. They were deep in conversation. Another hot spike of jealousy surged through me as I watched the two of them. There was no way around it—despite tonight's discovery, my Spring Break was not destined to end on a good note.

CHAPTER 27

For once, I wasn't woken up by the sound of tapping.

Good, I thought, rolling over and stretching. Now that the hiding place had been found, Lauren must have abandoned her annoying hobby. We could finally have some peace and quiet around here again. And with daily doubles over with, I could finally sleep in. I burrowed into my pillow again, preparing to do just that.

Before I could, though, there was a knock on my door.

"Lauren!" I groaned in protest. But it wasn't my sister—it was my mother.

"Girls?" she said. "We're getting ready to call Namibia!"

Mackenzie and I dressed in frosty silence. We hadn't spoken since last night. Downstairs, we found my parents and Hatcher and Danny already up, seated at the kitchen table with Pippa. There was no sign of Lauren.

Maybe Nancy Drew finally wore herself out, I thought.

"We're just waiting for Rusty and True," my father told us. "I sent your grandparents an e-mail last night telling them when to expect our call."

When my aunt and Professor Rusty arrived a few minutes later, it turned out they'd brought Professor Rusty's research assistant along with them again.

"Oh, hello, Felicia," said my mother. "Coffee?"

"Tea, please," she replied primly. "Earl Grey, preferably."

Hatcher kicked me under the table. I flared my nostrils at him.

My father sat by his laptop, keeping one eye on the kitchen clock as everyone got settled. "Oh-eight hundred," he said finally, and dialed my grandparents' number. A few moments later, Gramps and Lola's faces popped up onscreen.

"That's quite a crowd you have there, J. T.!" said my grandfather.

"The more the merrier."

"Your e-mail was awfully mysterious," said Lola. "Apparently you have something to show us?"

"Wait until you see," my father said, picking up his laptop and carrying it out of the kitchen. We all trooped after him. In the front hall, he passed the laptop to Hatcher, who held it with the camera pointing toward the staircase as my father lifted the squeaky tread.

My brother Danny shined a flashlight inside, and my father motioned to Hatcher to angle the camera toward the concealed room.

"What on earth?" I heard Lola exclaim.

"It's a hiding spot, Mom!" Aunt True's voice rose in excitement. "It's where our ancestors put the runaway slaves."

"Well, I'll be darned," said Gramps. "First a secret compartment and a long-lost diary, and now this. That's what we get for skipping town—we miss out on all the fun!"

My father showed my grandparents the telephone closet and explained about the false wall, and then we all went back into the kitchen and settled in for a chat.

"This is just remarkable," said Gramps, who sounded nearly as thrilled as Professor Rusty. "To think that I never suspected it was there!"

"So you really didn't have any inkling?" Aunt True asked.

My grandfather shook his head. "Not a one. No one ever breathed a word. I'm sure my father and mother would have told me, if they had known."

"Your father was Booth's son, right?" said Professor Rusty.

Gramps shook his head again. "Grandson. He was my great-grandfather. I knew him when I was a boy. Booth lived with us for the last few years of his life, and he used to tell me stories about his boyhood in Germany after the Civil War. But he never mentioned a secret room, or the Underground Railroad."

"What about his mother?" Aunt True asked. "Did he ever speak of her?"

Gramps's face clouded. "Such a tragic tale."

Beside me, I felt Mackenzie stiffen. Suddenly, I wasn't so sure I wanted to know the ending to this story.

"We know some of the details from the diary," my father said. "Ruth—the one Truly calls 'Mother Lovejoy'—died in the winter of 1862, apparently."

"That's right," said my grandfather. He glanced over at me. "Truly, why don't you go get the old family Bible? It's on the bottom shelf in the bookcase next to the piano."

I scurried off, returning a few moments later with a big, leather-bound book.

"If you open it to the front flyleaf, you'll see a record of births and deaths," Gramps said, and everyone crowded around, peering over my shoulder as I did as he instructed. "Do you see Ruth's name there?"

I ran my finger down the page and nodded. "Yes. It's the same date as in the diary. In fact, I think the original Truly made this entry in the Bible. It looks like her handwriting."

"That would make sense," said Lola. "Truly was the only Lovejoy in the house when Ruth died. Aside from Booth, that is, but he was a just a baby."

"What else do you see?" asked Gramps.

My finger moved to the line below, and stopped. My eyes suddenly welled up with tears.

How is it possible that I can feel such sadness about someone who lived—and died—over a hundred and fifty years ago?

I thought. The diary had made them all so real!

"When Truly got word that Matthew had been captured, she took the baby and went to Washington to try and secure his release," said Gramps. "The house stood empty for a while, Booth told me. His aunt—Matthew's sister Charity—would come up from Boston and look in on it from time to time, and she and her family often used it as a summer retreat."

I nodded. Truly had said as much in one of her final diary entries.

"Sadly, Truly's mission was not successful, and Matthew passed away in Andersonville that summer."

Professor Rusty went pale.

"Andersonville!" he breathed. "The worst of the Confederate prisons!"

My grandfather nodded somberly. "Truly was devastated. She returned to Germany to be with her mother."

"Did she ever get married again?" Mackenzie wanted to know.

"No," Gramps told her. "She died fairly young, too—of a broken heart, my great-grandfather told me. After her death, he finally came back to Pumpkin Falls to claim his inheritance—our home on Maple Street."

We were all quiet for a bit.

"He would have been too young to remember the runaways," said Aunt True slowly. I could tell that she was feeling sad too. We all were.

We all have to drink from the cup of sorrow, the original Truly had written. I glanced over at my father's arm. Our family had, that was for sure.

"Wouldn't his mother have told him about her involvement with the Underground Railroad?" asked my father. "It's not as if it were something to be ashamed of."

"No, but it was part of a tragic chapter in her life," Gramps replied. "She may simply have wished it to remain closed."

"What about the mysterious F, and the secret that Truly promised to keep?" I asked.

"What secret?" asked Lola.

"In the diary," I said. "Hang on, I'll read it to you." I retrieved the diary, then riffled carefully through the pages until I found the entry I was looking for.

"Here it is," I said. "May 15, 1862." I read aloud the passage about the bracelets.

"How odd," said Gramps. "A love token. *Our hearts are forever entwined* . . . It almost makes it sound as if Truly had fallen—"

"Wait, a bracelet made of hair?" Lola interrupted. She grabbed my grandfather's arm. "Oh my, Walt."

"Oh my what, Mom?" asked Aunt True.

Onscreen, my grandparents exchanged a glance.

"Truly," Lola said slowly, "I want you to go upstairs to the attic. I'm pretty sure it's in the second small bedroom on the left—"

"—one of the servant's bedrooms?" I asked, and she nodded.

"Somewhere in there amongst our things, you'll find a box marked 'Family Keepsakes,'" she told me. "There are a lot of boxes, and I don't remember exactly where I put it, but you'll find it. Bring it downstairs, would you?"

"I'll go with you," said Hatcher.

It took us a while, but we found the box. Back downstairs, my brother held it up to the laptop camera. "Is this it?"

Lola nodded. "That's the one. Open it up, would you?"

My mother helped me, and we carefully removed the contents—old photographs, mostly, and mementos from when my father and Aunt True were little. There was a crib-size quilt and some baby shoes and a Cub Scout sash filled with sewn-on badges, and some toys and a silver rattle.

"You're looking for a small, square, black velvet box," said my grandmother.

"Got it," I said, spotting it buried beneath Aunt True's debate team trophy. I plucked it out and handed it to my mother. "You open it."

"Are you sure?"

I nodded. My heart was racing, and I could hardly breathe. I was pretty sure I knew what it contained.

My mother lifted the lid. "Oh my," she said, echoing my grandmother. "Would you look at this, J. T.?"

"This has certainly been a week full of surprises," said my father, peering into the box.

There was a bracelet inside. Black hair and brown braided together, just as the original Truly had said, *so close in hue I almost cannot tell them apart*. I almost couldn't either.

"Look at that braidwork!" Aunt True reached out a finger and gently stroked the bracelet. "It's exquisite."

"Sentimental hairwork was a common handicraft in the Victorian era," Felicia Grunewald suddenly spouted, setting her teacup down with a rattle. "Bouquets, wreaths, artwork, and jewelry made of human hair were viewed as a way of showing affection—you were literally wearing part of a loved one—and honoring them, or of memorializing the dead."

We stared at her, stunned into silence. How was anyone supposed to respond to that?

"Eew," said Mackenzie finally.

"Your father's mother gave the bracelet to me when we married," Lola told Dad and Aunt True. "All she knew was that it had belonged to Booth's mother."

"But what does it mean, *our hearts are forever entwined by our ordeal*?" I asked.

"That, it would seem, is destined to remain a mystery," Gramps replied. He glanced at his watch. "I hate to have to leave you all, but we have an appointment with the builders over at the new library."

We said our good-byes and promised to call with any new developments.

Annie Freeman, rubbing her eyes and yawning, wandered

in as Mackenzie and I were starting to clear the table. She spotted the bracelet and frowned. She opened her mouth to say something, but before she could, my mother asked, "Where's Lauren? You girls must be starving."

"She probably has her nose in a book," said Hatcher.

Annie's brow furrowed. "She's not down here with you?"

My mother shook her head. "Nope."

"Maybe she went over to the Mitchells' to feed Bilbo," said Danny. "Isn't she ferret-sitting this week?"

Something about the expression on Annie's face caught my mother's attention, and she set the cereal box she was holding down on the counter. "What is it, Annie?"

Annie looked at her, wide-eyed. "Last night," she said, "after everybody went to bed. We stayed up for a while, and Lauren was reading—"

"See? I told you," said Hatcher.

"—and all of a sudden she got really excited. She said something about figuring out what happened to the packages. She wanted me to come with her, but . . ." Annie's voice trailed off.

"Go on," urged my mother. "But what?"

Annie's voice dropped to a whisper. "But she said it might be a little S-C-A-R-Y."

My mother's face went ashen. "And she didn't come back?"

Annie shook her head.

My mother grabbed her cell phone and punched in Lauren's number. We all stood there, waiting, as it rang and rang and rang. "Nothing," she said, pressing her lips together and giving my dad an anxious look. "It went to voicemail. Either she doesn't have her phone with her, or the battery ran out."

My father turned to Hatcher and Danny. "Upstairs on the double, boys," he ordered them crisply. "Check the bedrooms, the bathrooms, and the closets. Make a sweep of the attic while you're at it too—she's been spending a lot of time up there." He grabbed his jacket. "I'll go next door and check the Mitchells'," he told my mother. "I'm sure it's nothing. She's probably feeding Bilbo, like Danny said."

He returned to the kitchen at the same time my brothers did. They all shook their heads.

"No sign of her upstairs," said Hatcher.

"And she's not next door," my father reported grimly.

As my mother sank into one of the chairs at the kitchen table, my father turned to my brothers. "She's not in the attic? Are you sure?"

"I checked all over," Danny assured him.

"Check again," my father ordered, and my brothers immediately vanished.

My mother turned to Annie. "When did you see her last?"

Annie's face crumpled, and my mother put her arms around her. "It's okay, sweetheart, it's okay."

"I fell asleep!" Annie wailed. "I tried to stay awake,

waiting for her, but I fell asleep! She told me not to tell anyone. She said—"

Annie paused, gulping back tears.

"She said what?" my mother asked gently.

Annie wiped her nose on her pajama sleeve and flicked a
glance at me. "She said she was going to show those stupid
Pumpkin Falls Private Eyes," she finished miserably.

Across the table, Mackenzie's eyes met mine.

My sister was missing.

And it was all my fault.

CHAPTER 28

Owl eyes, I thought. *I need owl eyes and ears.*

Owls could find their prey without even seeing it, my new birthday book had informed me. Their round faces were shaped like a satellite dish, specifically designed to detect sound. The ring of stiff feathers surrounding their face channeled sound toward the ears, which were hidden at the side of the face. At certain frequencies, an owl's hearing was ten times more sensitive than that of humans.

If I were an owl, I might be able to hear my sister, or somehow sense where she had gone.

I hated the idea of Lauren out there somewhere, alone all night and probably scared out of her wits. She was a pest and she drove me nuts sometimes—okay, a lot of the time—but she was my *sister*.

What on earth had possessed her to run off?

My mother called Belinda Winchester to see if Lauren had

gone to visit the kittens. My father called Mr. Henry to see if she was at the library. They tried the General Store and the Starlite Dance Studio and Lou's. Nothing. Professor Rusty and Felicia went back to the college to scour the campus; Aunt True headed down to the bookstore and checked there and her apartment. But Lauren was nowhere to be found.

"She can't have gone far," my mother kept saying. "It's just not like her to wander off!"

In all the confusion, no one had remembered to feed Bilbo.

"Truly, would you mind?" my mother asked.

"No problem." It was the least I could do. I grabbed my barn jacket and slipped out the back door.

The Mitchells' house was quiet. The clock above the mantel in the living room ticked loudly. *Lau-ren. Lau-ren. Lau-ren*, it seemed to say.

"You haven't seen her, have you, buddy?" I asked Bilbo, passing him a ferret treat.

But if he had, he wasn't telling.

Back in our kitchen, I heard Aunt True on her cell phone enlisting Ella Bellow to activate the town grapevine. Professor Rusty was in the telephone closet talking to campus security. My father had called the police—well, our town's lone policeman—and my mother was talking with the *Pumpkin Falls Patriot-Bugle*.

"The boys are checking the barn and the backyard," my father told me after he hung up. "Your mother and I will probably need to go out, so I want you and Mackenzie to stay here at the house just in case anyone comes to the door or calls on the landline."

"Yes, sir," I replied.

My cousin, who was on her cell phone with her parents, nodded too.

Belinda was enlisted to babysit, and she and Augustus Wilde—still sporting his purple socks—came over to get Pippa and take her back to Belinda's house.

"The kittens will keep her calm," Belinda whispered to my mother.

Professor Rusty slipped his arms around my aunt. "We'll find her," he assured her.

Definitely boyfriend, I thought, watching them.

In the space of an hour, the entire town had mobilized to search for Lauren.

Mr. Henry closed the library. Ella closed A Stitch in Time, and Bud Jefferson closed the coin and stamp shop. The Freemans shut down their maple syrup operation, and Maynard's Maple Barn, and the General Store, Mahoney's Antiques, and Suds 'n Duds all closed as well. Only Lou's Diner stayed open, so it could serve as downtown headquarters for the search.

I texted the Pumpkin Falls Private Eyes to tell them what had happened, and they immediately offered to join in the hunt. Scooter Sanchez texted back to tell me that his father had offered us his colleague's video surveillance equipment, if we needed it.

All across Pumpkin Falls, friends and neighbors and complete strangers fanned out to look for my sister. But as the hours dragged on, there was still no sign of her.

"Lou's is handing out sandwiches to the volunteers," Hatcher reported as he and Danny swung by at noon with a plate for my cousin and me. "Mrs. Winthrop sends her love."

"Mackenzie! Lunch!" I called up the front stairs. She'd been staying out of sight up there somewhere all morning.

"Not hungry!" the answer floated back down.

I was, though. Grabbing a chicken salad sandwich, I paced back and forth in the kitchen. *Think, Truly, think!* I told myself. *Think like an owl hunting her prey.* Single-minded. Focused. Alert. Where could Lauren be?

Annie had said something about her reading a book last night. Which one, I wondered? Could it offer a clue? Leaving my half-eaten sandwich on the counter, I ran upstairs to check.

I found Mackenzie in Lauren's room, making the rounds of the cages.

"Her pets were hungry," she whispered, swiping at her eyes. "Nobody remembered to feed them."

All of a sudden I couldn't take it anymore.

"Mackenzie, I'm so sorry for how I've been acting," I blurted. "It was stupid! I don't have an excuse and I'm really, really sorry."

"Don't—" she began, but I plunged on before she could continue.

"I had no right to be snarky about Cameron McAllister or call you boy crazy. I'm an idiot and a total jerk and cretinous, just like Felicia Grunewald said! If you like Calhoun, that's fine. You can have him."

She looked at me, confused. "Calhoun?"

I lifted a shoulder.

"*Romeo* Calhoun?"

"Uh, yeah," I mumbled, frowning.

"What are you talking about? 'You can have him'? Why would I want Calhoun?"

"Um," I replied, "you said you thought he was cute."

My cousin pulled herself up to her full five feet one inch and placed her hands on her hips. "Is *that* what this snit was all about, Truly Lovejoy?"

Now I was the one who was confused. "Isn't it?"

"You're absolutely right—you *are* cretinous!" Mackenzie snapped. "I don't like Calhoun!"

"You don't?" I stared at her, astounded.

"Well, I like him, but I don't *like* him. You know what I mean. Besides, you're the only one he talks about."

I blinked. "I am?"

"He thought you liked Scooter."

My heart sank. Of course. The kiss behind the Freemans' barn.

"But I set him straight," said Mackenzie.

I gaped at her. "You did? When?"

"Last night. I knew you liked him, and I wanted to help."

So that's what she'd been doing when I saw them talking! "How did you know?"

She made a rude noise. "I've known you forever, you moron. I can read you like one of Lauren's books."

We regarded each other for a long moment.

"You're welcome," my cousin said finally.

I started to laugh, and a second later, she did too.

"I hated being mad at you!" I told her.

"I hated you being mad at me!" she replied. "You're my best friend in the whole world!"

"And you're mine!" I crossed the room and gave her a Bigfoot-size hug, lifting her off her feet and into the air. Then I set her down again and smiled. "Now, let's go figure out what happened to my sister."

CHAPTER 29

Lauren's room looked like a mini library. She went through books the way I went through sudoku puzzles. There were books piled on her dresser, books piled on her desk, books piled on her chair and on her bedside table and on her pets' cages and on the floor.

I didn't even know where to start.

So I called Annie Freeman.

Her mother answered the phone. "Any word yet about Lauren?"

"Not yet," I said. "May I please speak to Annie?"

Mrs. Freeman hesitated. "She's awfully upset."

"I just want to ask if she remembers what Lauren was reading last night. It might be important, Mrs. Freeman."

"Okay."

There was a pause, and then Annie got on the line. I repeated my question.

"Um," she said. "I think it was something about a house, maybe?"

I relayed this information to Mackenzie, who took a quick look around the room and then shook her head.

"Okay, Annie. If you remember anything else, call me."

Something about a house, I thought as I hung up. That rang a faint bell, but I couldn't put my finger on it. I tried Aunt True next, but that proved to be another dead end.

"Sorry, Truly—I honestly have no idea," she said. "Your sister devours books the way Rusty devours my Bookshop Blondies. How about Mr. Henry? Could you try calling him? Lauren's always at the library. He might be able to help."

"Good idea!"

Mr. Henry answered on the first ring. "Truly Lovejoy!" he replied eagerly when I told him who was calling. "Any news about Lauren?"

"Nothing yet," I replied. "Hey, I was wondering, do you remember if she checked something out recently about a house?"

"A house? Hmmm." He was quiet for a moment, thinking.

"It might have had something to do with the Underground Railroad," I added.

"Lauren didn't check anything out about the Underground Railroad, but there may have been something in that stack I brought to sock class for your mother. Tell you what, let me check the computer. I should have a list here."

It was quiet for a minute. I could hear him typing.

"Let me see . . . yes, here we are." He read off the names one by one.

"Nope," I said to each of the titles. "Nope. Not that one either."

He listed several more, then said, "Wait, was it *The House of Dies Drear*?"

I gave a little yelp. "I think that's it! That's the one I saw her reading the other night at dinner!"

"It has a black cover, as I recall."

"Thanks, Mr. Henry."

Mackenzie and I took the room apart. We finally found the book in the unlikeliest spot—stuffed down at the foot of Lauren's unmade bed.

Her bookmark was still in it. I opened to where she'd left off reading and scanned the page. *Snick!* The pieces slid into place as neatly as one of my sudoku puzzles.

I looked up. "I think I know where Lauren is," I told my cousin. "Sort of."

CHAPTER 30

I ran down the hall toward the stairs. Mackenzie was right on my heels.

"Obadiah, Abigail, Jeremiah, Ruth," I chanted as we flew down the stairs. My cousin joined in, and we singsonged the rest in unison: "Matthew, Truly, Charity, and Booth!"

I pulled up the stair tread that marked the entrance to the hidden room and shined my cell phone light into it. As I'd suspected, it wasn't exactly as we'd left it yesterday.

"Remember Professor Rusty told us not to touch anything until the history department had a chance to look everything over?" I said, and Mackenzie nodded. "Check it out."

She peered inside.

The tattered rag rug had been shoved over to one of the far corners of the cramped space.

"No one thought to look in here when Lauren went missing," I said, sitting down on the step above the gaping hole and reaching out a hand toward my cousin. "Steady me, would you?"

She did, and I climbed inside. A cloud of dust flew up. "I could use a little more light," I told her, coughing.

"Hang on, I'll grab the big flashlight. Danny left it on the hall bench."

She returned momentarily and aimed a strong beam downward.

"Much better." Kneeling down, I peered closely at the floor.

"What are you looking for?" Mackenzie asked.

"A trapdoor," I said, and explained about *The House of Dies Drear*, and how it involved this family who moved to a creepy old house riddled with secret passages and tunnels that runaway slaves had once used to hide in and escape.

"Wow, that must have been catnip to Lauren," said my cousin, and I nodded.

"Ha! Gotcha!" I crowed, slipping my fingers into a small groove in the wood floor. The trapdoor squawked as I lifted it, its hinges stiff from a century and a half of disuse.

"Wow," breathed Mackenzie. "No way! I can't believe we missed that yesterday."

"Professor Rusty would hardly let us touch anything, remember?"

My cousin squeezed into the hiding space beside me. We peered down into the darkness. "Where does that ladder go?"

"I guess we're going to find out," I told her, and taking the flashlight, I swung my legs over the edge.

The air grew colder as I climbed down. I waited at the foot of the ladder for Mackenzie, playing the flashlight beam around what appeared to be another small room.

"They must have walled this section of the basement off," I told my cousin, my voice echoing against the stone. Straight ahead, a tunnel curved past the fieldstone foundation. It was narrow and dark and brick lined, and the walls and ceiling were thick with cobwebs.

I froze.

Cobwebs meant spiders.

I couldn't believe that Lauren had had the courage to come down here by herself.

She'd come this way for sure, though. I could plainly see her footprints in the dust.

I had to go after her, even though every fiber of my body was screaming *Stop! Stay back!*

"Shouldn't we call your parents?" Mackenzie whispered, clutching the back of my sweatshirt as I stepped slowly forward.

"As soon as I find my sister," I told her, then called, "Lauren?"

There was no answer.

I called again, louder this time. My voice bounced off the brick walls, echoing weirdly back to me. I took a few more steps forward.

Mackenzie peered into the darkness. "Do you think this leads to the barn?"

"No idea."

We inched our way forward through the cobwebs and dust, following my sister's footprints.

"Which direction do you think we're going?" my cousin asked, coughing as she accidentally kicked up a cloud of dust.

I made a face, swatting at the strands of cobweb that clung to my hair. "Toward the Mitchells' house, maybe?" I guessed. It was disorienting down here in the dark.

"Didn't your mother say something about houses connecting in some communities? Maybe the people who used to live at the Mitchells' were involved with the Underground Railroad too."

"That would totally make sense!" I quickened my pace, buoyed by the thought of my sister so close at hand.

A few minutes later, I stopped. "Does the tunnel feel like it's getting narrower?"

Mackenzie grunted. "Maybe."

We pushed on. Now I definitely could feel the tunnel growing narrower. Panic welled up in me—Mackenzie was right, we should have told my parents.

And then we turned a corner, and I stopped short.

"Whoa!" said my cousin as she slammed into my back. "What is it?"

"The footprints," I replied. "They disappeared."

"Huh?"

I shined the flashlight on the floor. "They're gone. See?" My sister's trail ended at a pile of rubble.

Mackenzie stared at it, and then understanding dawned. "The tunnel caved in!"

We fairly flew back to the ladder. I called my parents the minute I clambered out of the hiding place. They arrived at the same time that Pumpkin Falls' lone police car pulled up. The rest of the town soon followed, and in the space of ten minutes our house looked like Grand Central Station.

My mother cleared off the dining room table, and my father got to work organizing the search and rescue teams. Before long, one crew was hard at work in the basement of the Mitchells' house, looking for a possible tunnel exit. Another crew was assigned to the tunnel beneath my grandparents' house, where they cautiously began trying to clear away the rubble.

Professor Rusty threw caution to the wind. "Nothing matters but rescuing Lauren," he said to the work crew as he followed them down the ladder in the hiding place that led to the basement. "Don't worry about damaging anything. Life always trumps history."

"What is taking them so long?" my mother asked a short while later, pacing up and down the front hall. "Shouldn't they have found her by now?"

"It's slow going," Professor Rusty reported when he emerged a few minutes later. "They're trying to avoid another cave-in."

By midafternoon neither the crew over at our neighbors' house nor the crew in our basement had found anything. I was heading to the kitchen to get myself some water when I saw my parents talking quietly in the dining room.

"Oh, J. T.!" I overheard my mother say. "What if she's—"

"We're not going to think that way, Dinah," my father told her firmly. "We can't. There's no reason to give up hope. Lauren is a Lovejoy, after all. And Lovejoys are made of strong stuff."

"She's a little girl, and she's down there somewhere in the dark," my mother whispered.

"I'm sure she took a flashlight with her."

"But how long can a pair of batteries last?" My mother leaned her forehead on the windowpane, watching the shadows lengthen in the yard. My father put his good hand on her shoulder and squeezed.

Tears pricked my eyelids. I backed away. I hated to think of my sister trapped in the dark too. But there wasn't anything I could do. It was up to the search and rescue crews now.

Friends stopped by, bringing food and offering comfort. Lucas Winthrop's mother and Mr. Jefferson arrived together with a fruit basket, and peeking out the window I was pretty sure I saw them holding hands as they came up the front path. Bud Jefferson's were back in his coat pockets when I opened the door to greet them, though.

The Abramowitzes brought a casserole, Scooter and Jasmine's parents brought a ham, and Mr. Henry came with what looked like a lifetime supply of his award-winning Maple Walnut Cupcakes.

I was in the dining room with my mother when Mrs. Freeman came in. "Dinah!" she said.

"Grace!" my mother replied, and the two of them embraced.

"I brought homemade bread," Mrs. Freeman told her. "I'll just leave it in the kitchen. And I have something I want to show you. I don't know why, but I think it may be important." She turned to me. "Something you said last night, Truly, made me think of it."

She drew a small box out of her jacket pocket. "It's a family heirloom."

She lifted the lid, and I stared at the contents, confused. Nestled on a piece of white velvet was a bracelet made of intricately braided hair.

A bracelet identical to the one that belonged to Lola.

There are two bracelets, Truly had written in her diary. The mysterious F had kept one, she had said.

"It was my husband's great-great-grandfather's," she said. "His mother gave it to him."

His *mother*! I thought. *Snick!* The last puzzle piece clicked into place.

Our hearts are forever entwined.

And all of a sudden I knew where my sister was. For real this time.

CHAPTER 31

"This way!" I cried, squelching across the backyard. My family and half of Pumpkin Falls were right on my heels. My flashlight bounced wildly off the birdbath and the evergreens that lined my grandparents' property. In the distance, an owl hooted: *Who cooks for you! Who cooks for you-all!*

Barred owl, I thought automatically, wondering if it was the same one Mackenzie and I had seen that first night she was here.

Which seemed like a million years ago now.

The original Truly had listened for owls too, a hundred and fifty years ago. She had listened, and responded, and saved lives. Could I save one now?

Lauren! I thought desperately. *Hang on! We're coming!*

This must have been what happened back in the winter of 1862. A cave-in. That must have been the disaster that Truly mentioned in her diary. Her two "packages," trapped beneath the earth. And no one able to dig them out for days, thanks to the slave hunters lurking everywhere. There'd been a happy ending to that tale—the runaways were miraculously unharmed, Reverend Bartlett had told Truly. Would there be another miracle now?

"Are you sure you know where you're going?" said my father, smacking at the underbrush with the Terminator.

"Pretty sure," I told him as my flashlight picked out the overgrown path that led from Gramps and Lola's property to the old Oak Street Cemetery.

The hill behind my grandparents' house was steep. We bushwhacked our way up, panting from the effort, and finally emerged by a line of tombstones at the back of the graveyard.

I grabbed Mrs. Freeman's arm. "Where's your ancestor's grave?"

"Which one?" she asked.

"The first Frank Freeman's."

She pointed her flashlight to the left. "Over there."

I ran over toward where her beam was shining. There it was! The sculpture on the lid of the tomb was unmistakable. I pointed my flashlight at the headstone:

FRANK FREEMAN
Two hearts forever entwined, one forever yearning to
be free

Frank Freeman was the original Truly's mysterious F! I was sure of it. *Our hearts are forever entwined by our ordeal*, F had written to her. It had to be Frank.

I looked over at Professor Rusty. "Remember William Still?"

He ran a hand through his hair as he pondered my question, then his eyes lit up. "Of course!"

I looked at the most-photographed grave in the cemetery, considering. I pushed on the epitaph. Nothing. I ran my fingers around the edge of the headstone. Nothing seemed out of place; nothing had any give.

It had to be the statue, then, the beautiful carving of the African American mother cradling her infant, which stood in the middle of the slab covering the crypt.

As my family and friends looked on in bewilderment, I nodded at Professor Rusty. He reached out and grabbed the statue by its base and gave a mighty heave. At first, nothing happened. He heaved again, and this time there was a loud scraping sound as the slab moved slightly.

"Some help, gentlemen?" Professor Rusty looked over at my father and my brothers. They leaped into action, crowding around.

All four of them heaved, and stone ground against stone with a mighty screech. With one final piercing squawk, the slab shifted, revealing the open crypt.

I flung myself onto the edge, hardly daring to look down inside.

My sister was huddled in the darkness beneath us, her pale face streaked with dirt and tears.

"Truly!" my sister sobbed as I lifted her out. "I knew you'd find me!"

"Lauren!" my mother cried out. "Oh, Lauren!"

We wrapped our arms around her, both of us sobbing in relief too.

"Can I be one of the Pumpkin Falls Private Eyes?" Lauren asked, gulping back tears. "Please?"

I nodded, hugging her fiercely. "Cross my heart and hope to fly."

EPILOGUE

April 12th

Dear Diary,

My sister is safe. She was cold, hungry, tired, and very, very frightened by the time we found her, but she's safe and that's all that matters.

Aunt True is right—nothing is more important than family. I know that now. Not world travel, not swimming, not owls, not sudoku or best friends or boys. Family is everything.

After the dust finally settled from the excitement of the search and rescue and the hoopla that followed—we got our press conference after all, though there was no mention of Bigfoot—Aunt True gave me this diary, and a fountain pen to go with it.

"We have to do something to celebrate," she told me. "And this seems appropriate."

Professor Rusty took the original Truly's diary to the college, where the museum's curatorial staff (including cretinous Felicia

Grunewald) is busy studying and transcribing its faded pages. It turns out the diary is a big deal. Several collectors have asked to buy it, but Gramps and Lola told them it's not for sale. I'm glad.

Our house is a big deal too, thanks to the hiding place and the tunnel. Aunt True is working with her boyfriend (she calls Professor Rusty that openly now, so it's official) to get it listed on the National Register of Historic Places.

I'm kind of a big deal too. At least our local newspaper thinks so. I was on the front page of the Pumpkin Falls Patriot-Bugle, along with Lauren, of course, and Annie Freeman says I'm a H-E-R-O-I-N-E for rescuing my sister, and for solving her family's mystery too.

The Freemans are still wrestling with the fact that their ancestor Frank Freeman was actually a she, not a he—a runaway slave named Frankie who was the original Truly's dear friend, and the mysterious F in her diary.

Like many other runaway slaves, Frankie had concealed her identity and passed for a man. It was safer for women that way, Professor Rusty told us. Part of the "ordeal" that she and my ancestor and namesake shared was the birth of Frankie's son. That's what the whole *our single package is now two!* riddle in the diary meant.

"You mean my great-great-great-grandfather was actually my great-great-great-grandmother?" said Franklin, who was incredulous when he first heard the news. "Why would someone want to keep that a secret?"

Professor Rusty explained that it probably started when his ancestor fled the South. "In the end, Frankie simply kept her disguise," he told us. "After reaching Canada, she probably stayed for a while, but her dearest wish was to return to Pumpkin Falls and her new friend Truly."

It wasn't easy for women to own property in those days, he told us—especially African American women. Frankie might have risked losing her farm if people knew she was a woman. So she'd kept her secret, but she left a clue: the statue on the crypt of a woman and infant. And sure enough, when Professor Rusty and his team of colleagues examined the statue closely, they found her name scratched in tiny letters on the bottom: FRANKIE.

As promised, Truly had kept her friend's secret faithfully, taking it with her back to Germany, and eventually to her grave. We'll never know for sure why she didn't tell Booth about Frankie, but the secret remained for us to discover.

Professor Rusty had DNA tests done on the hair in the twin bracelets, and they came back 100 percent positive as Freeman and Lovejoy, further proof of the activity of the Underground Railroad in our tiny town. Frankie's and Truly's lives were entwined back then, just as our neighbors' lives and ours are here in Pumpkin Falls still.

The whole sap rustler thing turned out to be kind of a big deal too. Scooter's surveillance video of the raccoon saboteurs went viral, and Aunt True made hay with it, designing a bookshop window that featured blown-up stills of the mama raccoon and her babies, along with cookbooks, picture books featuring raccoons, and more stuff on maple syrup. Lauren got in on the act too, adding Rascal, one of her all-time favorite stories.

My aunt really is a marketing whiz. Cup and Chaucer, her new micro café, is starting to take shape. The two little tables she set up are almost always occupied, even though she's only serving tea right now. The directions that came with the espresso machine were in Italian, and as soon as we get them translated, Aunt True is going to train Hatcher and me to be baristas.

Ella Bellow took pity on my poor pathetic socks, and I was invited to Stitch and Snitch—I mean A Stitch in Time—for a remedial class. "Free of charge," she told me. "I did advertise successful socks in a week, after all."

With her help, I finally finished them. They're kind of lumpy, and they itch, but they don't look all that bad, so I'm wearing them anyway. I worked too hard on them not to.

Mackenzie and I talk all the time, just like always. We video-conference a couple of times a week, and she loves to show me what Frankie, her new kitten, is up to.

Yes, Mackenzie took a kitten home. Belinda's persistence paid off. And yes, my cousin named her Frankie, after Franklin's ancestor. "That way I'll never forget our Spring Break together," she told me.

Like there's any chance either of us could.

My cousin is still crazy about Mr. Perfect Cameron McAllister, although I think she's keeping her options open with both Scooter and Lucas, because I've overheard them vying with each other about who gets more texts from her. She backed away from Franklin, though, after I told her that Jasmine liked him.

The two of us are cooking up a plan to get together this summer. Cha Cha and Jasmine might come along too. I can hardly wait.

I'm still adjusting to life as a teenager. I still cry unexpectedly sometimes, and I still find myself wishing I were a chickadee instead of an ostrich more often than not, but at least I don't wish I were twelve anymore.

Thirteen is just fine with me, thanks to a certain boy whose initials are Romeo Calhoun.

Mackenzie's little talk with him seems to have lit a bit of a fire under Calhoun, because he volunteered to go owling with me. I take this as a good sign. I'm hoping maybe there'll be another kiss, eventually, to erase the memory of that first disastrous one with Scooter behind the Freemans' barn.

I have to go now. There's a full moon in the sky outside—a maple moon!—and Calhoun is waiting. I'm wearing the owl earrings that Mackenzie gave me for my birthday, and I can hear a barred owl in the distance. Wish me luck!

Yours, Truly

AUNT TRUE'S
BOOKSHOP BLONDIES

Please ask a grown-up for help.

6 T. butter, softened

1 cup maple sugar

1 egg

½ tsp. maple flavoring

½ tsp. vanilla extract

1 cup all-purpose flour

1 tsp. baking powder

½ tsp. salt

1 cup chopped walnuts (optional)

Sea salt for sprinkling

• Preheat oven to 350° F. Grease an 8" square pan.

• In a large bowl, cream the butter and maple sugar together; beat in egg, maple flavoring, and vanilla. Whisk flour with baking powder and salt and add to egg mixture, stirring to combine. Add nuts.

• Pour into greased pan and bake for about 25 minutes, until edges are lightly brown and just beginning to pull away from pan.

• Remove from oven and cool on a rack. Sprinkle the top of the blondies with sea salt, if desired.

MISS MARPLE'S PICKS

The Canterbury Tales by Geoffrey Chaucer

The Hidden Staircase by Carolyn Keene

The Hobbit by J. R. R. Tolkien

The House of Dies Drear by Virginia Hamilton

Moses by Carole Boston Weatherford and Kadir Nelson

Rascal by Sterling North

The Sasquatch Escape by Suzanne Selfors

The Secret of the Old Clock by Carolyn Keene

The Westing Game by Ellen Raskin

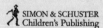